The Weekend At Longwood

Bill Dughaille

CONTENTS

Chapter 1: Returning

'Who do you think did it?' she asked.

He did not reply immediately. He had been thinking that the pre-war Humber was finally behaving itself, perhaps happier in the winding country lanes than the city streets. He had been day-dreaming, imagining that they were in an open-topped sports car, their hair streaming in the wind under the glorious August blue skies. Life had recently been very pleasant, despite the difficulties of the war's aftermath. He had been avoiding thinking about what they were going to.

'I don't know,' he said finally. 'Maybe it was you.'

'Beast. That's a horrible thing to say,' she replied mildly, as if knowing he did not mean it.

'It was a pretty horrible thing that happened.' He grimaced. 'Silly phrase, isn't it? "Pretty horrible". "Gruesome" would be more accurate. Especially compared with how relaxed that afternoon had been. But all I meant was that we all had a motive. For all you know it could have been me.'

'I wouldn't have married you if it was you, darling.'

He debated whether to reply to this, and decided not to.

'I wonder if she really knows who did it,' she mused.

'That's what she seemed to suggest in the invitation.'

She was silent for a few moments.

'An invitation to tea, four o'clock tomorrow,' she continued. 'Saturday. It was a Saturday when it happened. That Saturday night.' She looked at him. 'You know, if it has to be – well, one of us – it would be better if it was – well, it wouldn't be fair, but ... '

'You mean the dead can do no more harm? One of us who didn't make it? One of the nine?'

'Well, it would be easier. A lot has happened since then.'

'A lot of water under the bridge.'

'Not all of it water, either.'

'Hard to believe it's 1946.' He paused as he changed gears. 'Maybe tomorrow we will have an answer to that weekend. Maybe.'

'It's strange,' she said, staring out the window, 'it seems like a different world, yet ... at the same time, it feels like only yesterday.'

He smiled.

'I'm quite happy with today, my sweet. What more could a man want than a happy home and the love of a good woman?'

She smiled back.

'Or even that of a not-so-good woman?' she asked wickedly.

'There is that, too,' he acknowledged, chuckling softly.

August 1939

The last weekend of August, 1939. With the recent announcement of the Nazi-Soviet non-aggression pact, war seemed, barring a miracle, inevitable. Children were being evacuated from the cities. Business travellers and tourists were hurriedly leaving Europe. Georgina Riley, famed American novelist and socialite had her passage booked on the Northern Star leaving on Tuesday the 29th of August – but she was leaving not because of the looming war, but because of what she impishly called a "previous engagement"; she was due to marry her childhood sweetheart in New York in September. She would, she claimed, have preferred to stay in England had she believed war was coming. She believed passionately in England as those who have adopted another country as their spiritual home. She was also, however, one of the few who did not believe that there would be a war.

'After the Great War, who could be so foolish as to start another?' she asked in her twinkling voice, with barely a trace of her original American accent. She had invited a number of friends to stay the weekend, her last in England for a while, at the country house she had rented, "Longwood", a large mock-Tudor style house tucked into a fold in the hills close to the sea, not far from Portsmouth. They were sitting on the lawn in front of the house, Georgina leaning back on a blanket with her legs tucked underneath her, others in deckchairs or on the grass, enjoying drinks, the fading summer heat and the approaching sunset of the Saturday evening. The sun shone; the clouds loomed. It was a typical late summer's day in South-Eastern England. It might turn unbearably muggy as an Indian summer, the clouds might cool and burst as a prelude to the onset of winter.

They were almost all in their mid-twenties; younger people, she often claimed, were much more easy and tolerant, whereas the older English made her very aware of her American roots, treating her as an outsider. She was somewhat of a contradiction, thirty years of age yet with the attitude of an eighteen-year-old, long, loose blonde hair and childlike face, but wrote as if she was a wise old woman, stories of love, chivalry and honour in the United States' Civil War, while agonising about the tragedy and brutality of the Great War.

'I very much fear that Hitler and the Germans are special types of fools,' Nigel Johnson said morosely, lying on the grass, chin cupped in his hand, staring vacantly into nowhere. He was twenty-two, a self-proclaimed socialist and aspiring poet. He had a thin, drawn face, and a wispy moustache.

'Not all the Germans,' an accented female voice countered softly. Johnson blushed.

'Of course not, I never meant to include you, Frieda, obviously not. I was talking about the Nazis.'

Frieda Rosenberg did not reply. She was sitting close to Georgina, looking down at the grass she was absent-mindedly tugging. Eighteen, looking more late-twenties, a blonde young woman who could have been an advert for Hitler's Germany, had she not left after her Jewish parents had disappeared during Kristalnacht.

'The English like to claim good people as their own,' Georgina teased, leaning over and gently pushing Frieda's hair away from her face. 'All the others are nasty foreigners.'

Nigel looked abashed, like a chastened puppy, his eyes fastened on Frieda's face.

'Ah, but you're claiming Frieda for America,' historian Professor John Haskins said from his deckchair. He was unusual within the group, being at thirty-seven the eldest amongst them. The effect of smart tan slacks and shirt was offset by the way they were rumpled; an open smile under a beaten old bush-hat, which no wife would have permitted, confirmed his bachelor status.

He had referred to the fact that Frieda was to travel with Georgina to the United States, where Georgina had promised to get her citizenship. In England Frieda would be reluctantly tolerated as a refugee, she said, whereas in America she could be a free woman, accepted for what she was.

How, exactly, she would be able to overcome America's strict quota system for Frieda she had not said, if she had at all considered the problem. In Georgina's world people just did things for her. Problems happened to other people.

She smiled at Haskins, a teasing, mischievous smile.

'And I, my dearest Professor, will also be reclaiming our glorious General Ulysses Grant for the United States of America,' she said. Haskins smiled and raised a glass in wordless salute. His latest book had been a comparative history of the American Civil War and the Great War, *Lessons we should have learnt, Lessons we must learn* in which General Grant's orders had been unfavourably compared to the slaughter on the Western Front. Georgina had publicly stated that Haskins should leave fiction-writing to her, and that she would produce facts from the archives she normally used to prove Haskins wrong in a number of areas. Their friends had expected a great row, but he had merely laughed and wagered her a penny that she couldn't. His students would have been amazed at this mild reaction; for them he was "Professor Grim" behind his back.

'There won't be a war,' Johnson said, as if he regretted the lack, 'the capitalists won't allow it. Stalin was clever enough to realise that any war would be against Communism. Now that he's prevented that the capitalists are stymied.'

'There won't be a war,' Haskins corrected him sternly, 'because their military will not allow it. I spoke to some colonels over in Germany a few months ago. They do not want a war with the West, they know they can only lose. Hitler has been clever up until now, he has achieved what he wanted without any actual fighting. But as soon as he orders real action the generals will take over in a coup. They don't like the idea of war, you know.'

The look on Nigel's face suggested that this was an unlikely notion, but he remained silent.

'Which colonels were they?' asked Frieda. The question surprised the group. She looked up. 'I had a friend at school whose father was a colonel,' she explained. 'When I was young, and we were allowed to go to school and have friends. And parents.'

'I promised never to reveal their names,' Haskins replied gently, 'not to anyone. It could get them shot, you know.' Frieda seemed to acknowledge this, sadly returning to her contemplation of the grass.

'If there is a war,' Johnson declared as fiercely as he could, 'I certainly will not be taking part. I have no intention of risking my life to keep the capitalists with their snouts in the pig-trough.'

'There is such a thing as duty,' Haskins responded. None of them appeared to notice his nose twitch slightly, as if slightly doubtful of his own words, or perhaps knowing that such statements left hostages to fortune, and fortune has a bad habit of returning to collect the ransom.

'It isn't that I'm afraid to fight,' Johnson assured the world in general and himself in particular. 'I volunteered for the Republicans in '36. That was a cause worth dying for. But it was over before I could get there.'

'Not afraid to fight?' Haskins asked dryly. 'I am. I have a distinct aversion to people trying to kill me. But if it comes to it one has to do the right thing.'

'Hello, here come the young lovers,' Georgina announced loudly, hoping to end the disagreement.

A young couple were approaching along the path, he tall, tanned and fit-looking in white shirt and long white trousers, she, raven-haired, in a white blouse and light blue skirt, with a pert, slightly sunburnt face that suggested she spent most of her time indoors and was making the most of the fresh air and sunlight.

'Hello, you lot,' the woman called. 'Have you been gossiping about us?'

'Sadly not, Rose. This lot have been all morbid and talking of war. Grab yourself a drink.'

'I'll have a Moselle,' Rosemary Morely said to the man, who went to the basket to pour their drinks.

'I've already had my call-up papers,' he announced cheerfully. 'They keep sending them and then cancelling the orders. This time it looks like they've finally made their minds up.'

'Well, Peter, that will teach you fly with the reserves,' Rosemary said, equally cheerfully, making herself comfortable on the grass near to Haskins.

'Only way I could afford it,' Peter Henderby laughed. 'Don't earn much as a tennis coach these days. Pity my expensive education didn't equip me for a more rewarding job.'

'Ah, but what about all those rich women just dying to have you hold them firmly as you show them how to play the forehand?'

'They can carry on dying for all I care,' he said, handing Rose her drink and sitting down next to her. He took a sip of wine and sighed happily at the taste. 'That sort of thing can get a man into deep trouble. Firstly the woman becomes insanely jealous and demands all your attention, and then the husband finds out and, if you're lucky, gives you a sound thrashing and you lose your job.'

'That's the lucky option?'

'Yes. The unlucky option is he says thank-you, divorces the wife and leaves her on your hands.'

They laughed. Henderby was skilled at charming people and a gifted raconteur. The others rather suspected that he did occasionally take advantage of some of his clients, but no-one had yet complained.

'So what were you doing in the woods with Lady Parker?' asked Georgina mischievously. Henderby pretended to be alarmed.

'Oh, no, you won't tell, will you? I was merely attending to a slight sprain. Honest.'

'Funny place to get a sprain,' Georgina said.

Haskins looked at her thoughtfully. He wondered how much of a pretense it was. There was a Lady Parker, young and attractive, and Henderby was coaching her.

'Where did you leave your brother and whats-her-name? That anaemic thing.' Georgina asked Rose, changing the subject.

'Jessica? Rob had a creative moment and wanted to be alone with his muse.'

Georgina giggled.

'You mean they're alone musing?' she asked suggestively.

'Really, Georgy!' Rose giggled along. 'Actually, I feel a little sorry for her. She's hardly more than a child – and what a surname, Goodchild! Jessica Goodchild. The muse. Sounds almost indecent.'

'I wish I could be a muse,' Georgina said, sadly.

'You're a writer,' Haskins pointed out. 'You should have a muse, you can't be one. You know,' he smiled at her, 'I think of you more as a pixie.'

'A pixie!' She pouted. 'I am not a pixie!'

'An elfish little pixie, spreading mischief and mayhem,' Haskins continued, teasing.

'I am not!' she insisted. Had she been standing she would have stamped a foot. A thought suddenly struck her. 'I can't be a pixie. Pixies do not have tiaras.' She smiled triumphantly.

'A tiara?' asked Rose, surprised.

Georgina jumped up.

'I almost forgot about it. I bought it in London last week. I wanted something to cheer me up, what with all this talk about war, sandbags everywhere, everyone going around as if the world were about to end. I spotted it in a jewellery shop in Bond Street and thought, yes, I have to have that. I'll get it to show you. It's a really pretty little thing.' She danced off to the house.

Rose shook her head slowly.

'"Almost forgot about it"' she mimicked. 'I wish I could afford to pop into a jewellery shop for a tiara to cheer myself up. Unfortunately Whaitebeys don't pay their junior staff that sort of money, not even in ladies' lingerie.'

'Cheer up, old girl,' Henderby said, 'any day now you'll meet a rich old man who will fall in love with you and shower you with diamonds.'

'Any day now. Ha! What with Georgy going back to America – nobody else will invite me out. And she only does that because Rob's my brother. Our marvellous up-and-coming artist.' She sighed. 'Anyway, rich old men go for young twenty-year olds, pretty but brainless. I'm – almost as old as Georgie. On the shelf.'

'There were nine muses, you know,' Haskins said thoughtfully, not, apparently, having been listening to what she had been saying.

'Oh, great, now a history lecture from the great Professor!' Rose muttered sarcastically. Haskins frowned at her.

'The muses were the daughters of Zeus and Mnemosyne,' a loud voice announced from behind them.

'Rob! Where did you come from?' A heavy-set man in his mid-twenties but looking older, working his way to plumpness, red-faced, bushy-bearded with heavy eyebrows and a lowering look, wearing a panama-hat, and a thin bare-headed young girl-woman in a plain shift had appeared from the side of the house.

'We went the whole way around,' he announced. 'A red wine, Jessica,' he ordered, slumping to the ground like some heavy weight which could no longer stand. The girl obediently went to the drinks basket. 'A great view, gave me several ideas.'

'How's your latest work coming along? Venus and Hell?' asked Haskins. Rob Morley glared at him, suspecting sarcasm.

'Venus Descending, not necessarily into hell. It's the ambiguity that gives the edge. There are one or two aspects I am concentrating on. Conceptually. Have to get the concept right. That's what all great art is about.'

'And the exhibition?' Haskins asked. It was Rose's turn to glare at him. She knew Rob's work had received adverse criticism in the newspapers, and that Haskins thought him a fraud of no intellectual or artistic ability. She secretly suspected the same, but hated Haskins for needling her younger brother.

'Had some good offers,' Morley replied off-handedly.

He was spared further interrogation by the re-appearance of Georgina, a small, polished mahogany box cupped in her hands. She skipped into the centre of the group and knelt down. Carefully she opened the box, and slowly lifted out a semi-circle of diamonds, glittering in the rays of the lowering sun. There were gasps.

'Oh, Georgy, it's beautiful!' Rose whispered. Frieda's face softened. Haskins leaned forward, smiling. A look of greed passed Johnson's

and Morely's faces, to be quickly replaced with disinterest.
Henderby whistled.

'Nice stuff if you can get it,' he murmured.

'Go on, Georgy, put it on,' urged Rose. Georgina raised the tiara slowly to her head. Frieda leaned forward to help her. Rose smoothed her hair carefully. 'You look absolutely – stunning.'

'That's money for you,' Johnson grumbled.

'Money! The curse of the artist,' Morley pronounced, irritated that he was no longer the centre of attention. The thin young girl lay next to him, her head on his shoulder, her eyes fixed on Georgina's head.

'Wouldn't mind being cursed myself,' a woman's voice interrupted them. Georgina looked around and gave a cry of delight.

'Erica!' She jumped up, rushed over and hugged the new arrival, almost dislodging the tiara. 'You made it! I thought you weren't coming!'

'Not come? Don't be silly, my sweet. Where else would I get free drinks and eats? I've left my bags in the entrance, you'll have to show me where I'm sleeping.' She paused, looking at Georgina's head. 'Why on earth are you wearing that ridiculous thing on your head?'

While the newcomer was as slim and slender as the other women present, her mannish grey slacks, loose white shirt, forthright voice and bushy red-brown mop of hair gave the impression of a much larger force.

'Ridiculous? It's not ridiculous! It's my tiara. Don't you just love it?'

'Not my style, darling Georgy. I'd sell it and use the money for something useful. Like paper and typewriter ribbons. That's the price you pay for being in poverty.'

'Oh, Erica, I'm sorry, it's thoughtless of me. I'll put it away.' Georgina sheepishly carried it back to its box.

'Don't worry about me, girl,' replied Erica expansively, laughing. 'You've got the money, indulge yourself girl. You're only young once. I would if it was me.'

'Why a tiara, though?' asked Haskins. 'Not the sort of thing I'd think people would wear very often in America.'

'That's exactly why. Because it is so very English. I shall swan at parties like an English princess. I shall be the belle of the ball.'

'Won't be any balls around here. Not for a long time, anyway,' Erica said, helping herself to a whiskey.

'Why not?'

'There's going to be a war, or hadn't you noticed? Cheers!'

'The great professor disagrees with you,' said Rose, smiling evilly at Haskins. Erica had once been a student of Haskins, and, it was rumoured, more than that.

'The great professor has a good many misconceptions,' Erica replied, glass in hand, also looking at Haskins. He shifted uncomfortably in his chair, tugging at the brim of his beaten bush-hat. Rose enjoyed the sight.

'Oh, do stop bickering, you lot!' pleaded Georgina. 'It's my last weekend here, do try to be a little cheerful.'

Henderby jumped to his feet.

'Of course! Let's have a little fun. A party. A –' he looked around at them. 'An end of the world party. Let's party like there won't be another day! As if we don't care if we're alive tomorrow!'

'Good idea, Pete,' Georgina said, taking his arm, 'let's go indoors and get some music playing. And drinks. And I'll get Mrs Murgle to make something to nibble on.'

'After all, what are the peasants for?' muttered Johnson under his breath. He stood up and slouched after the other two.

'Come, Jessica, to party we go,' Morely ordered. She rose and followed him obediently.

'Why Georgina wants to go off to America to get married defeats me,' Erica said, sipping her whisky. 'Plenty of useable men around, swap them when you want. No need to marry one of the damn things.' She set off for the house, emptying her glass as she went, refilling it from a bottle in her other hand.

Frieda folded the blanket neatly, and then watched Haskins fold his deckchair. Rose was kneeling on the ground, putting the bottles back into the basket.

'How do you say in English? House-trained?' she asked. 'The others, are perhaps not so trained.'

'Privilege of wealth,' Rose replied, stretching for an empty wine bottle. Frieda looked at her, nodded thoughtfully, and turned towards the house. Haskins watched her go.

'Strange girl,' he commented.

'You'd be strange as well if you'd been through what she has,' Rose said. 'Apart from that, she's the sort of girl who looks fifteen when she's ten, and acts as if she were thirty.' She stood up. "Then again, you're a little strange yourself. What are you going to do with your love far, far away?'

'What on earth is that supposed to mean?'

'Oh, come on John, any fool can see that you're smitten by our American hostess.'

'Absolute nonsense.'

'If you say so, puppy dog.'

He tried glaring at her, but it didn't seem to work. He knew he had a soft spot for Georgina – they shared a mischievous sense of humour which he felt he needed to repress in his official life as a historian and professor – but also that he was not, as Rose claimed, "smitten" by her.

It was ironic, he thought, that there were two women here that he was attracted to, quite strongly. One was Erica; she had not been his student, but they had formed a relationship after meeting when she was doing post-graduate studies. Her possessiveness, he believed, had caused the breakup, something he still regretted, and often wondered whether perhaps he was partly to blame, the confirmed bachelor.

The other woman was Rose herself, but her continual digs at him – confusingly often followed by bouts of pleasantness – made him wary of saying anything which might be misunderstood or even misinterpreted. He was afraid that any suggestion of intimacy, even just inviting her out for dinner, would be met with a withering response, and the story would quickly become gossip.

'Do you really think there won't be a war?' she asked softly, her agreeable side coming to the fore. He stood with the deckchair in his hand and looked out towards the distant sea, the sun descending, a view of calm and peace.

'I sincerely hope not,' he said quietly.

'You were in the war, weren't you? The Great War?'

'Only just. It wasn't pleasant.' And he had been extremely stupid, in hindsight. He had lied about his age to get in, he remembered, pretended to his boarding school he was on his way to his parents' home, to his mother that he was staying at school. His mother had had the right contacts to eventually get him out, but not before he had spent two months in the trenches, just before the Armistice was declared. It was then that the patriotic jingoism inculcated into him by his elderly teachers had been undermined and then almost washed away, leaving him uncertain of many things, unwilling to commit to any firm beliefs. Had Johnson, when Haskins spoke of duty, asked the question one of the older soldiers asked him – "Duty? Aye, but to what? And to whom?" – he would have been hard put to answer. Sometimes he wondered whether that was why he had not married and settled down to a domestic life. Marriage would bring duties and responsibilities, and he wasn't sure that he hadn't had enough of both.

'I think a war could be fun, actually,' Rose said, standing up and picking up the basket.

'Fun? You must be mad. You don't know what it's like.' She smiled at him, walked over, and took his arm in hers. They moved slowly towards the house, as if reluctant to join the others.

'I was brought up to live in the good old life of luxury,' she said. 'Wealthy – well, upper middle class, I suppose – upright parents, public school, not the best, but quite respected, all that sort of thing. Pillars of the community, as everyone said. Up until Daddy lost it all in the Depression. And took his life when they discovered he'd been quietly committing vast acts of fraud to keep up the pretence. Mummy died of the disgrace. Now I'm stuck in an awful little job in a horrible little shop having to deal with customers who have absolutely no manners. And I find I now have very few friends – they seem to disappear very quickly when trouble comes and the money goes. A war could open up all sorts of opportunities. Look at the last one. Women took on loads of different jobs that they would never have done before.'

'And lost them straight afterwards. Anyway, I hardly think you'd enjoy working in a munitions factory.'

'I wasn't thinking of working in a factory. There will be opportunities, it's just a case of waiting for the right one and recognising it when it happens.' She chuckled. 'I might become a cat-burglar, or something. Who knows, maybe I've inherited some of Daddy's criminal side.'

It sounded like wishful thinking to Haskins.

They stopped at the French windows leading into the lounge. Inside Henderby was leafing through records, looking for appropriate music. Georgina was calling 'Emily! Emily! Where has that girl gone?' Erica was looking at a picture while feeding herself handful after handful from a bowl of nuts. Georgina looked at Morely. He had established himself in the largest armchair, brandy in one hand, cigar in the other. Jessica sat next to his legs, like an adoring dog. 'Rob, we need the couches and armchairs pushed back, can't you do that?'

'You called, Miss Georgina?' Emily was young and black, Georgina's maid from her home in New York. Haskins noticed both Johnson and Morley giving her appraising looks.

'Put this in the cupboard in my bedroom, Emily. Clean it first. I want it polished. We've put some nasty fingerprints all over it.' She handed over the tiara box. 'Then tell Mrs Murgle I want some nibbles. Snacks, Emily, Snacks. And more wine.'

'Yes, Miss Georgina.' The girl left and Georgina whirled around.

'Come on, Peter, slowcoach. Surely you must have found something by now. There's loads there.'

'I know, darling, that's what's taking time. Deciding on the perfect one for you.'

'Put on "We have No Bananas", I like that one.'

'But it's old hat darling. Ancient, in fact.'

'I like old hat. So there.'

Haskins looked at Rose next to him. She shook her head sadly, and looked up at him.

'Let's take these things around the side,' she said. 'We can leave them in the kitchen.'

They began walking along the path. While most of the garden was either lawn or wild undergrowth, to minimise the work required to maintain it, a gardener had planted red and pink clematis along the sides of the house, giving it, from a distance, the impression of resting on a bed of candy floss, almost as if an alien building had landed amidst the green fields.

'You don't seem too eager to join the party,' he suggested. She shrugged.

'Things are a little – how can you describe it? Bitchy, I suppose. Oh, yes, I know I've been guilty of some, and there's always a little of that going around, but it seems worse today, somehow. What with Georgina leaving and all this talk of war. It feels strange, like – well, a bit of a bad dream, almost. Combine that with a few drinks – and let's face it we've already had a few – and things are likely to get out of hand. I just have this feeling that something nasty could happen.'

'The thought had struck me as well. Waving that tiara around, in front of people who could desperately use some of the money, wasn't exactly the most diplomatic thing to do. I was planning on staying at a distance, observing from afar, just in case things get thrown. As an academic one has to take a purely neutral view – and stay out of the path of flying objects.'

She smiled at him.

'You don't think it's a coincidence, do you?'

'How do you mean?'

'All of us apart from you are short of cash. She enjoys parading her wealth in front of us. You – well, she likes digging her claws into you because of that history book you wrote. Frieda – her little plaything, a demonstration of her largesse.'

'That's a little extreme, isn't it?'

'You can't see it because you're smitten with her. And don't deny it. Everyone else is quite aware of their role in this farce, and they don't like it. If she pushes too far someone might just do something ... Well, let's just say I know what I feel like doing to her.'

He felt unable to reply, as they had come to the kitchen door, and Mrs Murgle, the cook was in hearing distance. 'Mrs Murgle,' Rose called, 'we've brought the stuff from the lawn.'

'Ah, that's sweet of you, my dear,' Mrs Murgle replied, busy with something on the stove. 'Just leave it all by the door and I'll get Emily to sort it out.' They did as bidden and began walking back.

'Such a beautiful place,' Haskins commented. The garden and the fields beyond were deep green, the sky just beginning darkening blue, the stormclouds had left, some wispy clouds in the distance suggesting a coming rich sunset. It was quietly peaceful, the seagulls and other birds silent, the only noise the faint sound of music coming from the lounge.

'So peaceful,' she agreed. She stopped and looked at the view, her arms wrapped around her as if trying to hold it to herself. He stood next to her, looking towards the sea. 'They were saying in London,' she continued dreamily, 'just before I left, that there will be a million casualties in the first few days, civilian casualties – if there is a war. And all the sandbags and trenches ... I just can't imagine it. Not here. It seems like ... some mad nightmare that just couldn't possibly come true.'

He looked at her and smiled. She seemed a mixture of woman and child, perplexed at the stupidity of man. She reminded him of Erica before they had split up. That was when Erica had abandoned skirts and blouses for a mannish look and dominating approach, something he hoped she would grow out of.

'What are you smiling at?' she asked.

'You. I was thinking how you look just like a child who cannot understand how adults can be so stupid.'

'I am not a child. I am a fully grown woman,' she replied with more than a trace of anger. 'And, if I say so myself, reasonably intelligent.'

'Oh, it wasn't a criticism. And I wasn't suggesting that you were being childish. I feel exactly the same way myself – quite often, really. In this modern world we all pretend to be so sophisticated, yet underneath, most of the time we're just perplexed and feeling vulnerable.'

'What will you do if there is a war?' she asked, walking on, apparently deciding that that subject had been exhausted, or just having tired of it.

'That's all settled. Someone I know has offered me a job in a new intelligence unit.'

'I wish I knew someone who could fix things for me.'

'Maybe you do. Can you type?'

'Sort of. Why?'

'If there is going to be a war – and that's a big if – they'll be crying out for all sorts of people. The section I'll be joining – if it happens – will need plenty of typists, clerks, you name it. I could probably wangle you a job there.'

'Typist? Not quite the opportunity I was hoping would come my way. Still, I'll bear it in mind.' They had reached the French windows. 'Party like we'll be dead tomorrow,' she misquoted Henderby. She grinned at Haskins impishly. 'Once more into the snake pit?' she asked mischievously.

Chapter 2: The Party

The road had led them into open country, autumn fields on either side, the old Humber given an occasional hiccough. They had decided to drive along as many country roads as possible, leaving early and taking their time. It was no great distance, and, as he had put it, "our world is changing – has already changed". London, Portsmouth, Manchester, Coventry and so many other towns and cities were riddled with gaps left by the bombing of the war. Soon the rustic villages of England would, he believed, succumb to post-war socialism. And not only England, but the other devastated countries in Europe, not to mention the trouble brewing in the remaining colonies. She thought he was exaggerating – she had always taken more of her views from people she met, whereas he tended to think academically, in terms of movements, organisations, theory and history – but she liked the idea of a country drive. It would be a mini-holiday.

Except for the reason they were going.

'You remember during that evening, in-between dances while someone was choosing the next music, how we discussed the nine muses, and which one would be appropriate for each of us?' she asked.

'I'd forgotten that,' he said, surprised. 'Yes, I do now. Georgina insisted on first choice, but couldn't decide between Calliope, Euterpe and Thalia.'

'I remember Calliope was the muse of epic poetry; what were the other two?'

'Euterpe, lyric poetry. Thalia, comedy – she wanted Thalia because she liked the name. Ironic, I suppose you could call it. Melpomene would have been a better choice – or more accurate, anyway.'

'Melpomene?'

'The muse of tragedy.'

The thought brought silence for a mile or so.

'I don't think I've ever been as drunk as I was that night,' she said.

'I think we all were to some extent.'

'Apart from one person. Someone was pretending, and we don't know who it was.'

'Apparently we will, shortly.'

She looked at him. Things had certainly not turned out as they might have expected, or even imagined, that weekend. He had changed since then – yet not changed, in a way. Matured, almost, yet into something that retained a little boy's mischievous sense of humour. Not now, as he concentrated on the driving, and the – ordeal? – that lay ahead. But, yes, he was so very different, they both were. They had been through a lot, having lost and found each other at least twice. But at least the last finding had stuck.

She wondered whether she should tell him of what she thought she had seen that night, something she had never told anyone else, not the police, not even him. It hadn't seemed important then.

Georgina's taste in music was almost entirely modern, popular, informal, and mainly jazz. It allowed the group to dance together, apart, as couples or as the mood took them. The mood took Morely to return to his armchair with another brandy and cigar as soon as possible after an obligatory dance with Georgina, claiming that an artist could not expend too much energy on such pastimes. Jessica sat on the armrest, a little-touched glass of wine in hand, looking enviously on at the others. Haskins noticed her wistful look, and pulled her gently but firmly into a dance. Her face lit up as she relaxed and indulged in frenzied movement, enthusiastic if unconventional.

'That was good of you to look after our little waif,' Georgina said to him a few dances later, when he found himself paired with her, off to one side. 'I declare you do try to be the perfect gentleman, don't you?'

She had added a faint Southern twang to her words. There was a certain mockery in her smile. For a second time he wondered how far it was gentle teasing, and how far she could go if she had the urge.

'But of course, my dear Georgina,' he replied in a similarly teasing vein, 'surrounded by such beautiful women how could a man not be a gentleman?'

And that sort of nonsense, a voice at the back of his mind said, shows that you have had a little too much to drink.

But it seemed to mollify Georgina, who was content to enjoy the rest of the dance, before handing him over to Rose, who had sat the dance out and had now put on the next record, Glen Miller's Moonlight Serenade, a record Georgina had brought from America.

'My, you do impress me, dear Professor,' Rose said, putting one arm on his shoulder, the other around his waist, pulling him in close and rubbing against him suggestively in a manner Glenn Miller had probably not intended. 'You dance so elegantly,' she continued, whispering in his ear, 'you're such a charmer with our hostess, and you succour young girls who so obviously want to join in the fun but need a helping hand. Why, I do declare, I'm sure you're fond of little children and gentle with kittens.'

While Haskins would never claim to understand women, he considered himself reasonably competent in the art of social banter, but Rose was proving to be a greater conundrum than he had encountered before. In a very short space of time she could change from being friendly, honest and open to baiting him with great enthusiasm, as she was doing now.

'Not little children,' he replied. 'Little children frighten me.'

She gasped in his ear.

'The great Professor? Scared of little children? You mean you do have a flaw? You are human?'

'They tend to ask innocent questions to which I don't know the answers,' he confessed. 'Unfortunately they seem to think adults have all the answers.'

'I thought you did have all the answers, isn't that why you're a professor? Don't you overawe all of your little students?' she asked waspishly. She must have felt him tense. After a pause she continued, 'I'm sorry, that was a little too bitchy.'

After a further pause she asked, pleadingly, 'Forgive me?'

'Of course. Nothing to forgive,' he replied, a slight catch in his voice revealing the lie. To his relief the music ended shortly thereafter, and Rose retired to the ladies' room, presumably, he thought, to freshen up for the next skirmish. He took the chance to sit out the next couple of dances, recover from the battlefield, and observe what other miniature social environments were evolving.

Erica, to his great relief, after a couple of failed attempts to re-visit their former intimacy, had decided that Henderby was her target for the evening. Haskins knew that she had a flaming temper and was quite willing to vent it on himself. With both Georgina and Rose having a go at him he hardly needed Erica to add to the witches' brew.

Henderby appeared to be coping reasonably well with Erica's advances. He threw himself into dances shared with her with physical gusto, displaying his athletic strength while keeping her at arm's distance as far as possible. In-between he occasionally managed to get Jessica on to the dance floor. Fortunately Georgina had invited her neighbours – in so far as people living a mile away could be termed neighbours – two retired couples, one of whom was energetic enough to wish to try out this new-fangled young music with Jessica. The other three sat rather bemusedly to one side, as if watching the rituals of a strange and rather frightening tribe from some far-distant and uncivilised land.

Frieda was somewhat of an enigma, he decided. Had a photograph been taken of the women present, it would be Frieda whom most people would have singled out as the likely leader, taller than the others, more robustly built, firm jawed. But here, although she joined in with some enthusiasm, it was also with a great deal of reserve. She kept to the side of the room where Georgina was, almost as if she needed her protection. Haskins had danced with her once, having decided that it would be impolite to ignore her, but she was not the one ignored; it was as if he had not been there at all.

Jazz had been one of the first things banned by the Nazis, Haskins recalled. For a jazz-loving young Jewess the trauma of the years up to

Kristalnacht must have been an increasing series of fears, undermining whatever confidence she might have started out with. He supposed this explained Frieda's strange contradiction.

Johnson had danced with Frieda quite early on, but presumably he had received just as little encouragement. He was not a good dancer, however informal the context, and it was plain he was not enjoying himself on the dance floor. He had now retired to the an armchair next to Morely's, presumably to set the world to rights from within an increasing haze of whisky. At one point Haskins overheard him loudly declaring that there were things worth dying for. Morely's equally aggressive response was that some things were living for, followed by some indistinct muttering about art and socialism, in which the former was presumably overwhelmingly more important than the latter.

Haskins' observations were interrupted by the arrival of Georgina demanding a dance, noting that the men obviously lacked stamina, and accusing him being an old fogey, a rather undiplomatic statement considering her neighbours were within earshot. Once out on the dance area it became apparent that Georgina had at least reached the tipsy stage. Previously deftly executed movements now had a dangerous air of just succeeding, and a couple of times Haskins feared that he might be propelled into a bookcase by her vigorous dancing. At not quite appropriate moments she would grasp him in a clinch, and whisper outrageous comments in a voice only the steadfastly deaf or drunk might miss. At one point she told him, not so sotto voce, 'That Rose is dreadfully jealous of me flirting with you like this, you know, I'm sure she'd like to strangle me. And Erica isn't too happy either, despite her pretending to go for Peter.' This was followed by an inappropriate giggle as she whirled away; Haskins noticed Rose watching them, having obviously overheard, a venomous look in her eyes.

Others came in for similar biting observations, but fortunately they were mostly either too far away to hear, or too engrossed in what they were doing. Johnson was a "nincompoop". Morely an amusing "fraud". Erica a "sad excuse for a writer". It was as if Georgina felt that her imminent departure for the States had left her free to say exactly what she felt. Erica had heard the comment about her writing, Haskins noticed as he was whirled around. The look on her face was, if anything, more filled with hatred than Rose's had been. And the way she was holding a wine bottle suggested that she was eager to employ it in a manner for which it had not primarily been intended. Had she been closer Georgina would have got it across her face. The large room was becoming increasingly hot in more than one sense.

To Haskins' relief she finally released him as the song ended, declaring that she was dying for a drink. Before Haskins could beat a retreat he found himself captured by Jessica, who, to his alarm was also showing the side effects of too much Moselle. Not only was she far more physical than previously, she was also given to revealing secrets.

'Georgy said I should dance as much as I want,' she said giggling, 'it irritates him.' "Him" was defined by a backwards nod towards where Morely was sitting, watching them with angry, bloodshot eyes, looking more than merely irritated. It was a look crossed with puzzlement, as if he wasn't quite sure what it was he was supposed to be angry about. It was a look that quite often preceded the owner beginning to ask other people what they were looking at and whether they wanted a fight.

Haskins wasn't worried about having to handle Morely physically, should the unfortunate necessity arise. What worried him was that Morely was, to his mind, the type who would not pick a straightforward confrontation with someone who was in a position to retaliate – he would choose either someone weaker, or a moment when the other wasn't prepared for it.

Suddenly the wish that Morely would start something came into his head, just enough so that he, Haskins, would have an excuse to belt the living daylight out of him. As the thought passed through his mind he knew the drink and the atmosphere were getting to him. Belt the living daylight out of him? You're supposed to be a highly regarded historian, not a street thug, he told himself.

It was just after eleven o'clock when that dance ended. The neighbours left, and Haskins chose the moment to go outside for a breath of fresh air and a cigarette. He sat on the edge of the verandah, drink next to him, and wondered whether he should make his excuses and go to bed, or just quietly disappear. It had been a long day in the hot sun, and he found the behaviour of the others both perplexing and understandable. The reaction to the threat of war was to be expected. The backstabbing he could not understand. The air of incipient violence did not sit with his idea of a fun time had by all.

But if he said anything about retiring he knew Georgina would have another dig about his being "too old", and she was unlikely to be the only one. A period of calm and peaceful reflection under the stars was appealing.

After fifteen minutes of admiring the peace of the night air and pondering the dilemma he found himself calm and relaxed. As he lit another cigarette someone sat next to him, rather clumsily.

'Oh, goodness, I do think I am drunk as a lark,' Rose said. 'Or should that be "lord"? Do you mind?' Holding his shoulder for support, she took his cigarette gently, took a deep draw on it, and passed it back.

'I didn't know you smoked.'

'Poverty is great for keeping one in a healthy lifestyle.'

'That reminds me of a joke.'

'What, poverty?'

'No, what you said about being as drunk as a lark. This defence lawyer is having a hard time with a judge, and he asks the witness, "Would you say the officer in question was as drunk as a judge?" And the judge says, "Mr Peters" – or whatever his name was – "Mr Peters, don't you mean as drunk as a lord?" And Peters looks at him and says, "Yes, my lord".' She smiled.

'That's quite amusing.' A pause. 'Do I sound silly, saying that? Amusing. The girls at the shop are always laughing at my accent. Posh, they call it. Poash.' She had surprisingly little difficulty pronouncing the sibilant for one apparently drunk as a lark, he thought. Can larks get drunk, he wondered.

'Not at all. Nothing wrong with correct pronunciation,' he said, hoping he wasn't sounding like a stuffed shirt, as he knew people sometimes took him to be. 'Whatever the modern world says. Some of my pupils' English is atrocious. You wonder how they ever managed to get into university.'

'Rich daddy and mummy,' she replied.

'I suppose so.' She leaned into him and they sat, watching the night sky, happily silent.

'What are your parents like?' she asked suddenly.

He paused before replying.

'My father was a major in the war. Got caught in a trench without his gas mask during a gas attack. I was told he went over the top, gun blazing, let the Germans finish him rather than die a slow death. I've never been sure that that wasn't just an embellishment to hide whatever really happened. My mother – she never really recovered. Died in '19 during the flu epidemic.'

'Oh, John, I'm sorry. It must have been terrible for you. You were still a boy. And you were in it too.'

A sixteen-year-old subaltern, he thought. Only just sixteen. In charge of men much older and far more experienced as soldiers. God help us.

He had always felt that somehow he had not seen enough of the fighting to rank as one of the others, one of the soldiers who fought the war. Yet he had seen more than enough to put him apart from those that never went. In a way he had always felt adrift from two generations.

'More or less,' he replied. 'You get over it. You haven't exactly had an easy time of it yourself.' He sighed. 'So, how are things going in there?' he said, changing the subject.

'It's a bit like being in a dream. Sort of Midsummer's Night, I suppose. Nigel was trying to have an argument with Rob – you saw that. Anyway, finally Rob called Nigel a moron, and promptly fell asleep on the snooker table. So Nigel went off to find someone to discuss politics with, had a long and involved one-sided conversation with Emily, the maid in the kitchen, tried to kiss her, received a slap for his pains, and went off to the drawing room to play the Internationale on the piano. Got through about two notes before falling asleep on the keyboard.'

Haskins chuckled.

'You know, you have a lovely chuckle,' she said, and snuggled closer, burying her head in his shoulder and closing her eyes.

'I thought you and Henderby –'

'Don't be silly, now, Professor Prim and Proper. Peter and I are united by upbringing and poverty, but we're hardly likely to fall for each other. So don't spoil the moment by petty jealousy. You don't have a white charger, by any chance?'

'Afraid not.'

'Pity. I'd rather like you to turn up on a white charger and whisk me away.' She sighed comfortably. 'Do you think Mrs Murgle has put anything funny into the food?'

'Not as far as I'm aware. Why?' He put his arm around her, holding tightly.

'Mmm, that's nice. It's just everything seems so dreamy. I thought maybe she'd slipped some funnies into the sandwiches.'

'I can't see Mrs Murgle in that role.'

Though it was indeed a strange evening. Perhaps Mrs Murgle had introduced mushrooms of dubious quality into their diet.

'Mushrooms,' he said. 'Must be mushrooms.'

'You know I've fallen in love with you, don't you?' she said softly, dreamily.

Haskins did not know what to say. His years as an easy-going bachelor had given him a fine sense of how not to get caught in such situations within relationships. It seemed to have let him down this evening.

'Definitely mushrooms,' he replied eventually, hoping Rose would think he was meandering drunkenly

There was no reply. She was fast asleep.

I wonder, thought Haskins, how she will feel tomorrow.

Women, in his experience, did not forgive men easily for allowing them to drunkenly declare their love for them. He had a slight scar on his jaw to prove it.

And then: I wonder what I'm going to do with her here? Can hardly leave her sleeping in the open. Which means carrying her to her room. Through the lounge. Through all the others. He'd be embarrassed as he went through, she'd be mortified in the morning. It was the sort of thing so-called friends would recall and recount each time they met.

He wondered if there was a side door open somewhere. That would mean leaving Rose lying there. Unless he could wake her up.

He gave her a shake. There was no response whatsoever. One hand fell limply down his front.

'Not there, girl,' he said, placing the hand in a less suggestive area. Maybe he could leave her in a chair in the lounge, laugh it off. Maybe the others wouldn't notice anything.

He suddenly realised that no noise had come from the lounge for the past few minutes. He laid her down gently and carefully padded to the window to have a peek. There was no sign of the others.

'Thank god for that,' he said quietly, and returned to where Rose lay. He picked her up in both arms, gently at first, then with increasing firmness. In films the hero sweeps the swooning heroine off her feet. Rose wasn't swooning, she was firmly built and a dead weight, and, having drunk too much, he was finding it difficult to get a decent hold without putting his hands somewhere no hero would do. Finally he gave up and picked her up in a fireman's lift. He still struggled, but it was manageable.

Inside the lounge he noticed that there were still people present – in a sense. Morely lay face down on a table in a corner, snoring loudly. Next to him Jessica jerked spasmodically, presumably in the grip of a nightmare. In another corner Henderby held Erica against a wall, his face locked with hers, apparently trying to eat her. She was doing as much to him. She saw Haskins, gave him a rude gesture, and waved a hand as if to say, "go on then, leave us to our fun". Haskins tried to tiptoe past, but found it impossible while carrying Rose. He settled for a slow scuttle.

He managed to make it up the staircase and into Rose's bedroom without hitting any part of her anatomy on balustrades or doorways along the way. With some relief he deposited her on her bed. He took a while to get his breath back, while deciding on his next move. Should he loosen her clothing? What if someone came in while he was doing it? What would they think? What would she think, tomorrow?

Finally he settled for taking her shoes off and putting a light quilt over her, up to her waist. It should be sufficient for the warm August night, he thought. And then he went to his own bedroom. He was not, he decided as he sank into bed, the type for this new kind of loose living. He preferred a little more decorum in his love affairs.

Rubbish, he thought to himself as he drifted off to sleep, you just don't like not being in control of things.

The following morning dawned gloriously sunny, blue skies without a breath of wind, green fields stretching to the sea, the early morning perfumed by the clematis, greeted by the calls of starlings, chaffinches and other birds eager for the early worm. Almost like Eden, thought Haskins. He had bathed early and set off for breakfast, humming to himself. Why he was in such a good mood he was uncertain – after all, when Rose awoke she was unlikely to be overly happy with what she had done, and it would be his fault. The words "biting" and "acerbic" would not do justice.

Still, that could take care of itself later.

He entered the dining room to find another early riser. Erica waved a hand as she concentrated on a full plate of egg, bacon, toast and fried tomatoes.

'I've never understood how you manage to stay so slim with your appetite,' he commented.

'Enjoy it while you can, that's my motto,' she said through a full mouth. He looked around for the source of breakfast. The baine-maries were empty. 'I had to hunt down Mrs Murgle,' Erica said. 'She wasn't expecting anyone to be up until noon.'

'It is unusual after a party,' a voice said from the door. 'Many things seem unusual this morning. Emily not around, her bed not slept in. The world is coming to a pretty pass.' Mrs Murgle, alerted by one early requirement had obviously kept her ears open for the next. She paused and regathered herself. 'The full breakfast, or just toast, sir? Few people seem to have an appetite for breakfast these days, especially after a party.' The word "party" was delivered with strong disapproval.

'The result of good, honest, healthy exercise,' Erica said, and choked on a piece of bacon while laughing. Mrs Murgle shot her an outraged look.

'A full breakfast, please Mrs Murgle, that would be excellent,' Haskins said.

'I'll bring some fresh coffee,' Mrs Murgle promised, closing the door. Haskins sat down a chair away from Erica, close enough to be polite, not close enough to be a prey.

'So you got a bit last night as well, did you?' asked Erica maliciously.

'I did not, as you put it, get a bit. Rose had too much to drink and I merely put her to bed,' Haskins said stiffly, investigating the coffee pot.

'Poor you. Wouldn't have stopped you before, from what I remember. Or maybe it's because you're besotted with our host?'

He wondered where she had got the idea that he was interested in Georgina. From Rose? From someone else? Had she mistaken his behaviour towards Georgina? There seemed to be a great deal of subtle social politics going on.

He also wondered how much of her act was an attempt to spite him for what had happened between them previously. Almost dragging Henderby to bed to prove that he, Haskins, wouldn't the only man in her life. He remembered how she had threatened various of his

30

female acquaintances with physical violence after their relationship had ended.

'Erica, I know you went through a bad time. It wasn't easy for me either. But that's in the past now. You're a grown woman. Can you kindly drop it?'

'Oh, don't take on so, John. I got over you ages ago. I just enjoy sticking the knife in every so often for old times' sake.' He wondered. He very much doubted that she would ever get over it. He often wondered whether he would. 'But there is something you could help me with, just to show we're just good friends,' she continued. He groaned inwardly. He knew what was coming. Her book. Her first book, *England's Victory*, a history of the Napoleonic Wars. To his mind it was bad history and unpublishable, but a good word from him could achieve results. The drawback was that, when it duly failed, it was his judgement that would be questioned. 'Please, John?'

He looked at her. The hard face was gone. She was again a semi-child, pleading for a favour. He thought of the heartache she must have gone through to turn herself into a ruthless hunter, all the rejection that had scarred her heart – his and others. When she looked at him like that he could feel an ache in his heart, and she became almost impossible to refuse.

He sighed.

'I will read through it again,' he said, amazed that he had managed to read it a first time, accompanied as it had been with continual exclamations about the veracity of several of her claims. 'I will make suggestions as to how it should be edited to make it readable – and vaguely conform to the accepted idea of historical fact – and if, and only if you make the required changes, I will put in a word with my publishers.' She squealed, jumped up and charged round to his chair, giving him a kiss and an enthusiastic hug. He managed to extricate himself before she hit her target, his mouth. She looked at him sorrowfully, her hands on his shoulders.

'I could be good for you, John, you know that. We could be the ideal couple. You know I –'

'Not interrupting anything, am I?' a voice came from the door. Haskins could have sworn. It was Rose, up unaccountably early, and she had obviously seen some of what had gone on. Erica returned to her seat, all smiles.

'Not at all,' she said. 'John has agreed to review my book and advise changes.'

'Oh, good,' Rose said, walking stiffly towards them, and sitting in the chair next to Haskins, away from Erica. 'John is full of surprises, isn't he? For such an upright and proper man.'

'Oh, I don't know, you just have to know how to handle him.' Haskins felt like he was a piece of cod being haggled over by two fishwives.

'I hear he was the perfect gentleman last night,' Erica continued with relish. Rose looked at her, and then at Haskins.

'Next time you may loosen my clothing,' she said, adding ominously, 'if there ever is a next time.'

'A bit stiff, then, eh?' asked Erica, and laughed uproariously. 'Course I never fell asleep on him. Not while I was dressed, anyway.' Both Haskins and Rose were ready with retorts when the door opened and Mrs Murgle entered. Haskins breathed out slowly. He was uncomfortably aware that his face was going red. He always found this easy "modern talk" embarrassing. Some things were best kept in private.

'Your breakfast, sir. And some toast and fresh coffee. Would you be wanting breakfast, Miss?' Rose looked at the plate in front of Haskins, three fresh eggs, crisp slices of bacon, sausages, tomatoes, mushrooms, a sprinkling of cheese.

'Yes, please. And while you're making it I'll share.' She picked up a fork and speared a mushroom from Haskins' plate. Mrs Murgle gave a frown of disapproval. Haskins looked at her and rolled his eyes. She chuckled suddenly.

'Very well, then, another full breakfast.' She left the room with an almost sprightly step. Erica sighed and lit a cigarette.

'This world is most unfair, you know. Here we are, two young women fighting over John, and he even has Mrs Murgle dancing attendance. We women have a bad deal.'

'I am not fighting over him,' Rose replied evenly. That could mean any number of things, Haskins thought, one of which being that she had already fought and won. He decided that the better part of valour was breakfast and tucked in.

'Butter me some toast,' he said to Rose, pointing his knife at the toast rack. She glared at him. He winked back, and she smiled suddenly, scooping up a slice of toast and proceeding to butter it generously. Erica stood up, a cynical look in her eye.

'Well, I'm off for a walk. But I warn you,' she said, looking at Rose, 'bad things come to those who get involved with him. I know. I understand him better than you do.' With a curt nod to indicate the truth of this she left the dining room.

'Sleep okay, darling?' Rose asked, putting the slice of toast on his plate, wiping her fingers clean and carefully smoothing his hair into position.

"Darling?" he thought. When did we reach the "darling" stage? This was only the fourth or fifth time they had met. He wasn't used to things developing at such a swift pace.

'I'm sorry I fell asleep on you. I promise it won't happen again.' She speared another mushroom and sucked it suggestively. For him, anyway. "It won't happen again" was also available to several interpretations.

'Mmmm,' he said, filling his mouth with egg and bacon. He hoped the "Mmmm" was sufficient for all possible interpretations. Such as the breakfast was gorgeous, thank you very much. He realised that she had her hand on his shoulder. Fortunately Mrs Murgle appeared, and she resumed a pose of more propriety.

'There you are, Miss,' she said, laying a full plate in front of Rose. 'Nice to see a healthy appetite, I say. Most times the young women who stay overnight are all peaked like. Can hardly handle a morsel.'

'I'm famished,' Rose said. She gave Mrs Murgle the full, grateful smile. Haskins, not for the first time, began to analyse male-female social relations much like he would the battle of Waterloo. Rose was sending the equivalent of a diplomatic request to Mrs Murgle to join her side. Unfortunately, in this scenario, he was Belgium.

'Aye, as I say, the waifs that I normally see, you'd think that their mothers would have fed them more. But it's the fashion, or so I'm told. London! Pah! What they want is good country living and a bit of a roll in the hay. If you don't mind me saying so, of course.'

Haskins paused, his fork halfway to his mouth. Mrs Murgle's moral outrage seemed rather flexible according to context.

'I fully agree, Mrs Murgle,' said Rose. 'You wouldn't happen to know of any haystacks nearby?' Mrs Murgle chortled and waved a hand at her.

'Now then, be away with yourself. You enjoy your breakfast and a good walk. Meantime, I have to be on with work. Miss Georgina will want waking soon no doubt.' A serious look came into her face. 'Young Emily's gone missing, some fellow, no doubt. Very unusual, she's always been most faithful to Miss Georgina. No good will come of it, mind, her being a what she is. Not that she's bad or anything, but they're different over there, those Americans. Anyway, times must.' She left them, full of busyness and energy. Haskins put his fork down. Rose picked it up, speared a segment of egg, and tried to feed him. He held up his hand to indicate that he was full. She ate the egg herself.

'What was that Mrs Murgle said? ' he asked, frowning. There was something in Mrs Murgle words which had raised a thought. It was there, somewhere, waiting for him to catch hold of it. Rose shrugged, not appearing to have noticed anything strange, and concentrated on her food. Haskins kneaded her shoulder absent-mindedly. Like some obscure phrase from a military report which changed the way an historical battle had been fought, Mrs Murgle has said something which changed his view of this house. But he didn't know what it was.

He decided to forget it. What should have been a relaxed weekend was turning out to be somewhat more complicated. Rose appeared to have fallen for him in a very short space of time. Not that he objected, but women, like Erica, seemed to demand some sort of ownership when that happened. Like Georgina. Like all of them. Even Mrs Murgle, who, having decided that he was a man for a full breakfast, would refuse to understand if he decided to have only coffee.

'I feel absolutely dreadful,' a weak voice came from the door. A pale apparition gradually resolved itself as Henderby as he moved slowly and cautiously, and sat, weakly, opposite them. Rose grinned.

'One or two too many then?' she asked.

He looked at her, and then at Haskins.

'I suppose you know. I caught a glimpse of you going past. Couldn't see anything else. That woman is an Amazon.' He groaned and lay his head in his hands. Rose poured a cup of coffee and placed it in front of him. Haskins put an arm around her to indicate his ownership above her concern. She squeezed his hand to show acceptance. Henderby groaned again and sipped the coffee. 'I shall have to marry her, you know. Can't do that sort of thing and not marry a girl, can you?' The coffee seemed to have revived him slightly. 'Could have sworn you were carrying something,' he said to Haskins, 'something heavy. Must admit, it's all a little of a blur. Damn woman must have put something in my drink.' Rose looked at Haskins in surprise.

'What on earth were you carrying when –' She paused, realising where the conversation was going. 'When you were supposed to be fast asleep?' she ended lamely.

'Our Professor doesn't sleep,' Henderby said, taking a deep draught of the coffee. 'He studies us. Like organisms. You think he's sleeping, but he is actually prowling around, doing god knows what. With god knows whom.'

'What on earth do you mean?' asked Rose angrily, looking at Henderby and then at Haskins. 'John, you weren't ... not with that woman?' Haskins leaned over and whispered in her ear. She looked at him, startled at first and then at Henderby, laughing outright. 'Oh, Peter! You didn't! Not with Erica!' He looked suitably abashed, yet smiled, possibly still drunk, or not yet recovered.

'Have to do the right thing by the woman,' he mumbled sheepishly.

'Peter, really, she had you. She set out to have you, you avoided her as best you can, and she had you. It's hardly your fault.'

'She's only a woman,' he said apologetically. 'My fault for being so attractive to the damned things.'

'Well, you carry on feeling sorry for yourself. I dare say it will pass.' She pushed her plate away and stood up. 'In the meantime, John and I are going to look for a haystack.'

'A haystack?'

'They're supposed to have loads of them around this time of year, but we haven't seen any. We are going to investigate this phenomenon. And have a good walk.'

'Ah, I see,' Henderby nodded slowly, as if afraid for his head.

Haskins was glad he could see. All, he, Haskins, could see was a great deal of trouble ahead. He had heard of the New Woman before. All it meant was New Trouble. He wondered whether he could find an excuse to leave. Suddenly. Urgently. Now.

It was a wry thought, the sort he used as a defence mechanism. It was also the last wry thought he would have for a while. For it was then that they heard Mrs Murgle scream.

Chapter 3: The Scream

They were driving along the side of a hill, fields falling to their right, slow-rising to the left. In the distance the sea could be seen, or at least imagined, in the blueish haze. They had stopped at the previous village for petrol and a break, hopefully for tea. There was no petrol, and no tea. Both petrol station and tea-room had closed during the war, and had yet to reopen, if they ever did.

'Where were you between the hours of eight p.m. and three a.m. on the Friday?' she asked.

'Friday? If I recall correctly we were together in Southampton for the day.'

'No, silly. I was thinking of the police – our friend Inspector Rudman.'

'Dear old Rudman. He should look like a bloodhound, he acts like one. All part of the act, I suppose.'

They contemplated the idea for a while. Then she shuddered at a memory, and drew her coat tighter around her.

'If it hadn't been for the war I don't think I would ever have got over the sight that morning,' she said.

'Yes. Ironic that. At the time I thought it was the worst thing I had ever seen since the trenches. Worse, really, because the trenches were impersonal.'

'You know – you know how they were lying there – well –' she struggled to find words.

'Yes, I know.'

She looked at him.

'Darling ... There's something I saw that night. Or I thought I saw. I was a little preoccupied at the time. And maybe I'd had a few drinks too many. I didn't think so at the time. But you don't do you?'

That's Mrs Murgle,' Haskins said. A loud scream came down from the first floor, and carried on, and on, monotonously unwavering yet piercing and blood curdling.

'Whoever it is, kindly ask them to stop,' Henderby pleaded, head in hands.

'Probably found a mouse,' Rose suggested.

'One hell of a mouse for her to make that noise,' Haskins commented, and set off towards the door, Rose following. As they got to the foot of the stairs Erica came racing in from outside.

'What the hell is happening?' she asked a little breathlessly. Mrs Murgle continued screaming.

'That's what we're about to find out,' Haskins replied, mounting the stairs two steps at a time. Rose and Erica followed. They raced into the corridor. Mrs Murgle was standing half-way inside the doorway to Georgina's bedroom at the end of the corridor. Doors were opening. Morely appeared in a deep red and blue dressing gown demanding to know who had woken him up.

'What's the matter?' asked Haskins as they reached Mrs Murgle. She had her face in her hands, terrified eyes wide, still screaming, white as a sheet.

'Mrs Murgle?' asked Rose. Haskins pushed past Mrs Murgle. He stopped.

'Dear sweet Jesus,' he said to himself.

'What is it, John?' asked Rose, coming next to him. Erica joined at his other side. Both their faces blanched, and Erica almost collapsed. Rose looked as if she were about to be sick.

'Take Mrs Murgle downstairs and give her some brandy,' he ordered, pushing them out of the room along with Mrs Murgle. 'Go on.' Rose looked at him as he took the key from the inside of the door and closed it, locking it. 'Go on. I'll phone the police.'

'It's not a – some sort of – sick joke?' asked Erica.

'No. Now get on.' Rose saw the serious set of his face, and put her arm around Mrs Murgle, Erica taking the other arm.

'Come on, Mrs Murgle. Let's get you back to the kitchen,' Rose said gently. Mrs Murgle was now whimpering, the screams having stopped once she could no longer see what had caused it. Tears streaming down her face as she stumbled along the corridor, the other two

38

women supporting her.

'What the devil's going on?' demanded Morely, blocking Haskins' path.

'You'll find out in due course. I suggest you get dressed.' Morely stood quickly aside as it was obvious Haskins was in no mood to stop. Down in the entrance hall he dialed the local exchange and asked for the police. A sergeant answered after two rings.

'My name is Professor Haskins, I'm staying at the Longwood house. There has been – I believe a crime has been committed. I think you will need to get someone here straight away. Quite a few people. Including a doctor.' He listened to the reply. 'Yes,' he said finally, 'it is serious, very serious.'

He put the phone down and went to the kitchen. Mrs Murgle was seated at the table, Rose and Erica on either side. Each had a glass of brown liquid in front of them. A bottle of brandy had been newly opened. Rose looked up at Haskins silently as he entered; Mrs Murgle was stifling low sobs, and Erica had an arm around her. Haskins picked up a glass from the sideboard and poured from the bottle on the table. He sat down. None of them said anything for a while.

'The police?' asked Rose finally. He nodded.

'Should be here any minute.'

They sat in silence until a loud knock at the front door announced the arrival of someone official.

'I'll get it,' Haskins said, putting down his glass. He opened the front door to find a middle-aged police sergeant and young constable.

'Professor Haskins?' Haskins nodded.

'This way.' He led them up the stairs and to Georgina's bedroom. 'The bathroom's over there,' he said, nodding with his head to indicate the direction as he unlocked the bedroom door.

'Bathroom?' asked the sergeant in puzzlement. Haskins opened the door.

'Oh Christ Almighty!' swore the young constable in a shocked voice. The sergeant took a sudden breath.

Georgina's maid Emily lay spread-eagled on the bed, nightdress half ripped from her body, lifeless eyes staring at the ceiling. The white bedclothes were drenched in blood, looking as if red were their normal colour and the white at the sides an intruder. On the floor in front of the bed Georgina was hunched face down in a foetal position, face against her chest, a knife slit along her throat, her nightdress and the white rug matching the bedclothes in blood. The young constable made a choking sound and rushed to the bathroom.

'Dead?' asked the sergeant.

'Looks that way. I haven't gone further in than this.' The sergeant carefully stepped over to Georgina and felt for a pulse. After a few seconds he shook his head and tried with Emily, averting his gaze from her body. Once again he shook his head and came back to the door. Haskins handed him the key.

'I'll have to make a phone call, sir. And I'd appreciate it if you could tell anyone else here not to think of leaving. Downstairs?'

'Yes. You can use the lounge. Or dining-room. Or wherever.'

He felt desperately like following the constable's example. Earlier he had thought the house and grounds were like the Garden of Eden. What he had seen was a sick and gross vision of a charnel house.

He went back down to the kitchen. It was in the hands of the police now.

Chapter 4: The Morning

She stretched in the seat beside him. He gave her an anxious look. He knew she did not like being cooped up in a car for too long.

'You alright, darling?'

She smiled.

'Yes, fine. Just a little stiff. I was trying to remember. Peter was the muse of comedy, wasn't he? That seemed an easy choice, with his eternal smile.'

'Thalia, yes, it seemed appropriate at the time.'

'Rob was a little offended. No specific muse for artists.'

'Yes, I've always wondered about that. Ancient Greek history isn't my main subject.'

'So you suggested he have as his muse – it sounded like an error.'

'Erato. Muse of love poems and mimicry.' She laughed.

'Good thing you didn't say that loud enough for him to hear, he would have mean most offended.'

They continued in silence. Then she decided to tell him.

'I told you that there was something that I saw – think I saw that night. I haven't mentioned it to anyone because I wasn't sure the next morning whether I'd imagined or not.'

'Go on.'

'It was about ten , maybe ten-thirty,' she said. 'I had to go to the loo, and on my way back I noticed two people close to the kitchen – it looked like they were kissing, quite passionately. I could see from the back that one was Frieda, and I wondered who the other was.'

'And? Who was it? Nigel?'

'No, that was the strange thing. If it were Nigel I would have seen him, he was quite a bit taller than Frieda. I was going to nip past quickly before they saw me, but then they stopped kissing and the other said something to Frieda, something in German. I was so shocked I stayed back in the shadows while they went back into the lounge.'

'So who was it?'

'Georgina.'

'Georgina? Are you sure they were kissing?'

'Well, no. At first that's what I thought it was. Then I realised one of them was probably whispering into the other's ear – they were half in shadow, it was difficult to see properly. But why do that? It wasn't as if there was anyone near to hear them – and what was so secret it had to be whispered?'

'There was a lot of whispering that evening,' Haskins said. 'Up until then I hadn't realised how really nasty Georgina could be. She was deliberately setting everyone against each other. She certainly told me what she thought of everyone else. No doubt she passed on some remarks about myself.'

She chuckled.

'I can't remember. I had other things on my mind at the time. But Frieda – if Georgina was trying some form of social power-play, how could Frieda help?'

'I've often wondered about Frieda. I don't think she was quite what she seemed to be. I've always felt that she was a lot older than the eighteen she claimed.'

'A spy? A German spy?'

'It's possible. A number of Americans were pro-Nazi. Possibly Georgina was one of them.'

'And you think Frieda could have killed Emily and tried to kill Georgina – because Frieda was a German spy? Emily found out? And Frieda couldn't risk Georgina telling the truth to the police?'

He knew his suggestion did not fully add up. The only support it had was that one of their group had almost definitely committed the murder – and Frieda had been one of them.

'No – well, not necessarily. I'm just suggesting a hypothesis to explain why they were whispering to each other,' he said.

'Didn't do Frieda much good though, did it? If that was the case.'

The morning was a blur for most of them. The initial shock of learning of the what had happened had increased when the doctor arrived, and rushed out of the bedroom after a minute, demanding an ambulance. Georgina, it seemed was still alive, but only by a thread. Falling forward in the foetal position, head pushed against her chest, had staunched just sufficient blood to keep her barely breathing.

This was followed by the arrival of Detective Inspector Rudman, a morose individual whose gaze seemed to suggest that he knew each one of them was guilty, if not of the murder, of something, which he would find out. Haskins recognised it as the approach of a professional. He very much doubted if Rudman was as morose as he made out.

The morning passed with each being invited into the dining room to give their personal statement of where they had been and what they had done over the previous twenty four hours. The probability, it appeared, was that whoever had murdered Emily and tried to murder Georgina had done it sometime between eleven in the evening and four in the morning. Most claimed to have little recollection of where they were during those hours. For most, it was apparent, this was true. But who was telling the truth, and who lying, was impossible to say. There was little social conversation as they sat in the lounge, either awaiting their turn, or having already been grilled, as Johnson put it, by the police.

Lunch, such as it was, was a miserable affair. Indeed, with Mrs Murgle in bed, sedated, there would have been none had it not been for Morely's grumbling, and the decision of Rose and Erica to throw something together in an attempt to restore some form of order. After lunch most went for a walk, in pairs, in different directions. There was a wind coming off the sea, a chill rather than cool breeze and Haskins chose a walk towards the beach. He found himself joined by Rose just outside the door, and he had a suspicion that Erica had been planning the same thing, only just being beaten to the point by Rose. At any other time he would have found the situation amusing, possibly even a boost to his ego, but not under those conditions.

'People don't seem very sociable today,' Rose noted with a touch of sarcasm.

'They're probably wondering who the murderer is, and hope they aren't walking with him or her right at this very moment.'

'Ah, but at least you know it wasn't me.'

'Not? How do I know you weren't faking it, and jumped up the minute I left you?'

'You surely don't believe that?'

'No, but it's what everyone will be thinking. Morely claims to have woken up, picked up Jessica, and stumbled off to bed around about three a.m. What I find difficult to believe is the bit about picking Jessica up. I think he would have left her lying there.'

'You don't like my brother, do you? And how do you know that's what he said?'

'I think you can guess what I think of him. I'm always amazed when I remember you're supposedly his elder sister. I think something must have been mixed up at the hospital when he was born.'

'You can be really beastly at times, you know.' She sighed, and added, 'Even if what you say is true.' She gave him a sideways look. 'Anyway, you haven't answered my question.'

'Inspector Rudman mentioned it. I think he regards me as an ally. Or possibly because I'm the only one who can remember approximately what he was doing last night. Or possibly it's some kind of double bluff. I think Rudman has a rather devious mind. Shall we sit down here?' They had reached an enclosed section of beach where the wind did not reach.

'You and Erica – you're the only ones who weren't absolutely pickled.'

'I think Erica was pretty far gone herself,' he said, sitting down. Otherwise she wouldn't have been so flagrant in her behaviour with Henderby, he thought to himself, she's not really that sort of woman. Rose looked at him sternly and sat down next to him.

'I hope you gave Inspector Rudman a decent version of what I did last night.'

'Of course. I was the soul of discretion. After all, you didn't do anything last night.'

'Apart from get stonking drunk and falling asleep in your arms. I doubt whether country policeman think very much of women who do that sort of thing.'

Haskins smiled. He debated whether to assure her that he had no objections to her getting tipsy and falling in his arms, but the falling asleep part of it was what he had a problem with. He decided it might not be a good idea.

'Rudman is hardly a country policeman, Rose. His patch – as they call it – is Portsmouth and surrounding areas. He comes across as being pretty competent. Devious, but competent.'

They sat in silence for a while in the sunshine. It was warm out of the wind.

'What sort of person would do that – to Georgina and Emily?' Rose asked.

'It's amazing what humans are capable of doing, given the right stimulus. Or, in this context, motive.'

'But that's just it. None of us have a motive.'

'We all do.'

'Oh? Such as?'

'Well, there's that good old and ancient motive, commonly referred to as Mammon.'

'But Georgina didn't have any money here, not enough to warrant that sort of thing.'

'But she did have a tiara, worth, I would say, several thousand. One that appears to have gone missing.'

'How did you – oh, let me guess, Detective Inspector Rudman.'

'Yes. I mentioned the tiara. He appeared to be surprised that no-one else had. But I don't think he was. People can fail to mention something purely because they've forgotten about it just as much because they don't want to highlight it. In your case, for example, I think you've put it out of mind because mentally, at this moment, it's beyond reach. Or perhaps because you have no wish to own a tiara.'

'Oh, you've been discussing my state of mind with the Inspector then?' she asked angrily.

'Of course not. I was just saying that to you.'

It was a message, she decided. He was telling her he was comfortable enough alone with her to discuss such things.

Otherwise he was being an arrogant and pompous ...

'Well, Erica and Peter are in the clear,' she said, suddenly chuckling. 'Though I'd imagine Peter wasn't too happy giving his statement.'

'Well, I agree with the second bit, but I doubt that the first is necessarily true. They could have been in it together. The scene in the lounge, and at breakfast this morning – well, they could have staged those. It does seem peculiar that Peter was up so early, after such a heavy night, and with a heavy hangover.'

'Peter's always up early. It's something of a thing with him. Fit young tennis coach can take heavy partying. That sort of thing. Anyway, I don't believe it.' She paused and looked at him. 'Can I ask you something personal? Very personal, I mean.'

'Go ahead.'

It took Rose a few seconds to find the right words.

'Do you still – I mean, Erica, you had a thing going with her at one time didn't you?'

'You mean, do I wish we still had?'

'Something like that, I suppose.'

He thought for a while.

'I'm never really sure,' he said finally.

Rose dribbled some sand through her fingers, and then looked up, out to sea.

'So who are we left with then? Nigel?' she asked, changing the subject.

'Johnson? Yes. Self-confessed socialist and down on his luck like most here. Stealing a tiara probably qualifies as winning a battle in the class war.'

'And murder?'

'The murder could have been an accident. The person or persons slip into Georgina's room thinking she's in a drunken sleep. They

46

discover instead that Emily is there, panic, and kill her. Georgina wakes up and they try to – indeed, believe they do – kill her.'

'So why was Georgina's nightdress so badly ripped?'

'Any number of reasons. The most obvious being that there was a struggle. Or it was done deliberately, afterwards, as a smoke screen. Then there's the other possibility.' He looked uncomfortable.

'Which is?'

'Emily was an attractive looking young woman in her own way,' he said carefully. 'Some people have very strange ideas about that sort of thing – forbidden fruit, that sort of thing. Someone capable of doing what they did last night – well, they'd be capable of a number of other things.'

'Rape, in other words. And Nigel had already made a pass at her.'

'It's a possibility.' He looked at his watch. 'I suppose we'd better be getting back.'

'I suppose we had,' she said reluctantly, and they began a slow walk back. 'What about you,' she continued, 'you don't have a motive – you have plenty of money yourself.'

'Well, I wouldn't call it plenty – sufficient, maybe. As for motive, Georgina was going to publicly denounce me once she had evidence to prove my theories about General Grant were incorrect. Very bad thing for an academic in my position.'

'Were you worried?'

'No, of course not. Mine is an academic audience. Georgina writes flamboyant romances set in the American civil war – an attempt to rewrite history, really. I doubt whether many of my readers have even heard the name Georgina Riley.'

'Still, there's one person who couldn't have done it – not in terms of motive, anyway.'

'And who would that be?'

'Frieda, our young Jewish friend. She won't be going to America anytime soon. God knows what she is going to do.'

'God knows,' he agreed. 'But that doesn't mean she didn't do it. Maybe Emily caught her doing something in the bedroom – hoping to steal the tiara, perhaps – Frieda kills her, Georgina walks in and she has to be silenced too.' Rose looked at him.

'I bet you could find a scenario for anyone.'

'I'm afraid that's the way it is at the moment – certainly the way Rudman will see things.' He had carefully kept away from mentioning the possibility that the attack had been a drunken and brutal reaction to Georgina's caustic commentaries on the others – which would mean that Rose and Erica would both have had cause.

'Still, we will find out when Georgina recovers,' Rose commented.

But Georgina would not be recovering for many months.

Chapter 5: Theories

It was their one concern about taking country roads; stuck behind a harvester in a narrow lane. But it was to be expected during harvest time, and neither was in any particular hurry to get to their destination.

'I wonder if any of the others have seen her since – since then.' She didn't want to say "since the accident", or any similar, silly phrase. It hadn't been an accident.

'I don't know. I wouldn't be surprised if they hadn't. After all, she was in a coma for a month.'

'And then couldn't remember any of what had happened.'

'Not surprising, really.'

'Do you think she's remembered now? And that's why she's invited us back to Longwood?'

'I rather doubt it. I have a feeling that this might be an uncomfortable weekend. I rather suspect the main item on the menu will be revenge.'

'Revenge? Against all of us?'

'If she doesn't know who the killer was, then, yes. Being murdered can leave a person quite bitter. And it was the cause of her wedding falling through.'

'And that's why we're staying at the village pub rather than Longwood,' she noted, 'not out of, as someone sitting close by claimed, thoughtfulness for her health, not wanting to overburden her, but because things might turn nasty.'

'A situation can be interpreted in several different ways depending on context,' he replied primly.

'Especially in light of your decision to bring along your service revolver. I knew that couldn't have anything to do with her health.'

'That's the thing. What if she's right?' he asked, wondering. 'If so we may well be in the company of a murderer. Or murderess. Or both.'

She shivered at the thought, but made no reply. After all they had been through, the times she had thought they would never be together as they were now, it seemed almost unfair having to face yet another danger.

Haskins and Rose returned to the house to find it in an uproar. Inspector Rudman had taken the decision to have the entire house and gardens searched while the occupants were out, without their knowledge. Morely declared it an outrage, several times. Jessica followed him around wordlessly, emotionlessly. Johnson was furiously denouncing the capitalist lackeys of the state, and, for some reason known only to him, announced that he would be writing to his member of parliament. Frieda sat on a couch in the lounge, hugging her knees to her chest, looking into space. Erica and Henderby sat sharing a bottle of wine, enjoying Morely's display. The idea of a search did not appear to worry them, though Haskins noted a searching look in her eyes as she saw he and Rose entering the lounge through the French windows. The look was quickly gone, to be replaced by one of unconcern.

'Puts me in mind of the story of a chap who wakes up in the night to find a burglar in the house,' she said to Henderby. 'He asks him what he's doing, and the burglar tells him he's looking for money. "Tell you what," says the chap, "I'll give you a hand and if we find any we'll share it evens"'. Henderby laughed. The wine appeared to have removed all traces of hangover.

'That's what it was. A burglar,' Frieda said suddenly and quietly. The others looked at her. She was still staring into space.

'Unlikely, I would say,' Erica said gently. 'At least the police don't seem to think so.'

'The police?' Frieda did not appear to think much of the police. 'I do not like the police.'

'I think we all think the same,' Henderby said. 'Otherwise why have we all being going around in pairs trying to avoid the others?'

'I have not been going around in – in pairs,' Frieda stated. Haskins noted that this was true. She had gone on one of her long walks in the direction of Portsmouth. It could be termed strange behaviour if she thought there was a murderous burglar in the neighbourhood. But most of Frieda's behaviour could be termed strange. Maybe it would have been thought normal in Germany, but he doubted it. He suspected that Frieda craved open spaces. He knew she hated being in a room with the doors and windows closed.

'Do you think they will find it? The tiara, I mean?' asked Rose of Haskins. The others looked at him, realising that he was, in a way, now leader of the group.

'Possibly. I doubt whether it will prove anything if they do. Not initially. Say they find it in Erica's room; she will claim she never put it there.'

'I most certainly would,' Erica said, as if shocked at the idea.

'The same goes for all of us. And it could well be true. If the murderer did take it – that's presuming Emily didn't put it somewhere hidden away, and it hasn't been found – then it's unlikely they would be silly enough to leave it somewhere where it might cast suspicion on them if discovered.'

'You're presuming that it was a well thought out crime,' pointed out Rose. 'What if it was something done on the spot – the opportunity came up, things went wrong, as you suggested earlier.'

'Sounds like we've all been playing detective,' Erica noted.

'To be expected,' Haskins said. He turned to Rose. 'I take your point, and, yes, that might be the case, but even so I can't see any of us being stupid enough to think we could hide the thing in our rooms. If the motive was money then the person in question is bound to have thought about where to hide the tiara. After all, if it was only a question of the tiara going missing, the house would have been searched anyway.'

'But what if the – whoever it was – was drunk,' Rose persisted. 'After all, most of us were.'

'That is something that has been worrying me, and, I suspect, Rudman. Remember the blood in the room? Whoever did it must have been drenched in the stuff. If they were drunk, they weren't drunk enough to leave any incriminating evidence – hand prints on the walls or such.'

Rose and Erica shuddered at the memory, and the image of the walls covered with finger and palm prints..

'You said, "if the motive was money" – well, what else could it have been?' Erica asked. For all the bluntness she had developed she still had little imagination about the seamier side of life. There was an embarrassed pause.

'Um,' Rose started tentatively, 'maybe someone had pursued Emily a little further than they should have, Georgina walks in, the person panics, kills Georgina – or thinks he has – and then kills Emily to keep her quiet.'

'And we all know who that would be,' Henderby said thoughtfully.

'Speculation,' Haskins said. 'It could turn out that it was from someone outside, though personally I doubt it. I'll see if I can have a word with Inspector Rudman tomorrow.'

'I have to leave tomorrow afternoon,' Rose said sadly. 'Back to the weekly grind on Tuesday morning.'

'If the Inspector lets you go,' Erica pointed out.

'I hope he doesn't, in a way.' They exchanged understanding glances which puzzled Haskins. Under the circumstances he would have expected a certain enmity, but there had been hardly any of that between the two.

'Anyone heard any news of Georgina?' he asked.

'Apparently she's still unconscious but stable, whatever that means,' Erica said. 'If she recovers consciousness tomorrow she should be able to tell the police exactly what happened. In the meantime – what say we rustle up some dinner. We could all do with something to eat and an early night.'

'Behind locked doors,' agreed Henderby, looking nervously sideways at Erica. She turned and gave him a suggestive look, raising her eyebrows coyly.

'Some people just don't know when they're well off,' she said.

Haskins suspected she wasn't addressing the remark to Henderby.

It was a new feeling. Never before had he felt himself pursued by two women at the same time.

Chapter 6: The Muses

'This journey could have taken us half an hour, an hour, maximum,' he mused.

'Well, it's taken us seven years, darling. A little more time is hardly likely to hurt.'

'True enough.'

'What was Jessica? Which one of the muses?'

He thought for a while.

'Urania, if I recall correctly. Astronomy, astrology and prophecy.'

'That's it. If anyone looked like they might suddenly come out with dire predictions it was her. Like – oh, who was it, Agamemnon's slave?'

'Cassandra. Good analogy, she seemed a bit like a slave to Rob. Though actually I thought Urania was more apt because her mind seemed in outer space the whole weekend.'

'Darling, really!' She giggled.

'It was interesting that they never found the tiara,' he said thoughtfully.

'Pity. It was such a beautiful thing. Not that I'd want one, but it was pretty.'

'Yes. Yes it was. But I was thinking more on the significance. Was it still in the house? Had someone concealed it so adroitly that no search uncovered it? Or did they spirit it out somehow, and then sell it, broken up diamond by diamond? Or was it really a burglar in the end?'

'Maybe it's still there today. After all, Georgina was in a coma, and when she was pretty much recovered – as much as she could be – the army had taken over most of the house. She lived in a couple of rooms for the war. Now that they've left ...'

'That's an interesting thought,' he said. 'After all, she did buy the place in – when was it, '43?. You'd have thought she would have wanted to distance herself from it, rather than actually buying it.'

She smiled at him. He could be infuriatingly pedantic, but he never failed to acknowledge another person's ideas, even if from a woman.

To him, the idea was the thing. To others, as she knew from experience, the source was more important than the idea, and women were the lowest source available.

'So maybe she's found the tiara – and the police have found some fingerprints on it. '

'We're speculating again.'

'We did a lot of that over that weekend.'

'Yes. I can't say that those days were the best days of my life. Probably the worst. At the time, anyway.'

She squeezed his arm gently.

'Nothing. Not so much of a hint of a sparkle.' Rudman said with disgust.

'So it could have been a burglar?' Haskins asked. They were alone in the dining room. It was Monday afternoon. Everybody else was either packing before leaving, or had already left.

'That is a possibility, but not a very likely one.' Rudman frowned. 'I might be based in Portsmouth, but I know this area. I know Sergeant Finchley, the sergeant who answered your call. He's a local, knows this place inside out. Longwood House is isolated to a certain extent, which also means people can't approach it without been seen. And Finchley reckons no locals were spotted wandering around here, nor any strangers. Most people are too worried about the likelihood of war to be floating around these parts. Going north, going to Canada – anywhere but the South-East of England.'

'No murder weapon?'

'One of the constables found a knife in a clump of bushes a distance from the house that could have been involved – could have been thrown from an upper window – but it turns out the blade is too short to have been used in the murder – some type of pruning knife that someone must have lost. Mrs Murgle vaguely recalls the gardener complaining about one going missing.' Rudman screwed up his face as though he didn't believe it. 'Strange it hasn't any finger prints on it, though. Almost as if it had been wiped clean.'

'A gardener would wear gloves, wouldn't he?'

'I suppose so.' Rudman, Haskins thought, was a little too desperate for evidence to allow even the least hopeful item to escape.

'And you've eliminated the neighbours, as it were?' he asked.

'Both couples walked home together, each gives an alibi for the other spouse. I can't see either couple being such good actors that they could do what was done without giving the game away. And retired couples aren't normally the types to do what was done here.'

'So your gut-feeling is that it was one of us.'

'As is yours, I reckon.'

Haskins looked him in the eyes.

'Why is it that you don't suspect me?' he asked.

Rudman returned the look.

'What makes you think I don't?' he returned the question.

Good point, thought Haskins.

'I have never seen anything like this since the war,' Rudman continued, looking at the ceiling. 'No, not even then. This was personal. Brutal. Deliberate.' Haskins nodded agreement. Rudman caught the nod and asked, 'Were you in the war? You seem a bit young.'

'Last few months,' Haskins said. 'Infantry. By that time they would take in anything out of nappies, no questions asked.' Rudman nodded slowly in understanding.

'We're going to seal this place up tight,' he said, looking at the table-top in front of him, as if he were thinking aloud. 'I've arranged for a forensic team to come down from London, they'll be here midweek – latest technology, that sort of thing.' He paused, and then looked Haskins in the eyes. 'I want to get the bastard who did this,' he said. 'Normally I would say "no matter how long it takes", but that might mean a little longer in this case.'

'How do you mean?'

'If there is a war – and I believe there will be – we'll lose a lot of men. To the army, I mean. I know, it's supposed to be a restricted occupation, the police force, but some will volunteer, others – well, we'll have to do all sorts of things we wouldn't normally be responsible for. The strange murder of a coloured maid of an American will take second place.'

'What makes you think there will be a war?'

'You're a historian, Professor. Hitler's a dictator. Dictators have to keep moving by conquest.'

'True. But personally I think he will suffer the fate of dictators – he will be ousted, in this case by his generals.'

Rudman gave him a cynical look.

'Not if they start winning,' he said.

'The Maginot Line will stop them. We have the time.'

'Professor, I'm a copper, and, I reckon, a good one. When people repeat time after time that something is true I begin to have doubts. And there's been too much talk of the Maginot Line. I don't trust it. I don't know why, but it sounds like people are repeating things, hoping that repetition will make them come true. Fooling themselves, in fact.'

'And what have people been repeating about the murder?'

Rudman stroked his jaw.

'That it was a burglary gone wrong, an outside job, impossible that anyone here could have done it.'

'Yet you're letting us all leave?'

'Apart from the Jew. She hasn't anywhere else to go to. Poor b – thing. I've got all your addresses, we can pick you up when we need. Anyway,' he smiled at Haskins grimly, 'you lot keep on getting under our feet. We've got all the information we need, it's just a case of putting it in the right order.'

'But no fingerprints.'

'No fingerprints, no. None unexpected, at any road, so far.'

Haskins nodded slowly.

'Well, I suppose I'd better be off. I do have a great deal of work to do for my students.' He stood up and Rudman followed suit. They shook hands. 'Good luck, Inspector. Any chance of keeping me up to date with any news?'

'I dare say I might need to consult your memory from time to time.'

'Thank you, Inspector.' He left the room, confident that Rudman would at least be in touch occasionally. Outside the dining room Sergeant Finchley stopped him.

'Professor? I was asked to give you this.' He took the envelope. It was addressed "To Dear John". He opened it as the sergeant slipped politely away.

"My darling John

I couldn't face a goodbye scene. It was fun while it lasted, but, let's face it, I'm hardly your type of woman. You either need the staid, boring type who will make you a good wife, or someone like Erica, who adores you and will make life hell until you make a decent woman of her. My advice is, go with Erica. Peter means nothing to her. She was just trying to make you jealous.

I can't see that we'll meet again. You're a successful professor and writer – and ever so morally upright. I'm just a shop-girl with the morals of a – well, I can't write such words down, now can I?. And I do think that there will be a war, despite what you think, what you hope for. I hope that it will give me the opportunity I spoke about. Maybe we'll meet again when I'm rich and your equal – well, sort of, I can't see my wealth, if it happens, coming from honest toil. I'm sure you'll despise me. But I can't help myself; I want to have fun in this life while it lasts. It would have been nice if you had been part of it.

Look after Erica. She's really soft at heart. And she'll look after you.

Love

Rose"

He read it twice, slowly, in the corridor. Finally he folded it carefully, and put it in his jacket pocket.

'Bad news?' He looked up to see Erica standing in front of him, suitcases ready. There was a mocking look in her eyes. 'I saw her slipping away quietly. I don't think she loves you, you know.'

'Know?' he asked angrily. 'You know nothing.' He saw the look in her eyes. Sudden hurt. A child who had been chastened.

'Please, John. Please? I'm sorry about –' She waved her arm to indicate Henderby, the irrelevance. She put a hand on his arm. He shrugged it off and strode away. Suddenly he stopped and turned around.

'Apparently I'm wrong. Again. Apparently there is going to be a war. In which case, I don't think we will meet again.' He turned and left. She watched him go, angry tears in her eyes.

'Need a hand with these, Miss?' asked a gentle voice next to her. Sergeant Finchley, no doubt unaccustomed to carrying young ladies' suitcases with his rank, had seen a requirement.

'That's very kind of you, sergeant.'

'Reckon as how kindness is going to be in short supply for a while,' he said. 'Constable!' he called one of the men, 'give me a hand with these bags.'

Upstairs Haskins was angrily throwing his things into a suitcase. He was a bachelor, happily so, though the thought had occurred to him recently that maybe it was time to settle down. He found Rose, with her spirited approach to life, extremely attractive, both physically and personally. He could have seen her as a potential settling-down partner.

And then there was Erica.

Had they seen him randomly and furiously filling his suitcase his students would have been amazed; they knew him as precise, analytical and detached. They respected him for that. He applied the same approach to relationships. Every time he had broken up with a woman it was with careful forethought and rationality.

Then the thought struck him. Perhaps, just perhaps, it was because it was not he who had decided on this break.

He resumed his packing with even more viciousness.

Perhaps Erica was the right woman for him after all.

It was hardly likely to matter.

None of them would be meeting again, not now. Even less likely if there was to be a war.

Chapter 7: War

They were on another hill, parked in a lay-bye. She had made sandwiches and two boiled eggs. She had read somewhere that boiled eggs were the least fattening. While that wasn't relevant for herself, she had decided that his diet was her concern. Everything about him was her concern, she had once decided, and she intended to make sure things remained that way.

'The police never found anything, then?' It was, in a way, surprising that they had never held this discussion before. But then, with the war, there had never been time.

'Not enough to arrest anyone,' he replied. 'I remember Rudman predicting that a war would interrupt the investigation. He was certainly right there. The specialist team from London never made it. Kept promising "next week", but "next week" never came.'

'All of us scattered within six months.'

There was Portsmouth, he thought, and there was London. And there were two women who seemed to have been so much part of his life during those years.

The other day she had found him sitting listening to a recording of Vera Lynn's "We'll meet again". He must have been tired, for there were tears in his eyes. She had sat next to him, and they had held each other tightly for some time after the record had ended.

'Everyone was getting out of the South East,' she said, interrupting his thoughts. 'Getting away from London. And Southampton, Portsmouth, Dover. Getting as far away as possible. Those who could afford it. Somehow I just felt I had to stay. Even while we were waiting for the Germans to invade.'

'I thought we would never see each other again, that weekend' he said.

She squeezed his hand, not wanting to linger over the memory.

'We seem to be the lucky ones. From that weekend.'

'Funny word to use when you think of what we've been through – lucky. I doubt whether I would have used it often over the past years.'

'But apt. Now.'

'Apt? Yes. Now. Since we found each other again.'

The Germans invaded Poland the weekend following that of the murder, Friday the 1st of September, 1939. By Sunday lunchtime France and Britain were officially at war with Germany. Polish forces were falling back along the front.

On the Monday Haskins reported to his new unit. He found that sufficient confusion reigned for him to take the rest of the week off to finish off his business at the university. He doubted that there would be a great requirement for history professors until the war ended, and, if the last war was anything to go by, it would go on for years. But this time there would be no jingoistic flag-waving or calls to march on Berlin. In many ways he found it almost impossible to believe that war had been declared.

The Monday after that he began his war duties. A Colonel Martins called him to his office. he was a rather florid, blimp-like man, who had apparently been rescued from a dead-end job as an insurance salesman – a very bad one – to resume his military career.

'I don't want you to get any ideas, Haskins,' he ordered, glaring at him as he sat opposite. 'We aren't cloak and dagger boys. Our job will be more in line with the police, black market stuff, smelling out sabotage if we can, interrogating refugees to make sure none of them are Nazi spies in disguise, that sort of thing. We will be working very close with the police, and I don't want anyone stepping on their toes. Understand?'

'Of course, sir.'

'Sorry to dash any hopes you might have had.'

'I can't say that I did have any hopes. One just has to do what one can.'

Martins' glare turned slowly into a smile.

'Good for you. I was a bit worried, I must admit. Some of the people around here are coming up with some very bizarre ideas. Parachuting into Germany dressed as German officers, without being able to speak as much as two words of the language, would you believe? And that's one of the more sensible suggestions.' He gave Haskins a quizzical look. 'I'm told you're very highly regarded.'

'As a history professor, perhaps. But I can hardly go back in time to spy on Nero or Napoleon.'

'No, that would seem a little tricky.' He studied Haskins for a few moments. 'I'll be honest with you. I don't think anyone really knows what our job is supposed to be. Some idiot decided there was a requirement for an intelligence unit at middle level, so they created our department. Quite simply put we can write our own rules until somebody starts asking questions. By then we have to be in a position where it'll be too difficult to change anything. Understand?'

Haskins nodded. Empire building, he thought. Martins appeared to read his mind.

'No, Haskins, not empire building. I want this unit to have a definite purpose and to do it well. So while we have the chance we identify what we can do well and accept that. Anything else someone else can take on. It's what I call efficiency. Last time there was just too much damned muddle.'

'I see.' It was a new definition of efficiency as far as Haskins could see. But he wondered if there wasn't a good deal of logic in it.

'We have a great number of things to do, and in a very short time. I've no doubt the French will invade Germany in the next few weeks, a month at the most – while Germany are busy with Poland, it would be military lunacy not to grasp such an opportunity. Then we can expect trench warfare, in Germany this time. By the time that happens we need to have identified exactly what part of the war effort we are undertaking. And I want the right staff by then. Don't worry about that from your side, I'm used to the sort of games the army plays as far as that goes.'

He gave Haskins another glare to indicate his disapproval of army tricks. Haskins rather suspected that Martins new every rule in the game book, and how to break them.

'Now, our area is the South-East. What that means is open to interpretation. I want us to do the interpreting. I want you to contact the Chief Constable, or whatever there may be, of every large town or county on the coast between the Thames Estuary and Bournemouth. Further on, if you have the time, which I doubt. Find out what they expect from a unit like ours – remember, black market, refugees, suspected sabotage – and anything else. We will make their requirements our responsibilities. The ones we accept, of course. Can you do that?'

'I'll need a car. A driver. Petrol. All the rest of that sort of stuff.' Martins waved his hand impatiently.

'Speak to McGowan. Used to be my Sergeant-Major in the war. He will organise any requirement you may have. Let me see, you were a subaltern in the war. At the end.'

Haskins was impressed. Obviously the army still held a file on him, somewhere.

'You'll be a major in this unit. I don't like promoting over ranks like that, but a captain probably wouldn't impress the police sufficiently. It will be temporary, you understand.'

'Yes. Of course.' Haskins had hoped to avoid a uniform. Martins granted him his wish.

'No time to have a uniform made up. Get one later, when you have time. Anyway, it's not that type of job. You'll have proper ID. And besides, the police don't like other people in uniforms, they think it's competition. When can you start?'

'Right away. I'll have a word with Sergeant-Major McGowan.'

'Good man. Oh, and Haskins, just one point. Try to remember, when other people are around, to say "sir" every so often, eh? Old habits die hard.'

'Of course, sir.'

He stood up. Martins looked at his desk somewhat dreamily.

'You know what?' He looked up with a grim look on his face. 'I suppose I'll have to get used to saying "the last war" when I mean 14-18. Do you think this one will turn into another world war?'

'I doubt it. The Russians will steer well clear – Stalin's no fool. The Americans definitely have no interest in getting involved in another European conflict. Spain is still recovering from their civil war. I think it will be just us, the French and the Germans. Mussolini is too fly to get involved, no matter how much bombast he spreads around.'

'A bit of the old boys club, then.'

For Haskins the next six months seemed to go by in a flash. After initial introductions to the Chief Constables he concentrated on making the acquaintance of the people he would be dealing with at an operational level, Superintendents, Chief Inspectors and Inspectors.

Most of them were happy to see him; for the majority of people the important area was what was once again called the Western Front, this time the Rhine and Germany's western border, and South-East England was not at the top of priorities. Poland had surrendered after a few short weeks, invaded by both the Germans and Russians, and German troops were now concentrated against the Maginot line. An attack was expected at any moment. Little attention had been paid to local issues, and some people were glorifying in the opportunity to report spies, parachutists, even the German navy landing close to Eastbourne. All this had to be investigated, overwhelming the available police forces, and the option of having a specially trained body to call upon for assistance was welcome – especially as the officers he spoke to were convinced almost all, if not all, of the "information" they received ranged from over-vivid imagination to outright hoaxes.

Haskins did not disabuse them of the idea of anyone being "specially trained". He was quite sure that, like many others at the time, Martins back in London was making things up as he went along, while damning the "incompetents" who had failed to start an attack on Germany while Poland was still active.

Haskins was in Portsmouth in mid-April 1940 when he bumped into Detective Inspector Rudman. They adjourned to the police canteen for a cup of tea. Haskins expressed surprise that he had not seen Rudman since the previous September, as he had met most of the others of his rank. Rudman gave a smile, a rare, friendly one.

'I've heard about your lot. And I've been avoiding you. Nothing personal, mind, just I have no intention of getting involved in all this malarkey if I can avoid it.'

'All what malarkey?'

Rudman waved a hand dismissively.

'Investigating strange lights which only the informant can see guiding German bombers which don't exist. Strange foreigners at the docks. Death rays passing through orchards. Suspiciousness nuns – suspicious because they look just like nuns. And they're Catholic nuns, of course, must be traitors. That sort of thing. Honestly, some of the nonsense people come up with. In peace-time they'd probably be locked up for their own good.'

Haskins nodded understanding.

'You aren't alone. How's the serious work going?'

Rudman frowned.

'You mean Miss Georgina Riley?'

'Well, not specifically, but yes, now you come to mention it. Any news?'

Rudman shook his head.

'She was in a coma for four weeks. Now she can't remember a thing. So, no new evidence. We took the place apart piece by piece after your lot left – well, we did that eventually; that London lot never arrived.' He tapped his fingers on his desk irritably. 'I've gone through everything a hundred times, but still – well, not nothing. But nothing conclusive. Nothing I can take to court without some lawyer demonstrating that it didn't necessarily have to be "X". And now all the "X"s are all over the place. I've been officially told to drop it for more current work, wait until Miss Riley starts remembering things.'

'Is that likely? I would have thought she would have recovered her memory ages ago. It's funny really – strange, rather. I think I presumed she had recovered, but – well, these have been a hectic few months.'

'Amen to that. I'm just glad they're having this war in a different country. It would make my job impossible if we were surrounded by soldiers busy shooting each other.' He looked at Haskins' new uniform, acquired a month before from Moss Bros, which he had chosen to wear to impress a certain Inspector who had maintained a wish to join the "fighting forces". 'Looks good on you, mind.'

'Sheer camouflage,' Haskins grinned. 'So what about Georgina?' he repeated his question. 'When is she expected to remember?' He wondered if Rudman had ignored the question deliberately. Rudman shrugged his shoulders.

'Next week. Next year. Maybe never. The doctors haven't a clue. She had lost a hell of a lot of blood, and gone through a hell of a shock. Apparently you're more likely to get an answer from a psychologist, and they don't know either.'

'I saw some cases of shellshock in the last war. Apparently sometimes there's no explanation. One man can go through a near explosion with no affect, another is paralysed through fear. Or something.'

'Talking of explosions, I see the phoney war has ended,' Rudman commented. 'That idiot Chamberlain claims that Hitler has missed the bus, next thing you know all hell breaks loose.'

'Denmark and Norway? Yes, I don't understand that. I can see he needs to protect mineral supplies from Scandinavia, but wasting troops in a neutral country when he needs them against us and the French? I think he's going to regret that one. Our boys are already throwing them back in Norway. Pity we can't help the Danes.'

Rudman pursed his lips as if not entirely agreeing, but did not follow up the subject.

'So, you here with Miss Morely? Or is it Mrs Haskins now?'

Haskins looked at him in surprise.

'Rosemary? I haven't seen her since – since that weekend.'

'Really? Sorry, for some reason I seem to remember you two were – well, courting, if I can use such a word.' Courting, thought Haskins, was not quite the word he would have used. 'Anyway, I've seen her around, so I put two and two together and came up with five. Silly me, and me a copper and all.'

Haskins suspected that Rudman did not quite believe him.

'Rose here in Portsmouth? Where?' And why am I asking, Haskins wondered.

'Drives a delivery lorry for various wholesalers, sort of on an independent basis. Must be earning a good wage, what with shortages of drivers, and food being in such demand.'

'It sounds as if you suspect something fishy is going on.'

'No, not as far as Miss Morely is concerned. Anyway, as I told you, not my area at all. And I have no intention of making it one, either.'

After a few more minutes discussing events on the continent Rudman took his leave, claiming an urgent appointment elsewhere. Watching him go Haskins wondered whether this chance meeting had been so coincidental after all. For over six months he hadn't met Rudman, which was itself surprising since he had met almost every other inspector in the area, and then suddenly Rudman is looking for information and appears out of nowhere. But what had he really been looking for? He could not remember anything new coming up, apart from Georgina's lack of memory, and that had told them nothing.

Haskins gave up trying to work out Rudman's intent, and thought of Rose. He debated whether or not he should try to contact her. He was in Portsmouth for two more days. He could get one of the wholesalers' name from Rudman.

Give it up, man, he thought to himself. He was acting like a lovelorn schoolboy after what wasn't more than a single weekend's foolishness. If Rose had wanted to contact him it would have been easy to get his address in London.

It reminded him that Erica had also not contacted him since that weekend. He should have been relieved, but somehow was not. Maybe, he thought, he should give her a call when he returned to London, just to make sure she was safe. Not to resume any relationship, he assured himself, but because he did still care for her as a person. Yes, he finally decided, he would do that. Because he did care for her as a person, not for any other reason.

He finished his tea and left the canteen. Leaving the police station he was about to cross the road when a lorry pulled out suddenly and almost ran him over.

'Sorry, love,' came a woman's voice, 'almost had you there, I did.' He gave the woman behind the windscreen a frosty glare, and was about to walk on when something struck him. He walked around to the driver's open window.

'Rosemary Morely, well, well, well. And what are you doing in Portsmouth wearing working overalls, driving a lorry, cigarette in mouth and using a fake cockney accent?' She grinned and threw the cigarette away.

'Image, my dear John, image. The others I work with – my dear clients – think a cockney sparrow more acceptable as a driver than some young lady talking poash.'

He smiled ruefully, shaking his head in admiration.

'You are full of surprises. Why the job?'

'Pays well – better than that old shop, anyway. So long as I deliver on time I'm free to plan my own day. It's all groceries and canned goods as such, so there's never any really heavy lifting. Any number of reasons. Anyway, you didn't seem surprised to see me. Not as much as I would have expected.'

She sounded slightly put out. He tapped the side of his nose knowingly.

'I get to know a lot in my job, nose to the ground, you know,' he assured her. 'Anyway, I have an appointment in – oh, five minutes ago. What say we meet up for a cup of tea or a drink or something?'

'Six o'clock,' she agreed, 'I'll be waiting for you here. Don't be late.' She gunned the engine and drove off, wheels skidding, to show she could. He watched her go, wondering.

Wondering what it was that he was wondering.

Chapter 8: Portsmouth

'Clio,' she said, 'you were Clio, I've always remembered that. That was the easiest one of all. The muse of history.'

They were back on the road again, having finished their picnic lunch.

'Funnily enough that seems to be the one that most historians agree on. The other muses all have subtle variations according to interpretation and translation.'

'Definitely you. The historian. Pedantic as hell, but fortunately also impulsive at times.'

'When did you decide to marry me?' he asked suddenly.

'What a strange question.'

'I would imagine so, normally. But under the circumstances ... '

'Yes, under the circumstances,' she echoed. She thought for a moment. 'I was convinced I would marry you the first time I saw you. But that changed, of course.'

'Yes, didn't it just. And then?'

'Then I decided to marry you when I knew I couldn't.'

He thought about that for a while. It was obviously some philosophical conundrum.

'Go on, explain.'

'You know me, darling. When everything looks lost I decide on the impossible.'

He laughed.

'All that time,' he said.

'All the people. Everything.'

'Difficult to believe, really. But, in a way, it was fun.'

He had been in front of the police station at five to six promptly, having taken time to change back in civilian clothes. It was darkening rapidly, and he wished he had brought a torch. London was bad enough, but blackout regulations were even more strictly enforced in coastal areas – if that was possible – and Portsmouth was one of the stricter.

She arrived at six p.m. almost to the second, driving a polished Hillman. It was another thing he hadn't thought about; he had dismissed his driver and car, thinking that they could get around in taxis. It was pre-war London thinking. Taxis were rare on the ground here.

'Jump in,' she called, and he got into the passenger seat.

'Smart car,' he said, wondering how she could afford it. He noticed that she had exchanged the overalls for a patterned frock covered by a smart duffel-coat, her hair carefully done, bright red lipstick on her lips, a little garish for his taste. He debated with himself whether she had done so because she was meeting him, but decided that that was unlikely.

'Sweet little thing, isn't she?' she said enthusiastically. 'It's called a "Melody Minx". Just the thing for me, I like good music and I'm a bit of a minx. Got it off a woman going to live somewhere north, Scotland, I think. More money than sense, she didn't even know how much it was worth. I told her I'd take it off her hands before the military requisitioned it, but insisted on paying her at least a nominal fee.' She laughed. 'Some people, as the saying goes, don't have the brains they were born with.'

'Is that a new saying? Sounds rather, I don't know, from the Midlands.'

'There are hundreds of new sayings, darling. You really should move with the times.' The "darling" was said off-handedly, as if she called everyone darling these days.

'Really?' he asked rhetorically, irritated. This young flapper-type Rose was not what he had expected. Previously she had been what he would have termed a little brash, but this was verging on the brazen. He was beginning to wonder if it was a big mistake, agreeing to meet up like this.

'Oh, come on, John, don't sulk. I'm just enjoying myself while I can.'

'Where are we going?' He wished he had brought his service car. Now he was more or less at the mercy of her whim.

'Cumberland Hotel. They have a nice saloon bar, gorgeous dining room, and also do evening meals for non-residents – not many worth it any more.' To his relief he noted that they were almost at the hotel.

At most he would have an hour's walk home, if necessary. She parked the car in front, and they got out. She took his arm and kissed him on the cheek.

'Come on, silly. Let's have a few drinks, some good food, and gossip about everyone else. Please?'

'Very well. But no strange accents.'

'Keine strange accenten,' she agreed.

Inside the public bar was plush and well stocked. Haskins settled for a whisky, Rose for a gin and tonic. She raised her glass.

'Mud in your eye,' she said.

'I wonder how long this will go on,' he replied, looking around at the deep armchairs, polished tables, velvet curtains. The curtains hid the tape that criss-crossed the windows, to prevent extensive scattering of shards of glass in the event of an explosion.

'Hopefully forever,' she said, 'but with all those ships being sunk ... I don't really want to think about it.' There was a pause before she continued. 'Did you know, Rob volunteered.'

'Rob? Your brother? He didn't strike me as the sort to volunteer.' She grinned.

'He isn't. He knew he had flat feet, and a note from his doctor saying he had a heart condition. Thought he'd make a great fuss about how heroically he tried to do his bit, but they wouldn't take him, etc, crying heart etc. So they put him into a propaganda unit as an ordinary private instead. Famous artist does his bit, that sort of thing.' She laughed. 'Poor old Rob.'

There didn't seem much sympathy in the laugh.

'I thought you always stuck up for your younger brother.'

'I used to. It seemed the sort of thing an older sister should do. But everything's changed now, hasn't it? We can do what we want to do, not what we should. After all, we might be dead tomorrow.' She sipped her drink. 'And there's what he did to Jessica.'

'Jessica?'

'His muse, remember? The adoring little puppy dog following him everywhere.'

72

'Ah, yes. Strange girl.'

'Not really. Girls that age do that sort of thing. Men like Rob take advantage of it.'

'So what did he do? To Jessica?'

'Started hitting her around. A few cuffs to start off with. Then a black eye, two. Finally he threatened her with a carving knife one night when he was drunk. So she came to her senses and left.'

'A carving knife. Interesting.'

'You're thinking of Georgina. And Emily.'

'He was drunk that night as well.'

Rose fell silent. It was as if she still retained a certain sense of duty to her brother, no matter what her suspicions were.

'I hear Frieda was interned,' she said finally.

'Interned? Not surprising, I suppose. Nobody's quite sure what the rules are. Some areas exempt what they class as refugees. Others exempt only Jewish refugees, and others intern only Jewish refugees, for reasons which are totally beyond comprehension. I suppose Portsmouth – well, as a harbour town, they're full of spy fever. I'll have a word with Rudman. He should be able to find out where she is.'

'Have her released?'

'I doubt it. But some of the camps they're holding them in – no planning, no resources, too many people, too few tents, toilets, soap, everything. And yet some newspapers report that they're living in luxury. Maybe Rudman could get her moved if she's in one of them. Though I wouldn't count on it, he's intent on avoiding the refugee question. Doesn't think it's proper police work.'

'You spoke to him? Did you discuss ... last August?'

'Briefly. He's no further forward. Georgina's memory has gone. I should have asked him where she is. Could go visit sometime.'

She smiled.

'You think that's likely?'

He grimaced uncomfortably.

'Maybe write her a letter, at least.' If he were honest he knew he would neither visit nor write any letters. There would always be something else to do. 'What about the others, any news?'

'Erica's had her novel published. It's supposed to be fiction based on fact, now. Not very diplomatic, publishing a book about defeating Napoleon, but apparently they think the French won't mind. She and Peter are living in Camden Town at the moment. I think they're planning on getting married.'

'Well, well. Published, eh?' he commented, caught between two different emotions, hoping that neither showed. News of her marriage-to-be should have pleased him, yet somehow it did not. On the other hand Erica had not made him fulfill his promise of promoting her book, for which he had been grateful. It saved him from promoting what he thought was jingoistic, bad history, more fiction than fact.

Yet he was strangely proud to hear that she had achieved success.

Rose chuckled.

'Apparently there is a greater requirement for books which, how can I put this, inspire patriotism? Factual approach not necessary. Indeed, completely unnecessary.'

'Well, good luck to her. Just glad I'm not involved. But Henderby – I thought he had been called up.'

'As far as I know he was. They sent him home because they didn't have enough barracks or aeroplanes or uniforms or something. Then they called him up again. Last I heard he was on two weeks' special leave, which is why I think they're going to be married. If only I had her number I could call and have a gossip for old times' sake.'

'Very unpatriotic. Blocking all those important military telephone calls waiting to get through.'

She wriggled her nose thoughtfully.

'I don't feel very patriotic.' She looked him in the eye. 'I don't see why women should be patriotic. We only get the scraps men are prepared to leave us. We can't get equal pay or decent jobs. We end up as old workhorses if we aren't lucky enough to be born into wealth, and even then we're just trophies for some man to marry, or baby-bearers, something to produce the heir. We're desperately wanted during a war, but straight after it's business as usual, shut up and do as you're told, get back into the kitchen. Why should we be patriotic about that?'

'Whoa, whoa, old girl, I'm not the entire male race. No use blaming me. I'm just a history professor, remember?'

She smiled ruefully.

'Sorry. I listened to some ridiculous talk of a woman's role in the war on the radio the other week. What a complete load of utter tosh.' She sighed. 'I'm beginning to sound like a suffragette, aren't I? A sort of female version of Nigel, our dear pet socialist.' She paused at the memory. 'I wonder where he is now.'

'Probably locked up for refusing to fight in a capitalist war, I would imagine.'

'I don't think he'd have the nerve. All talk, no action.' She sighed. 'Funny how different things seem to be. Oh, well. Come on, let's have some dinner to cheer us up. I think it's roast lamb tonight.'

'Sounds good. As you say, might as well enjoy it while it lasts.'

'Will you be in Portsmouth often? We could do this whenever you're down. Maybe take in a film? There's a Bob Hope film I wouldn't mind seeing, The Road to Singapore.' He smiled.

'I'm rather partial to Mr Hope's work myself. I dare say I could find reasons to be in Portsmouth on a regular basis.'

Chapter 9: A converted Fyffes' banana van

'So you promised you'd be in Portsmouth at least once a month. But didn't return for four.'

'We were hellishly busy at the time. And then there was Norway, and then Dunkirk, and all the rest. I telephoned every week.'

'Very unpatriotic,' she said, her eyes twinkling, 'blocking all those important military calls.'

'You like teasing me, don't you?'

'I love teasing you. It is fun.'

He grunted. Revenge is sweet, he thought.

'Good thing nobody nominated Urania for me,' he said. 'Prophecy definitely wasn't my forte. I think I got almost everything wrong. First of all whether there would be a war, then what the armies would do, and what countries would be sucked in.'

'It's funny, that. At the time we all believed every word you said – well, it's not surprising, really. After all the guff they gave us in the newspapers and on the radio.' She looked at him. 'But in the end you got the most important predictions right, didn't you?'

They smiled together.

Yes, he thought, I did get the important things right. The most important thing.

'Any prophecies about Longwood?' she asked.

'None whatsoever. I've given up on prophecies.' He sighed. 'I wonder how many of the others will be there.'

'I can't see Rob going. Not if what they say is true.'

'God knows where Johnson is these days. If he's still alive.'

'And of course Frieda won't be going anywhere ever again.'

'Yes, poor Frieda.'

'Yes. Poor Frieda.'

At the time it seemed as if a capricious fate had decided that Haskins should be kept away from Portsmouth forever more. No matter what reason or excuse he came up with, Martins found other towns more deserving of his presence, and with the chaos in France in May, and

Dunkirk in June, there was little counter-argument to be made.

On the 11th of July 1940 Portsmouth was heavily bombed by the Luftwaffe. Despite his best efforts he was unable to get away, and spent evenings fretting over Rose's safety, his calls either not getting through or remaining unanswered, and he was becoming increasingly worried. Eventually, three days later, she answered the telephone to reassure him that she was perfectly well and unharmed.

'I've been trying to get through to you since the eleventh,' he had said. 'You never answered the telephone.' It was an admonishment, and he felt guilty about making it.

'Things have been rather busy,' she had replied stiffly, obviously angry at his tone.

'I'm sorry, Rose, I shouldn't have said that. I've just been a little worried about you.'

'Only a little?' she asked. He could sense the amusement now in her voice.

'Well, I am rather fond of you, you know. Listen, I'll find a reason to get down as soon as possible.'

There was a pause, and he wondered if she were trying to think of an excuse to say no. Perhaps he should have used a stronger expression than saying he was "fond" of her. He wasn't quite sure of exactly how deep his feelings were. Even less of hers.

'Saturday would be nice,' she said finally. 'I won't have any free time before then.'

'Saturday it is, then. One way or another.'

In a marvellous act of serendipity Martins told him the following day that he had been asked for in Portsmouth. He left immediately, arriving on the Thursday, looking forward more to the Saturday.

'Glad they sent the right person,' Rudman said, shaking his hand as he entered the police station.

'You asked for me specifically?'

'Yes. You're basically a civilian, even if you choose to wear uniform on the odd occasion. Civilians I can work with, not the army. It's unnatural. In peace time we know a soldier's a soldier and hand him over to their people. In wartime most of the soldiers are really civilians. For example,' he continued as they entered his office, 'if I find you, in your uniform, selling army kit on the black market, who takes charge?'

'The military I expect.'

'Exactly. Have a seat. Nice and clear-cut. But supposing I find you selling civilian meat and veg on the black market, who takes over?'

'I confess, I have a pound of apples in the car that I bought off a farmer.' He had stopped off to buy them for Rose, presuming that Portsmouth was increasingly hit by rationing as London was.

Rudman grinned.

'In that case I'll have to hand myself in, I get all mine from my cousin. He has a smallholding just outside Eastbourne. But it does show you. Why should I waste precious time chasing petty criminals over a few slices of bacon?' He sighed, a sound Haskins found unexpected from the Inspector. 'You know, in my job we often face moral questions. You can't just apply the law down to the letter, quite often you have to take into account circumstances – say you catch a hungry little boy nicking apples. Best thing, if you can't pretend not to have seen it, is to give the little urchin a lecture, and maybe a gentle kick in the pants, more for show for the shopkeeper than anything else. Now we're supposed to come down heavy on anyone selling half a potato more than they should. And in wartime people suddenly find that everything's black and white. And you just know that it will be little people who end up doing time, the lords and ladies will still be enjoying their quail in aspic, or whatever it is they enjoy.'

Rudman was, Haskins decided, a rather more complex man that he liked to portray. It rather reminded him of himself and the way he acted before his students. Uncomfortably so. Playing a role he wasn't sure he believed in.

'I thought you were going to stay out of that sort of thing?' he asked.

Rudman grimaced.

'Orders from on high. My chief caught me investigating a refugee, and gave me a roasting. "Not our job", he said. "Henceforth and for all time you will concentrate on the black marketeers", end of story. Chase the cheese, hunt the haddock, trail the tea.' He made a sound of disgust.

'Why were you investigating a refugee? I thought that was another area you intended to steer clear of.'

'Not just any refugee. Your Miss Rosenberg, as she called herself.'

'Rosenberg? Doesn't ring a bell.'

'Fraulein Frieda Rosenberg.'

'Ah,' Haskins nodded. 'I meant to ask you about her. I heard she'd been interned. I wondered whether there was anything I could do for her.' Rudman looked uncomfortable.

'Close, were you?' he asked.

'Not at all. I hardly knew her. She seemed a strange sort of person. But you feel you should do something for refugees, after all they don't really have any friends or family as it is.'

'Yes. Unfortunately – you heard the news of the Arandora Star?'

'Sunk a few days ago? I read something about it. Only civilians on board, no military reason to torpedo it. I wondered whether it was being used for propaganda purposes. Difficult to tell when you're being lied to, in the middle of a war.'

'Yes, they do it more subtly in peace-time.' Rudman grimaced again, as if facing up to something unpleasant. 'Frieda Rosenberg was aboard the Arandora, along with a few hundred other refugees. They were on route for Canada. Churchill, I believe, in his own inimical style, gave the order, "collar the lot" – in other words arrest all aliens and send them to Canada, or Australia, or Outer Mongolia or somewhere. Bloody ridiculous, serves no good purpose and just creates more work for us – and hell for those caught up in it.'

'I heard something to that effect. I heard of a Joint Intelligence Committee report that stated that the lack of enemy sabotage was proof that they were waiting to co-ordinate their sabotage.'

'A bit of old Occam's razor, then,' Rudman commented. Haskins was surprised. Rudman did not strike him as a philosopher.

'Precisely,' Haskins agreed. 'The reason I know there is a tiger on the verandah is that it runs away whenever go outside, to avoid being seen, that sort of nonsense.' He sighed. 'Everyone's got invasion fever. Now it's no longer German spies, it's paratroopers disguised as nuns. With Italians or bogus refugees signaling them in from hilltops. So where is Frieda now?'

'She didn't make it. As far as I can work out. I'm sorry.'

'Good God. Poor child.'

'Child? Didn't look much of a child to me.'

'Well, she was only eighteen.'

'She said she was only eighteen. To my eyes she looked at least twenty-five. There was definitely something wrong there.'

'You think she was actually a German spy? But surely that isn't your department.'

'No, murder is my department. She was at the scene of a murder – and an attempted murder. I don't care – I didn't care – whether she was a spy or not. If she was a murderer then I wanted her hanged as a murderer. Then they could hang her as a spy.'

Rudman, Haskins thought, was somewhat fanatical about Longwood. 'Have you been keeping tabs on all of us?'

'Yes,' replied Rudman simply. He paused, and then added, 'There's someone missing in this whole case, have you thought about that?'

Haskins thought about it.

'I can't say I have. Who do you mean?'

'Precisely. Who do I mean? Where are they? Who are they? That's the problem. They're missing. They're not there. There's a gaping hole where someone should be.'

Either he himself was being especially obtuse, thought Haskins, or Rudman was being extremely cryptic.

'Think about it,' Rudman said, as if ending the subject. He took a deep breath before continuing. 'Now, the reason I asked you down here is this black marketeering nonsense. If we have to do it we might as well do it properly. We're thin enough on the ground as it is. A spot of assistance from your lot will be helpful on the odd occasion.'

'We'll do anything we can.'

'And it will allow me to continue to keep tabs on you.'

Haskins was uncertain as to how far Rudman meant it as a joke.

'From what I've seen the city seems to have taken somewhat of a pasting,' he commented, changing the subject.

'You can say that again. Bastards claim they were aiming at the docks, a legitimate military target, supposedly. Most of the bombs hit the Kingston area. Took out more pubs and houses than anything else – Blue Anchor, Keppel's Head, Row Barge. Every stayed at the Totterdell's?'

'Never heard of it.'

'Totterdell's Family Hotel. Won't be taking in any more guests. It's been gutted.'

'It must have been pretty terrifying.'

'It was, and none of the bombs landed close to where I was. Interesting, though, to see how people react. Your lady friend was quite a revelation.'

'Rose? In what way?'

'Volunteered to drive an ambulance. Well, a converted Fyffes' banana van, would you believe. Kept driving the whole way through, as the bombs were dropping. More guts than I would have had. And she's been doing the same almost every night since then, helping with the clearing up and what have you. She won't survive this war if she carries on like that.'

So that's why Rose had been so busy, Haskins thought. He would have some apologies to make.

On the Saturday evening he met Rose in the bar of the Cumberland. Already the room seemed somewhat dowdier, as if cleaning had taken a second place to everything else. He had made his apologies early on in the evening, and expressed his admiration and concern at her actions, which she had laughed away as being "quite safe so long as you drive fast enough", something that he was tempted to point out was not logical, but had decided, in the interests of peace and his own physical safety not to mention – he had seen the slight twitchiness in her eyes and over-excited manner showing that she was not as blasé as she pretended. When he mentioned the bag of apples waiting in his car she had seemed somewhat startled, but had quickly thanked him with a kiss, but assured him that things were nowhere near bad enough for him to plague innocent farmers with requests for fruit.

'So how did you manage to convince your Colonel Martins your presence was required here?' she had asked, changing the subject.

'Rudman has his eyes on a group of black marketeers,' he explained. 'He hopes to catch them in the act. Wants me there along with a couple of soldiers, partly as backup, but also because he's been ordered to keep the army involved. He doesn't see me as regular army.'

'Darling, it sounds exciting – you won't be in any danger, will you?'

He grinned.

'I have my newly-issued service revolver with five rounds. It's all they could spare. Everything else is given to the few troops we have to stop the invasion. Though I have a suspicion the five rounds have come from the last war's storerooms. I'm not even confident that they'll work.'

'So where and when is this thrilling stake-out?'

'Tuesday evening, the railway bridge on the London road. Don't worry, the police go in first. Rudman doesn't really want us there in the first place. Just manpower if it's needed. He's short on men himself.'

'Funny thing to do while the Germans are across the channel,' Rose commented. Haskins agreed, and they discussed the likelihood of invasion for a few minutes. He told her about Frieda.

'Poor Frieda,' she said. 'Does Rudman really think she was a spy?'

'He thinks she could have been – at any event he doesn't believe she was what she claimed to be. He's keeping tabs on all of us just in case.'

'Sounds like he's become besotted with the case. Though that's not the right word, is it? Fanatical?'

'That's exactly the word that crossed my mind. Either that or obsessional. I have this image of him in twenty years' time still haunting the police station corridors, noting down exactly which of us is where, doing what.'

'Twenty years' time. I can't even think twenty months' ahead. Hardly twenty days. Did he say where everyone was?'

'Eventually.' Haskins had had to grill Rudman rather subtly to get the information.

He now began ticking off the fingers on his hand. 'Frieda, well, we know about her. You, here in Portsmouth, myself traveling around the South-East pretending to be a soldier. Morely in a barrack room in London, having managed to escape a prosecution for assault.' He looked at Rose. 'Seems he had another go at Jessica. Found out where she was living, slipped out of camp, got drunk, and demanded – well, what he demanded doesn't appear to be too clear. Anyway, this time she was the one who picked up the carving knife. He had to have ten stitches. And once he's recovered he's got to explain the little problem of being absent without leave.'

'Good God, little Jessica. You wouldn't think her capable, would you?'

'I'm fortunate in having studied history. People do unexpected things in unusual circumstances.'

'And the others?'

Haskins resumed his ticking off.

'Georgina, still in a nursing home, no change – according to Rudman her wedding fell through after she didn't show up, so that can't have helped much. Erica, even more triumphant in London, with a second book published – a lusty and bawdy romance of Georgina's style, but set in a different period, so I'm told. Henderby, posted to Bexhill, flying Hurricanes – he'll be having a hot time of it.' He had resisted the temptation to call on Erica to deliver his congratulations on her forthcoming marriage, if that was what was to be. He felt that, while

Henderby was undoubtedly a decent man, Erica could have made a better choice. He was not prepared to admit to himself that he thought he himself would have been the better choice. 'Johnson,' he concluded, 'well, you won't believe this, but apparently he was among the troops who came back from Dunkirk.'

'Nigel? Surely not! There wasn't even enough time for him to become a soldier.'

'A good few months between last September and this May, more than enough time. It seems, from what Rudman told me, that Johnson had some sort of Damascene conversion after that weekend, and when war was declared. Either that, or he was running away from something. But he has received several mentions in despatches for courageous – or foolhardy – actions.'

'My goodness. Who would have thought it. Nigel, of all people.' She paused. 'Inspector Rudman seems awfully well informed, doesn't he?' Haskins nodded.

'About us, anyway. He isn't so sure about the black marketeers, though. Thinks it's all a wild goose chase.'

'You will be careful, won't you, darling?' she said, squeezing his hand suddenly, surprising him.

'Of course, Rose. I won't be in any danger whatsoever.'

This prediction turned out to be almost true. After waiting for several hours on a wet night without anyone turning up, let alone criminals, Rudman gave up and they went home. Two of the constables caught summer colds.

Chapter 10: Erica, London

The Humber had decided that it wanted a rest. She stood outside and leaned against the door, breathing the fresh country air in deeply as he tinkered with the engine. Tinkering made no difference to the it, but it helped him feel better. After fifteen minutes rest it would be happy to carry on.

'Frieda was Melpomene,' she said. 'Everyone agreed that her muse was tragedy. Which turned out in the end to be true.'

'She wouldn't have it. She wanted to be Terpsichore,' he said from under the bonnet.

'Dance and – what was the other?'

'Choral singing, I think.'

'She said she had had enough tragedy, and wanted only singing and dancing for the rest of her life.'

'She was a little tipsy then, I think,' he said. 'Actually almost smiled once or twice. Forgot the past, I suppose.'

There was an oath from underneath the bonnet.

'Are you alright, darling?'

'Yes, just banged my thumb. Usual stuff.'

She smiled, stood upright and stretched.

'If you think of in terms of money – say whoever it was did steal the tiara and sell it – then none of us seemed to have a lot of it afterwards,' she said.

There is one, he thought, but decided not to say. Reminding your wife of such things was probably bad form, as well as dangerous to the health.

'Not easy to dispose of a tiara, I would imagine,' he replied instead.

'I could imagine any number of ways of selling it,' she replied.

'Yes, my darling, you have a wonderful imagination – but that's not quite the same as actually doing it.'

'I bet I could,' she insisted.

'Maybe it was Peter,' he suggested. 'Maybe he didn't have time to cash in before he went missing.'

'You can't really believe that Peter could have ... The idea is ridiculous!'

He looked out from behind the bonnet. An oil stain on his cheek would have seemed humorous had it not been for the grim look on his face.

'Well, someone did it, didn't they?'

That was the problem. He had used Henderby's name as an academic example, and now he wished he hadn't. But the fact remained. Someone was guilty.

In September 1940 Haskins had been in the West End, browsing for a present for Rose. There was no special occasion, but he found himself in London with a day of little to do, and the idea of a present had struck him as sat in his office staring at the ceiling. 'And why not?' he asked himself, and promptly set out, determined to avoid any fruit stalls he might come across.

Oxford Street and Bond Street had yielded nothing – nothing he could afford or thought suitable. In the end he was strolling through the side streets when he came across the bookshop. It had a sign outside: "Special book-signing by Miss Erica Ringold, twelve until two". On the second impulse of the day he entered the bookshop. Once accustomed to the gloom he saw Erica sitting at a table, chatting to an old woman while a small queue of other women holding copies of her latest book waited their turn. He slipped past, using bookshelves to keep his distance, thinking he would wait until the others had gone before making his presence known. He found himself in front of the famed authoress's works. With reluctance he picked up Erica's second novel and began reading the introduction.

'Hiding from me?' a voice behind him asked. It was Erica. The bookshop was empty. He realised that he must have been reading for at least fifteen minutes. 'Or are you reading it here so that you don't have to undergo the embarrassment of buying a copy?' She was teasing him.

'I have to admit, it is compelling stuff,' he said reluctantly.

'But more fiction than fact.'

'Yes. More fiction than fact. But well written. I'm impressed.' She blushed.

'Coming from you, John, that is praise indeed. Though I'm aware that, were it not for the war, I wouldn't have had the first published.' There was an uncomfortable pause, uncomfortable at least for Haskins. He'd forgotten how appealing she could be; the aggressive look had completely gone, to be replaced with careful makeup and a somewhat tightly fitting dress covered with a light overcoat. He'd forgotten how she could give him a certain look which made him ache to take her in his arms. She seemed to have put on a little weight, which, if anything, made her look more attractive. 'I tell you what, John, I'm finished here. Let's get a taxi to Claridges and have some tea. My treat. I know how poor you soldiers are.'

'Claridges? You seem to be doing well.' She winked.

'The publishers pay for it. They think it's good publicity. Personally I wouldn't have tea in Claridges if I had to pay for it, even if I had millions in the bank. Claridges was never really me.'

'That's true,' he said as they walked towards Oxford Street. A taxi passed and he hailed it. 'You've always struck me as dreamy in your writing and down to earth in life.' He noticed that she got into the taxi with a little difficulty, and realised that the good life was putting a lot of weight on her than he had originally thought. She sat down and patted her stomach.

'Little Ben is growing into Big Ben,' she said, smiling.

'You're not – '

'Yes I am. Didn't you notice? I'm like one of those barrage balloons. Except they can be deflated. Which I will be in a few months, give or take a few weeks.'

'Well, congratulations.'

He wanted to say, 'I presume Henderby is the proud father-to-be?', but it would sound extremely rude. He tried to surreptitiously look for a wedding ring. She laughed and showed him her hand, small diamond on an engagement ring, gold wedding ring.

'All legal and honest. I am now Mrs Peter Henderby. Honestly, John,

I can read your face. You looked so guilty about asking.'

'Well, I had heard that you might have married.'

For some reason he couldn't fathom he felt more than a little jealous. She was obviously happy, and he was happy for her.

'And which gossip told you that? Or have you taken up reading the social columns recently?'

'No. I happened to bump into Rose Morely a few months ago, in Portsmouth. She mentioned it.'

'Rose! How is she? Oh, you are a fibber! Bumped into her? I bet you still have the hots for her. She had you in her sights right from the first time she saw you. Not that I'm saying I didn't, but then I suppose she has better aim.' She looked at him critically. 'Wandering the streets of London. I saw you outside, when you came out of that jewellers. Looking for a present for someone, mmm?'

'As it happens, yes.' She patted his knee.

'Oh, John, you always were such a prickly man. Relax. I hope you'll be very happy together. Peter's maybe not Prince of the Beautiful Kingdom, but I've decided that he's the right sort of man for me, especially since I couldn't have you.' The taxi had reached Claridges.

'How is Henderby?' he asked, helping her alight. An old doorman wearing medals from the Great War came limping to help them, and then turned to open the door. There was a pained look on Erica's face.

'I worry about him. All the time. You know he's at Biggin Hill?'

'Someone told me it was Bexhill.'

'Biggin Hill. Flying Spitfires. He's loving it, always enjoyed flying, says they were really lucky to get Spits – he calls them Spits – instead of Hurricanes. I don't know what the difference is, but he's happy as anything. But he must be in the thick of it. I hardly sleep these nights.' Haskins would have liked to have told her not to worry, but there seemed little point. With German attacks on radar installations, airfields, random attacks on harbours, bombing of shipping in the Channel, it was obvious that everyone was at risk, even more so the pilots who flew off to intercept the Luftwaffe. 'That's one thing I've

90

always liked about you, John,' she said as he helped her to sit down, 'you never lie. Other people tell me that he's safer than many civilians – they must think I'm a fool.'

'Unfortunately Hitler has to destroy the RAF and then the navy before he can invade. Being a fighter pilot is one of the most dangerous roles at the moment. There's no way you can argue out of that.' She smiled.

'Good old John. Now, help me worry less by telling me all the gossip. What are you doing in that smart uniform? How is dear Rose? Are you going to marry her?'

Avoiding the last question he brought her up to date with everything he knew. She was amazed that Rudman was still pursuing the case, "under current circumstances". She chuckled at the idea of Rose driving a delivery lorry. She frowned at the report of Morely's behaviour, "always thought he was a bit of a bully". Johnson's actions brought a whistle of astonishment. Frieda received clucks of sympathy. She claimed to envy his constant movement – imagine, Southampton two days ago, Bournemouth tomorrow!

Afterwards she took him to a little jewellery shop close to Soho, where he found a gold bracelet at an affordable price.

'Send her my love as well,' Erica said when they parted. They had exchanged telephone numbers, and he had promised to call her whenever he was in London. He was looking forward to the idea. Erica had never been just a lover to him, in the physical sense, he now realised, but also a friend and companion. In a strange way, now that she was married, he felt even more comfortable in her company.

A week later he returned to London, to find a message waiting from a Doctor Hampton from Charing Cross hospital regarding Mrs Henderby. He telephoned immediately.

'Premature, I'm afraid,' Hampton told him when he finally got through. 'Couldn't save it. You heard about her husband? I think that was what brought it on.'

'No, what about her husband?' Haskins almost shouted down the telephone. It was a bad line.

'Killed in action. Somewhere over the channel.'

Haskins was silent. Peter Henderby, the charmer, the man who decided to make an honest woman of Erica, dead. It seemed impossible. A week ago he, Haskins, had been sitting having tea with Erica. A week ago she had been happier than he had ever seen her.

'Hello?' asked the doctor over the phone. 'Professor? Are you still there?'

'I'll be over straight away,' he shouted, and put the telephone down. Doctor Hampton didn't have time to point out that Haskins was not family, and it wasn't visiting hours. He shrugged. Families seemed to have been broken up these days. Visiting hours, like many other rules, seemed to have gone out the window.

Erica was asleep when he arrived. She lay in a spartan room, an antiseptic, lifeless hospital room. He sat on a chair next to her bed and waited. Her face was pale and listless. He wondered whether she had lost the will to live.

Erica. Always full of life, laughing, seeming so much – yes, larger than life. He had loved her at one stage, or so he thought. Then ... he felt deeply guilty at his treatment of her. At the time it had seemed the right thing to do. Then she had found love with Henderby, and his jealousy was overladen by the happiness she seemed to have found. Now – fate had not dealt kindly to Erica.

After a few hours his eyes grew heavy and his head began to sink. He had had few hours sleep in the last twenty-four, and was beginning to feel it.

'John? How long have you been there?' She looked sleepy, confused. He looked at his watch automatically.

'Oh, two, maybe three hours.' She smiled.

'Dear John. Dear, dear John,' she said, and began to weep. He stood up, sat on the bed, and took her in his arms. She held him tightly, racked with sobbing. A nurse looked in, decided they were best left alone, and departed. After ten minutes or so she had calmed down.

'I'm sorry,' she said.

'Don't be daft, my sweet. You need it.'

'It's the war. This bloody, bloody, bloody war.' She wept again. He stayed silent until she spoke. 'I have to be ready for the funeral on Friday. I must pull myself together.' She spoke automatically, emotionlessly.

'I'll be there, darling,' he promised. 'I know how much Henderby meant to you. I'll be there for you.' He smoothed her hair gently.

'Not Peter,' she said. 'Not Peter. Little Ben. I made them promise I could have a funeral for little Ben. They never found Peter.' She began weeping again.

Chapter 11: London Blitz

The Humber had completed its rest and was once more on the move, almost purring at a gentle pace.

'Do you remember the funeral?' she asked.

'Vividly,' he replied. 'As if it were yesterday.'

'I will never forget that day.'

'No. Not the sort of thing one forgets easily.'

'A cold October afternoon,' she mused. 'That's what I remember. The vicar wanting to rush the service – wanting to finish before the air raid sirens went.'

'Yes, good old Hitler's decision to flatten London. And they did come that night.'

'I've never been so frightened in my life. Well, apart from ... '

'Yes, apart from.'

'You saw Inspector Rudman the following week, didn't you?'

'Yes. Rudman took it almost personally, the war. As if Hitler was robbing him of his suspects, one by one.'

'Rudman was mad, I think. Still is, I would imagine. He is going to be there?'

'I'm sure of it. I'm pretty sure he's the one behind this invitation, this – charade.'

She leaned towards him and stroked the side of his face tenderly.

'Still, we have good memories as well as the bad, don't we?' she whispered.

'Yes. We do have those. Good memories as well as the bad.'

The day after the funeral Haskins had driven Erica up to an aunt in Yorkshire. It was against her wishes; she would prefer to stay in London amidst the bombs, maybe join an anti-aircraft unit to help shoot the Germans down. But she was too weak to stand her ground against both Haskins and Rose. Rose had come up for the funeral, to give Erica any support she could. She stayed overnight at Haskins' house, intending to leave for Portsmouth the following day. He was surprised to find her still there when he returned.

'I thought I could spend a few days in London,' she said. 'There are some people I promised to look up. You don't mind, do you?'

'Not at all,' he replied, trying but failing to hide his delight. 'It's a strange idea, staying in a city being bombed every night, but I'd be happy for you to stay. As long as you want.'

'Portsmouth has had its fair share. If it has got your name on it ... '
She had no need of finishing the widely held saying.

That night the Luftwaffe came again. Haskins was lying in bed, willing sleep to come in the darkness when the air-raid sirens began. He got out of bed and opened the blackout curtains. In the distance he could see the searchlights playing across the sky, the lights giving the bedroom an eerie blueish glow. There was a knock at the door.

'Come in,' he said. Rose slipped in, closing the door behind her. She came up and stood beside him, watching the sight.

'Shouldn't we be down in the Anderson?' she asked, her voice low. They were speaking quietly as if the coming bombers might be able to hear them.

'Not yet, maybe when the bombs start dropping,' he replied. He had spent his spare time over the previous few days in the garden, digging a hole to take the Anderson shelter, semi-circular lengths of corrugated iron sheeting, covered with the soil from the hole it was in. Apart from the exercise he felt he had achieved little. The shelter looked puny when compared with the thought of the explosives the Luftwaffe was dropping. He and Rose had discussed whether he should convert the garden into a vegetable patch, and decided that it was his duty to do so, though his knowledge of vegetables was minimal.

'Have any come close?' she asked softly.

Her matter-of-fact question surprised Haskins, though he wasn't sure why. Her actions during the bombing of Portsmouth had shown her to be fearless, if he had ever doubted it.

'No,' he replied. 'This part of North London is too far north to be in any great danger. They're going after the docks, a legitimate, as the saying goes, target of war, though I don't buy that one. There are too many civilians living there to use that excuse.'

'But we're only a few miles away,' she pointed out.

'They have quite sophisticated bombing devices which can place a bomb within yards of the target, so they won't be troubling us.' He paused, and added: 'That's the theory, anyway.'

'And the practice?'

He grimaced.

'Our anti-aircraft guns will tear them apart. They will weave to avoid them, and might decide to jettison their bombs anywhere. And there's the chance their bombers will be too damaged to do anything but fly on and crash – and they're headed in our direction. And there's another thing called historical precedent.'

'This isn't going to be a history lecture, is it?' she whispered in his ear. It tickled.

'No, it's just a phrase. You remember when they bombed Portsmouth a few months ago?'

'Yes?'

'According to the theory they should have been able to drop their bombs with pin-point accuracy on the docks. Instead they were all over the place – some people say that the docks were the safest place to be, though I rather doubt that. I'm beginning to believe that everything we've being told about aerial bombing is a load of ... rubbish, I think the polite word is. I don't think they really know where those bombs are going. We may not be in direct danger, but I suspect people are going to die out of pure bad luck.'

She slipped an arm around him. He could feel the warmth of her body, and realised that she was wearing only a thin silk nightdress.

'Well, if we're going to die tonight we might as well enjoy ourselves,' she said softly, pulling him to her and kissing him. He felt her hand slip underneath his pyjama top, and she drew them towards the bed. He did not resist.

Though the little boy in him said that he would have preferred to wait to see the first bombs drop.

The following months he spent his time divided between London and Portsmouth. He knew he should have given other areas more attention, but Rose was in Portsmouth, and Erica had returned to London, filled with hatred and hoping the invasion would come so that she could "get a couple of them for Peter and Ben". In Portsmouth Rose joined him at whichever hotel he was staying in. In London Erica stayed at his house, being unable to face the idea of her lonely home in Camden. She busied herself with cleaning the house and cooking meals, muttering about men who couldn't look after themselves. She took over the planned vegetable garden with a passion, preparing it for the coming spring. It was her way of dealing with life.

'You need to get back to writing,' he tried telling her.

'I will never write another word again.' It was a final reply.

It was also a delicate situation. He innocently told Rose about Erica's living in his house while they were in bed in his hotel bedroom, registered as Mr and Mrs Haskins. He was amazed at the response.

'I see,' she had said, sitting up in bed, lips pursed. 'A woman in every port, then? Keeping the grieving widow warm at night, are we? Keeping the home fires burning?' She had rolled out of bed, switched the light on, and was angrily putting her clothes on.

'Rose, it's not like that at all. Erica doesn't want to go back to Camden, I've got a house which is empty most of the time. And Erica needs company. It is nothing — nothing at all like what you're suggesting.'

'Nice stuff if you can get it. What happened to Mr Prim and Proper? I suppose you think the war makes it all right. Is that it? Or maybe it's just you. Maybe you're the sort of man who would do that anyway.'

'Rose, please, I —' She was about to walk out.

'You know, now I understand what you meant by anyone being able to commit murder under the right conditions. Only I can't decide which of you to murder. Both, probably.' He got out of bed, realised he looked silly naked, and quickly put a dressing gown on, standing between her and the door, eyes blazing.

'Right. Now you listen to me Rosemary Morely. I have an idea, and it's a corker. It'll solve this problem in one go.' She looked at him in fury, but didn't interrupt. 'Erica needs company, you don't trust her and me. You actually like Erica. London is more dangerous than Portsmouth at the moment. You have some spare rooms, you told me once. So why don't we get Erica to stay with you?'

'Stay with me?' She sounded puzzled.

'Well? I think it's the perfect solution. And she'll keep the place clean for you, she's developed a passion for domestic chores.' He was about to add, jokingly, that Erica could also ensure that Rose remained loyal to him, that other possibility having crossed his mind a few times, but realised that it might not have been taken in the spirit it was meant.

'She can't stay with me. Not at the moment.' Rose sat down on the bed, as if the idea had dazed her.

'Why on earth not? Look –' Rose had held up a hand to stop him, her eyes closed. He sat down next to her. 'Very well, so she can't stay with you. But surely there must be a house or flat to rent nearby? You could go for walks together every so often, have tea, visit the cinema.' She opened her eyes and looked at him, smiling and shaking her head slowly.

'Walks? Tea? The cinema? Oh, dear John, you are so sweet.' She stood up, unbuttoned her skirt and let it drop to the floor. 'I'll trust you with Erica. We can talk about her coming down some other time. Let's go back to bed.'

He took his gown off, climbed back into bed and surrendered to her caresses, wondering, not for the first time, whether he would ever understand the female mind. At least it meant he wouldn't have to try to talk Erica out of London and the vegetable patch.

Two days later he was out with Rudman again, on another futile watch for black marketeers.

'I don't believe this lot exists,' Rudman said, back at the police station, sipping a hot but tasteless cup of tea. 'We've caught others, nearly caught others, but every time our so-called informants give us a tip about this lot it turns out to be duff information. I think someone is giving me the run-around.'

'It certainly looks that way,' Haskins agreed. He was thinking that he could be with Rose instead of freezing in the night air along with a couple of soldiers and several police officers. 'I wonder when this war will end?' he asked, thinking aloud. Imagining himself back at the university, with Rose ... where would Rose be? Would she settle down with him? She seemed to be enjoying a carefree life. It was certainly one she had no intention of giving up at the moment, not even for him.

'Maybe it will never end,' Rudman replied grimly. 'Germans chasing us around Africa. Japanese raising hell in China. The Russians sitting quite pretty on the sidelines, making a profit out of the Germans. The Yanks happy to sell us munitions until our money runs out. Yes, maybe that's our best hope, that it simply won't end. Hitler will invade in the a month or two, mark my words. If we can beat him off we can keep going for another year or so.'

'That would mean you having to keep tabs on us a little longer.'

'Don't worry. I can wait.'

Chapter 12: Barbarossa

'What was Nigel?' she asked.

'How do you mean?'

'In terms of muses. Which one was he given?'

'Polyhymnia, I think – sacred music and pantomime.'

'Is that what she is? I'm sure you said something differently that night.' He chuckled.

'I might have left out the pantomime bit. It seemed appropriate that evening.'

They had to slow down to wait for a shepherd to herd his flock of sheep to the side of the road to allow them through. They waved as they passed, and he returned a short nod of acknowledgement.

'What you said about Inspector Rudman being there,' she said, 'reminds you of what he said to you – when was it, '41? "I can wait".'

'And so he did,' he said.

'And now we're going to meet him again. Can't say I'm looking forward to it. Not my most favourite person in the world.'

He laughed.

'Well, I suppose he wouldn't be. Personally I think the war drove him a little mental. He needed something to hold on to, to make sense of a world collapsing around his ears – we all did. Only in his case that something was a murder case, a particularly nasty one. In a normal world he would have become resigned to closing the book on it.'

'I doubt it. I remember you telling me about the look on his face when he got that wonderful news a little while later. You said he had actually smiled. Smiled, like a wolf seeing a lamb, you said.' He shivered slightly.

'Yes. Made the hairs stand up alright.'

It was six a.m. on the morning of Sunday, June 22nd, 1941. Rudman, Haskins and assorted constables and privates had spent another fruitless night, crouched amongst bushes heavy with a summer dew. Rudman's mind had appeared to be on something else altogether. He had shrugged off the failure, and insisted on returning to the police station where he expected important information.

'Any messages come in overnight for me?' he demanded of the desk sergeant as soon as they entered the building.

'Yes, sir, it's on your desk. But, sir, there's something else –'

'Later, sergeant,' Rudman said sharply, and almost ran off towards his office. Haskins was about to follow when he noticed the sergeant jerking a thumb pleadingly towards the back.

'Well?' he asked, wishing to go back to the hotel, hoping Rose would not have left by the time he got there.

'On the news, sir,' the sergeant said. Haskins realised that he had been gesturing towards a civilian radio.

'Yes? What about the news? Come on, man, what is it? The invasion?' The sergeant dumbly leaned over and turned the volume up. An announcer's voice came over, neutral, unemotional.

'German sources have confirmed that German soldiers crossed the Russian-German divisional line in Poland early this morning. They have cited what they term "irreconcilable differences" and "Soviet intransigence" for the move. At this point it is unclear to what extent Soviet forces have been able to oppose them.' Haskins looked at the sergeant in surprise.

'He's gone? Gone into Russia?'

'It would appear so, sir.' The sergeant was grinning.

'Bloody hell. Bloody hell!' He was too shocked to say anything else for a few seconds. 'We've got the little bastard!' he said finally. 'He's made the same mistake as Napoleon! And he'll suffer the same fate. We're going to win, you realise it, we're going to win!' He was quite staggered at the news. Rudman returned as he tried to take in the enormity of Hitler's actions.

'Got him!' Rudman said triumphantly.

'You can say that again,' Haskins said enthusiastically.

'Henderby. He's not dead. He's a POW.'

'Eh?' Haskins had a sensation of floating in a sea of confusion.

'Henderby. He wasn't killed. Came down on a French field just off

102

Wissant, plane was a wreck, he was badly injured. Spent three months in a French hospital commandeered by the Krauts, until someone realised he was well enough to be in a POW camp. Managed to slip away before they could do that and spent the next few months hiding, trying to reach Switzerland. Caught by the Germans who didn't believe he was a POW – apparently the hospital tried to bodge the records to show they had already sent him off. Finally sent to Stalag Luft whatever and the Swiss Red Cross informed. Henderby is still alive.'

'Does Erica know?' asked Haskins, trying to take it in.

'Erica?'

'His wife.'

'Dunno. War Office will inform her, I suppose.'

Haskins looked at him with some distaste. To Rudman all Henderby was was a suspect. He wanted him alive in case he had to hang him.

'I'd better go,' he said. 'I have an urgent telephone call to make.' He slipped out of the door before Rudman could say anything further. Outside his driver took the injunction to "drive like hell" to heart. Haskins was back at the hotel in fifteen minutes. He took the steps two at a time, bursting in on Rose. She had been sleeping. She looked up with dream-laden eyes.

'John? What's happened?'

'Henderby's alive, Rose.'

'Alive?'

'Yes.' He was frantically searching his suitcase for his private address book. 'I have to telephone Erica. They won't know she's staying at my house.'

'Alive?'

'Yes.' He turned and smiled. 'And the Germans have invaded Russia.'

'Russia?' He found his address book, leapt over to the bed and kissed her forehead passionately.

'One, Alive. Two, Russia.' He left the room, racing down the stairs to the front desk. The porter whose job it was to man the desk in the morning hours watched in surprise as Haskins dragged the telephone towards himself and urgently requested connection to a London number. Just as suddenly he put the handset down. 'But what if Rudman is wrong?' he asked the porter. He drummed his fingers on the reception desk impatiently. 'Too early for the War Office to be up,' he informed the bemused porter. 'But we could make London by the time they are.'

'We?' asked the porter as he raced back up the stairs.

'Russia!' shouted Haskins back at the porter.

'Russia?' asked the porter in bewilderment.

'Alive!' Haskins replied just before turning into the corridor.

'Lucky beggar, then,' the porter muttered. 'Alive and in Russia.'

Rose had arisen and put on a dressing gown.

'Are you sure?' she asked as he threw clothes into his suitcase.

'No. I'm going straight back up to London to find out. And I want to be there when Erica finds out – if it is true. She won't know what hit her.' He slammed the suitcase shut, and kissed her briefly. 'I'll try to be back this evening.'

'But John, it's Sunday. Surely there won't be anyone around?'

'Don't you know there's a war on?' he asked jokingly. 'There is bound to be someone, somewhere. And with the news of Russia the offices will probably be heaving with people who think they ought to be there, but don't know what to do.'

She hugged him.

'I suppose so. Yes, you should go. I've got some deliveries to make today anyway. You go take care of Erica. She'll need it.'

'Deliveries? On a Sunday?'

'Don't you know there's a war on? Deliveries are no longer Monday to Saturday.' She smiled. 'I hope it is true. Really I do. Give her my love whatever happens.'

In the end it did turn out to be true, though it took Haskins a morning of badgering everyone he could find, before a helpful young woman took him to the right department and the right desk. He kidnapped the young woman with the Swiss Red Cross letter to prove to Erica that it was true – or at least official. Erica took longer

104

than Rose to understand the import of what he was saying, but finally it sank in. To his relief she did not need him there.

Eventually she smiled and kissed him.

'Thank you, John. Thank you for everything you've done. Now you get back to Rose. I've got some letters to write. And tell her I said thank you to her also. I couldn't have made it without you two.'

He left the young woman with her just in case. He spent the journey back to Portsmouth patrolling his emotions; Henderby alive, brilliant news; Russia invaded, marvellous, possibly not for the Russians, but Hitler would have gone for them sooner or later; Rosemary waiting for him, how much better could a man wish for?

And Rudman.

Of Rudman he was not very sure at all.

Chapter 13: Yorkshire

They were back amidst hedgerows, their view limited to the curving road ahead, a strip of sky and borders of green.

'Are we getting close?' she asked. 'I don't recognise any of this.'

'No, I can't say I do. But then, we were only here the once.'

'Strange that. Georgina had this place for, what, three years? Invited us to all her parties in London, but that weekend was the first time in Longwood.'

'Seems to have a special attachment to the place. I mean, buying it even though the army were in residence.'

'Maybe her mind flipped. I wonder what she's like these days.'

'Difficult to imagine Georgina as anything but a young girl having a laugh.'

'Darling. You can be so naive. You still think she was merely being kind to us.'

'People can be kind, you know.'

'I do know. I married one.' She kissed him gently on the cheek. He felt himself begin to blush. She was the one person who could wind him around her little finger if she chose. As it was her he didn't mind. Strange thing, he thought, this love business.

'What about dear Aunt Edith? She was a kind person.'

'True. Kind, but a little daft. I wonder if the two go together.' Probably, he thought. 'I shall never forget that January,' he said. It was as if we were in a sheltered little winter paradise, far from everything else. Mostly.'

Erica had suggested a holiday. The word sounded incongruous amid a world gone mad. The latter half of December 1941. A new ally had been added to the war, the United States of America. The addition of a new enemy, Japan, hardly seemed an addition at all; Japan had long been effectively their foe. Russia appeared to be so close to the verge of collapse it recalled memories of 1917.

'She says that, if I would like to come up for a week or so with some friends I would be more than welcome,' Erica had said, waving a letter. Since the news of Henderby Erica had become transformed. She was a whirlwind of committees for this, that and the other, glad to have her name on board. Fund raising, succouring the bombed-out, POW support, everything seemed to have "Erica Ringold" attached. She had given up on "Erica Henderby" in public; people wanted the authoress, not the wife. A judicious letter from Haskins to Henderby had brought him up to date on Erica's writing career, which was nil. Rose had helped him suggest, diplomatically, that he should ask her about her writing. Her evasive reply gave Henderby the chance to admonish her about her laxness, and, without actually saying so, suggest that he would be hard pressed to support both of them when the war was over.

'I think his injuries were worse than he has said,' Haskins commented, having read the letter. Erica always showed off Henderby's letters, few and rare as they were. Haskins wrote to Henderby once a month on a regular basis. Erica wrote every day, but could only post once a week, with no guarantee of when or if anything would get through. Rose apologised that she was not a natural letter writer.

'Send him my love, please?' she had implored Haskins and Erica.

'Don't worry, Rose my darling,' Erica had replied, putting her arm around her, 'we all have our own abilities. Mine is to write fiction and John's is to write boring.'

'Boringly,' Haskins corrected. Erica stuck her tongue out at him, and Rose giggled. She and Erica were now like sisters; in Erica's company she reverted to certain girlish – what he thought of as girlish – behaviour. He wished she could be the same with himself. But that would be to deprive her of an independence she had fought for and made herself. She needed that veneer of tough exterior to keep the world at a certain distance, including him.

It was probably about that time that the thought struck him that it might be his fault. It was only a few weeks before – less, just before Pearl Harbour – when she had suddenly exclaimed, 'Why can't you use everyone's Christian names? It's "Peter", not "Henderby"! And

"Morely", for Christsake! What makes me "Rose" and Robert "Morely"? Honestly, sometimes you're such an old dinosaur!' He would have written it off as "one of those women's things", but the arguments had been increasing lately. It was stress. The war going badly, and seemingly never-ending, rations at a premium, working long hours – the list could go on and on.

'What's Yorkshire like this time of year?' he asked after Erica's suggestion of a holiday.

'Terrible. All snow and hills and dales. Snug little pubs. Roaring log fires, good grub – well, compared to London, it is a farm after all.' She paused. 'My aunt has said we'll need to help with the minor household chores, most of the maids and what have you are gone, but I'll look after those while you two take long lovers' walks in the fading twilight.'

'Not good enough,' Haskins had boomed – in what he thought was his "booming" voice. 'We'll all take care of the chores, and you will take your typewriter along and pen purple prose while we take those lovers' walks in the twilight.'

And so it was agreed. The only slight problem turned out to be Haskins and Rosemary.

'You will have to be a married couple,' Erica informed them. 'unless you want single rooms. Dear Aunt Edith is somewhat Victorian in her ways. The war hasn't reached her part of Yorkshire yet.' This was hardly a major problem; for over a year they had been signing into hotels as husband and wife. He knew that countless other thousands were doing the same thing. He wondered whether, after the war, things would return to the old mores.

Slipping into bed alongside Rose that evening in London the thought struck him, not for the first time, that he was ready to marry. Looking at Rose's firm jaw as she read a novel, he accepted, as on the other occasions, that she was not. He longed to ask her what she hoped from their relationship. He also suspected that it was a tenuous one; if he pressed her on it she might decide it was time to move on.

They left for Yorkshire early in January. The festive season had been miserable. 1942 had started on a gloomy and downcast note, despite Churchill's hectoring. The latest National Service Act had laid down conscription for unmarried women between twenty and thirty-one, obliging them to take jobs in war-industries or auxiliary military services if so directed. Rose's work as a volunteer ambulance driver meant that she was unlikely to be conscripted, but it had not improved her temper or her feelings.

Looking at the suburbs as the train chugged slowly out of London, they could see broken buildings and open spaces left by the Blitz and later random visits by the Luftwaffe. Rose sighed as they finally entered open countryside.

'God, I am so glad to get away from it all for a while.' She echoed Haskins' thoughts. He knew Portsmouth had its own share of bombed-out spaces. Erica looked as if she had changed her mind and wanted to go back to help the war effort. Taking a break meant that she wasn't doing what little she could to help end the war and bring Henderby home, and even that little paled into insignificance at the thought of what would be required before the war could be brought to an end. It would require the defeat of Germany and its allies, and that seemed at times almost an impossible task.

The journey took seven hours, and required three changes of trains. The railway network was suffering badly from the effects of the war, and Haskins was relieved that austerity meant they travelled relatively lightly. Twice they had to change platforms at a moment's notice, lugging their suitcases up and down stairs. But somehow there was little complaining. It was almost, he thought, like an adventure. It was a relief to be away from large cities and the danger they posed.

At the train station closest to the aunt's farm they were met by an old man driving a pony and trap.

'Rationing,' he explained. 'Can't get petrol nor diesel for love nor money.'

But the three were delighted by the slow, bumpy journey; the fields were recently covered with snow, late afternoon sunlight throwing the landscape into relief, bright white and dark shadows.

'It's like a fairy tale,' Rose exclaimed, clapping her hands. She and Erica chattered happily about the sight. Haskins had been tempted to point out that, if they had to live and work here, it would be no fairy tale. Advisably he kept the thought to himself, and relaxed and enjoyed the journey and the chatter.

They were greeted by Dear Aunt Edith, a blazing log fire in the lounge, and mounds of sandwiches in case they were "peckish". Aunt Edith had made up for a lack of children by dedicating herself to the creation of wholesome country food.

And so began two weeks of walks, food and log fires, with a dash of domestic dish-washing thrown in. For Haskins, who thought in terms of "holidays" as a chance to research in Paris, Berlin, Venice or a number of other locations, it was the best time of his life. The war was far, far away, isolated from them in their winter retreat.

He had never seen Rose so happy, and Erica also showed signs of her old self, though punctuated by silences in which she was obviously thinking about Henderby.

Haskins was a man who observed and thought about other people, but rarely realised that they did the same about him, so he would have been surprised at a conversation between Erica and Rose on the third evening. Aunt Edith had gone to bed, Haskins had volunteered to fetch a jersey for Rose, and Rose and Erica sat in the lounge in front of the large fire.

'He's a sweetie,' Erica commented.

'Yes, he is,' Rose agreed absentmindedly, looking into the fire.

'He loves you, you know,' Erica continued. It was a potentially dangerous conversation to be having, but one Erica thought would have to be had sooner or later.

'I know,' Rose replied quietly. 'And I'm in love with him.'

Erica leaned forward, holding her hands out to the fire. Rose obviously did not want to pursue the issue, but Erica seemed intent on carrying on.

'I'm surprised you haven't made him propose yet,' she said.

Rose appeared to think about this for a while.

'Maybe one day,' she replied eventually. 'It's difficult at the moment – what with the war and everything.'

She was making excuses, Erica thought. It was almost as if Rose did not want to marry John. Or maybe she was thinking about her and Peter, and what she had gone through when she thought Peter had been killed. Or maybe she wanted to retain her independent life, but also keep John within it. She wanted to say something to Rose, not to leave things until too late, but felt uneasy about it. When she had kept house for John it had not consciously been an attempt to bring him back into her own life.

Or so she told herself.

She decided to let the issue drop.

It was that day that Haskins and Rose had visited a local country house, the gardens of which had been open to the public at specified times before the war. Now it was overgrown and deserted, the driveway up to the front gates needing attention, the front gates themselves rusting. Despite this they had passed the day speculating where various borders had been, what plants would have been grown, and whether or not they could take it over and grow vegetables to support themselves. It was a pipedream, making a dream future for themselves, the sort to have on a break from the war and real life.

In the second week, on the last Friday, they decided to return to the country house to re-enjoy the dream. Haskins had decided that he would ask Rose to marry him. He didn't have a ring – he had little thought that things would come to such a pass – but it would be the best and most propitious opportunity for a while.

But this time access at the gates was denied by an armed sentry, brown serge uniform with a "commando" flash on the top of the arm. The gates had been cleaned and oiled, restored to act as solid barriers, a small guardhouse built next to them..

'No entry to civilians, sir,' the soldier said politely but firmly.

'But we were here just a week ago,' Rose began to point out

'I'll deal with this, Bates,' a voice came from the guardhouse.

'Yes, sarge,' the soldier said, and appeared to lose interest. The sergeant appeared at the entrance to the guardhouse. He was young, of medium height, whippet thin, and looked the part of a particularly vicious soldier, bayonet on his belt. Haskins exclaimed in surprise. Rose followed suit.

'Johnson!' he said, 'Nigel!' remembering Rose's injunction. 'My goodness! Fancy meeting you here in the middle of nowhere.'

Johnson nodded, seemingly unsurprisable. The look in his eyes was hardly friendly, more neutral, but ready to be aggressive.

'You have your ID with you?' he asked.

Haskins looked back in surprise, but handed over his identity card. Rose did the same, looking put-out. Johnson saw the look on Haskins' face.

'We have to formally check the identity of anyone who comes to the gate,' he explained. 'Hmm, a major then. Sir.' He handed the cards back.

'I wouldn't worry with the "Sir" bit,' Haskins said. 'It's only nominal, and I'm in mufti now anyway. So what brings you here? Or am I not allowed to ask?'

'I wouldn't ask if I were you,' Johnson replied. 'I'll walk you back to the road.' They began to stroll back, Haskins partly intrigued, Rose irritated. 'So, seen any of the Longwood lot recently?' he asked conversationally, as if he were trying to be polite while escorting them away.

'We're at Erica's aunts farm, Erica's there.' Haskins gave him a summary of where the others were, as far as he knew. 'And Inspector Rudman is still on the trail,' he concluded.

'Still on the trail?' Johnson echoed in surprise. 'What's his problem? People dying every day, and he's still on about that stupid woman and her darkie?' Both were surprised at the change in Johnson, his attitude and his language. He obviously had no further interest in the workers of the world uniting.

'I suppose he doesn't like people being killed,' Rose suggested somewhat sarcastically. 'It goes against his job.'

'Plenty of people killing and being killed these days,' Johnson remarked with a sneer, 'easy enough when you've done the first few.' He slapped the bayonet at his side to emphasize the point. 'If you see Rudman again, suggest he comes with us on our next outing. He might learn something.'

They came to the end of the entrance road, and Johnson stopped.

'Right,' he said briefly, 'this is as far as I come without being AWOL. If they got me for that they wouldn't let me out to kill more Germans.'

He threw them a mock salute and strode away. They watched him go, and then turned, heading back the way they had come.

'He seemed to be trying to tell us something,' Rose said. She shivered and he put his arm around her.

'Yes, he was telling us he's a mean and nasty soldier who will kill at the drop of a hat, and we should be afraid of him. I rather suspect he's always been a bully. Or, at least, aspired to become one.'

'It's not just that, it's – when he said that about being easy after the first few – do you think he was referring to Emily and Georgina? That he had done it and was boasting about it?'

'God knows. Could be, or maybe he was just trying to suggest that he might have, to frighten us. I do think that he's the sort of person to avoid. Fortunately I don't think we're likely to meet him anywhere civilised.'

'He reminded me of a wild animal.'

'Yes. A ferret, I thought.'

'I was thinking of a rat. A particularly nasty rat, starving and hungry.'

The walked in silence for a while.

'Can we go back to the farm?' she asked. 'I don't fancy a walk anymore.'

'If we do that we've allowed him to win his silly little game. Let's go to the other side of the village, along the path by the oak tree.' She nodded reluctantly.

Once past the village she cheered up at the memory of a snowball fight they had had under the oak tree on the third day. They had another now. The exercise and childishness cheered them both up. But it did not quite clear the gloom Johnson had brought. The war had returned. Longwood house had returned.

And Haskins had missed his chance to propose.

Back in London Haskins made what he believed were discreet inquiries about Nigel Johnson. Various locations around the country had been taken by secretive army units, but that same secrecy allowed criminal gangs to dress up as soldiers and thus evade scrutiny. He didn't think Johnson was one of those, but it would be better to be safe.

Three days later Martins called him into his office.

'I hear you've been trying to dig up information on a someone named Nigel Johnson who is apparently a commando on training in Yorkshire,' he commented. Haskins nodded. 'Well, you can take the bloodhounds off. I've had a very loud reprimand from someone very high up about areas of jurisdiction. You're to forget you ever saw this Johnson.'

'Sorry. I was trying to be diplomatic about it. Didn't want to make any noises if he was the real thing.'

Martins nodded.

'I understand. Part of the job. And very discreetly done, I must say.' He opened a desk drawer and took out a bottle of whisky and two glasses. Have a seat, John. Time for a pre-evening tipple. Have to learn to relax, you know.' Haskins eyed the bottle. It looked suspiciously like one from a consignment that had been confiscated a month before in Brighton. Martins caught his look. He winked. 'Compensations of the job,' he said.

Haskins sat down and accepted a glass a third full. The whisky tasted good, unlike some of the poison that was being made in home distilleries, and that made him feel more uncomfortable. Six months previously he had been about to bring a private soldier up on charges after the man had been caught pilfering two tins of bully beef. In the end he had settled for what he called a "severe reprimand" and a lecture about duty and the sacrifices others were making to get food through, what, had he known, the soldier in question had referred to as a "right bollocking and a bloody long sermon". Later he had learnt that the man was trying to support a pregnant wife, and he found himself vastly relieved at his earlier decision.

But he personally had never taken anything. Now he began to wonder how much Martins was helping himself to.

Indeed, whether Martins was doing something more than helping himself to the occasional bottle of whisky. It was a standing order that he inform Martins whenever he went out on a raid. The sort of information that could be used to alert someone else.

It could well explain why certain of the raids he and Rudman went on had proved fruitless.

Chapter 14: Number 26

The Humber, he thought, was sniffing at the tractor trailer, saying to it, "Get out of the way, I'm a Humber and much faster than you. Indeed, in my young days I was five times as fast as you."

'Jessica turned out to be somewhat of a surprise, didn't she?' he said aloud.

'Ah, but that's because you always underestimate a woman's strength. You think we're all such meek and mild things, love little kittens and couldn't hurt a fly.' He grinned ruefully.

'I promise never to think that ever again.'

'She had Urania. Maybe Calliope would have been better – "epic".'

'The muse of epic poetry, mmm,' he pondered. He glanced at her.

'You wanted to have Terpsichore, Euterpe and Polyhymnia. All music and dance. I was surprised by that at the time.'

'I had to choose one. In the end it was Terpsichore. I liked the notion of music and dancing, wasn't sure about the name.' She sighed. 'Funny how, over time, we went from manic dancing to singing "There'll be blue skies" and then on to that American Boogy-Woogy stuff.'

'It was the nature of the times,' he said. 'First over-confidence, then dark desperation. And finally the belief that it would take time, but we would win. Eventually.'

'And Frieda was left with Euterpe. Lyric poetry. It didn't really suit her. She hardly ever said a word.'

'She was certainly the odd one out. Not an easy achievement considering how odd some of the rest were.'

'Including me?'

'Of course not, darling,' he replied, lying.

She watched the bushes go by, humming a tune from the war, "Yours" a favourite of Vera Lynn.

'Which Jessica did you prefer?' He grimaced.

'I didn't think much of her as Rob's muse. But then I'm not overly fond of the other Jessica. That is, very admirable, but somewhat frightening.'

'Very frightening,' he added after a pause.

September 1943. Haskins had long settled into a routine between London and Portsmouth. He was bored. He felt he was no longer contributing to the war effort, if he had ever been. Rommel had been chased out of North Africa. Sicily had just been invaded by the Allies. German armies in Russia were suffering huge losses. The Americans had stopped the Japanese and were beginning to push them back. Out there real soldiers were fighting a real war.

'I'm supposed to be going out with Rudman tomorrow night,' he told Rose in the Cumberland bar. 'He has a hot tip on a house in Nelson Avenue, wherever that is. I think I might tell him I have a previous engagement.'

'Nelson Avenue? That's where my little house is. What number? Can I expect to be raided? It would make a change, life is a little dull these days.'

'Of course, I'd forgotten that. Number 26, if I recall correctly.'

'Oh, goody. next door.' Her face dropped. 'Not so goody. That place has been empty for months. Years in fact. The previous owners objected to the noise of the bombing. I don't think I've ever seen anyone go in.'

'Another no-go. I shall pass the information on.' He sat moodily regarding the dust on the tables. The time was long past when the hotel had sufficient staff for daily cleaning. 'Rose?' he asked.

'Yes, darling?' She seemed preoccupied.

'Where are we going?'

'How do you mean? Tomorrow? I thought we'd agreed on the Odeon.'

'No, generally. Us.' He looked at her. 'Rose? Will you marry me?' he blurted out suddenly. It was out at last. Marriage would be something to plan for, something to make all the boredom acceptable, or at least bearable.

'Now don't be silly, darling. You will want to settle down into a nice little married life, with me at home waiting with your pipe and slippers.'

'What's so wrong with that?'

'I'm not quite ready for it. I don't think I shall ever be. At least, not while the war's on.'

'So the answer's "no", then,' he remarked gruffly.

'The answer is "definitely not yet".'

Not ever, he thought.

'I think I shall apply for transfer to an active unit,' he decided. 'I've had enough of this play-soldiering, semi-policeman nonsense. There's hardly anything happening these days anyway.'

'Don't be silly, John, you're too old for that sort of thing.'

'Just old enough for pipe and slippers,' he remarked sarcastically.

'Be patient, sweetie,' she pleaded. 'I do love you, you know.'

He shook his head sadly. He did not understand it. But if he pursued the matter it would only get worse.

That night was almost intolerable. He had passed Rose's information to Rudman, but Rudman had merely muttered something about "has to be done". At midnight they stood in number 26 reviewing an empty lounge by torchlight, having visited an empty kitchen, empty bedrooms, empty bathroom and all the other empty rooms. The only item of furniture, if it could be called that, was a large mirror attached to a bedroom wall upstairs, presumably left because it was too difficult or heavy to detach. The electricity had been turned off somewhere, probably by the electricity board after non-payment. Haskins wondered what on earth he was doing in an obviously empty house at midnight and how it might possibly be considered productive.

'There's something wrong with this dust,' Rudman said. Haskins looked at the dust in the torchlight. It looked pretty much as all the other dust that seemed around these days.

'Are you going to arrest it?' he asked. Rudman gave him a sour look.

'I'll come back in the daylight,' he said. 'Things look clearer then.' He tapped his jaw thoughtfully. 'You say you told your girlfriend – Miss

Morely – about tonight? Anyone else you might have mentioned it to?' It was obvious to Haskins that Rudman thought someone had been alerted to the raid and quickly disappeared, just like on so many other occasions. He didn't like the way Rudman had said "your girlfriend". It sounded almost lewd.

'Colonel Martins,' he said. 'I have to get clearance each time in case he decides it's not in our remit.'

'I would have thought you'd be able to take those sort of decisions yourself by now.' He tapped his jaw again. 'Trust him? Your Colonel Martins?'

Haskins thought back to the bottle of whisky. He thought back further, at his impression that Martins was creating his own little empire. At his insistence on being alerted whenever a raid would take place, no matter how minor. At how often tip-offs had resulted in nothing. Circumstantially the evidence did suggest that Martins was in a prime position to control events.

So, yes, that was the question: did he trust him?

'He is my superior officer,' he said finally. Rudman nodded slowly.

'In other words, you don't know. And you don't strike me as a man who is often undecided about something. Leave it to me, I'll make some inquiries. He isn't my superior officer.'

Haskins thought he should protest, but he didn't have the energy nor the enthusiasm. If Martins was a crook in uniform, let him have what was coming to him.

'Would you arrest him if you had to?' Rudman asked suddenly, looking Haskins in the eye, his own eyes bright in the reflected light, in the shadows across his face.

'Of course. I think my duty would be quite plain.' Rudman nodded.

'Thought so. You're one of the old lot, like me. Know our duty. These days people seem to think anything goes, so long as they can get away with it.'

Haskins expected him to say something about not knowing what the world was coming to, but Rudman appeared to have finished with that subject.

They returned to the station, Haskins hoping he could quickly return to his hotel. Rose seldom complained when he slipped into bed next to her, mainly because he made sure he didn't disturb her sleep – not after the first time.

He was to be disappointed. The duty constable on the front desk – it had been a sergeant previously, manpower was being further stretched – was clearly agitated.

'Inspector Rudman, thank God,' he gabbled. 'An aeroplane has come down near Creech Wood. They think it might be a German one, dropping a spy.' Rudman sighed and looked at the ceiling.

'Wainwright, you know that's an army matter. Get the local unit out. The Home Guard or someone. God's sake, Creech Wood is next to Denmead, we can hardly be the closest people to handle this. Isn't there a unit at Fareham?'

'They can't get there before dawn,' the constable pleaded, 'they asked us to get there as soon as we could, before they got away.'

Rudman sighed again.

'You mean they think it's a false alarm and don't want to get out of their little warm beds, more like.' He looked at Haskins. 'Your lot still outside?' Haskins nodded. 'Well, I suppose since we're already up we might as well go for a ride. Right then, Creech Wood, here we come.'

Having established the exact location – the exact reported location – they set off. Haskins checked his service revolver. He still had only five bullets. He wondered, not for the first time, if they would still work. Considering how old they were they might explode in the barrel.

Would he be prepared to pull the trigger if it became necessary?

He thought he would. If it became obviously necessary.

That was the rub. If the time came it would be unlikely that it would be obvious.

Rudman watched with ill-concealed cynicism.

'You don't suppose it might be a false report, by any chance?' he asked. The pair of them had similar views, decided Haskins; they both thought reports of German spies of dubious value. But while

Haskins little believed that there would be a German spy at the end of this chase, it could be a German pilot downed on a nuisance raid.

'Always pays to be prepared,' he murmured.

Rudman's mouth curled.

'Dib-dib-dob,' he said.

When they reached the nominated part of Creech Wood Haskins noticed against the dark of the sky what appeared to be a plume of smoke arising from a few hundred feet within. He pointed this out to Rudman, who, he was pleased to note, immediately checked his own revolver.

Haskins' four troops dismounted and mounted bayonets. Along with Rudman's constables they formed a line of torches and began moving into the wood. If it was a German they were after, Haskins decided, with the noise they were making they might have as well have sent a telegram. Still, his lot were all rated as being unfit for active service, and the constables no doubt felt that it was not part of their job to go into a wood unarmed against what could well be an armed enemy – after all, in legal terms, he hadn't committed a crime.

The smoke trail became more evident, and they entered a clearing to find a young woman sitting on a log, dazed, holding her left shoulder. She saw them and called out in French. Before Haskins could say anything the line of men converged on her. One overweight and badly dressed soldier reached her first, put his rifle in his left hand and used his right to pull her up.

'Parlez le Francais, do we little mademoiselle? Or maybe even German as well, eh?' he asked sarcastically, clearly believing that he was just about to arrest an alien spy. It was a bad decision. Before the others could move he had his arm whipped around his back, forced between his shoulder blades, and a knife appeared at his throat. The girl shouted something in French, something clearly a threat. The soldier wisely did not struggle, his eyes wide with fear. The knife was already beginning to draw blood.

There was something about the girl that looked familiar to Haskins. Suddenly he called,

'Jessica?'

'Who are you?' she asked with a pronounced French accent. It was clear to Haskins that she was stunned for some reason, and going on instinct alone. He moved slowly forward, directing his torch on his face, downward.

'We met a couple of years ago. At Longwood House. Remember me? John Haskins.' He heard Rudman utter an oath. Jessica looked at him, her eyes darting around at the troops, as if expecting danger from all sides. She looked as if she was high on drugs.

'What are you doing here?' she asked, as if in a dream. She was losing strength, the knife pressing closer into the soldier's neck.

'You're in England,' he said, suddenly realising what she might be thinking.

'England?' she asked, dazed.

'Yes. If you put the soldier down you will notice he is wearing a traditional Tommy helmet, none of your German scuttle-bucket nonsense.' Silently he prayed he could talk her around before the knife went deeper.

'You promise?' she asked. The French accent had gone.

'I promise.'

'You are John Haskins and you promise?'

'Yes, I am John Haskins and I promise you are in England.'

With an effort she threw the soldier aside. He scuttled away gratefully on all fours. She sank back onto the log, tired beyond caring.

'What the hell is all this about?' Rudman asked furiously, having restrained himself while the soldier's life was at risk.

'I think you can leave it up to us, now,' a voice said. A trenchcoated major appeared out of the darkness, accompanied by a civilian whose eyes and firm jaw seemed born to command.

'And who the hell might you be?' asked Rudman, full of fury.

'Good question,' said Haskins, ' I think you should ask them for their identity documents, and check them.' He sank down next to Jessica on the log. He realised his heart was beating rapidly. 'Before anyone else gets almost killed,' he added. The major looked at his uniform, into his eyes, and nodded. He handed over an identity document to Rudman.

'You have a radio in your car?' he asked. Rudman nodded. 'Your Chief Constable will confirm who I am.' They moved off back to the vehicles. Haskins noticed that Jessica was shivering. He took his jacket off and put it around her shoulders.

'You,' she said, eyes staring feverishly in front, 'you were the only one I trusted.' Haskins wondered what she was talking about, and whether or not to put a comforting arm around her. He decided against it, leaning forwards, his elbows on his knees. 'It was hell over there,' she said.

'Don't say more than you need to, old girl.' She looked at the back of his head in front of her.

'Should I call you Professor or Major?' She giggled hysterically, and just as suddenly composed herself. 'The network was blown. They were waiting for us. I had to kill two Germans to get away.'

With a knife, no doubt, thought Haskins bitterly.

'I managed to contact another group. They wouldn't believe me, but eventually they arranged a Lysander out. Unfortunately he seems to have lost his way. I think he's back in the wreckage.' She seemed unconcerned at the pilot's fate. 'You know how I killed them? The Germans?' she asked, suddenly again full of energy. Haskins did not really want to know. The details, he thought, could wait. 'I thought of them as Robért, The bastard!'

Robert. To his sister, Rob, to Haskins, Morely. To his muse, Robért – pronounced in the French manner.

'I was only seventeen, for Christsake!' she shouted. Haskins took this as an indication of how Morely – Robert? Robért? – had taken advantage of her. He did not know how to respond. He heard the approach of returning feet. Quickly he wrote out an address and a telephone number on a scrap of paper.

'You can contact me here if you want to.' Automatically she slipped the paper into her clothing. She too had heard the others coming back. Her face had become neutral.

'We'll take it from here, Major, if you don't mind.' The anonymous major and civilian had returned with Rudman. Haskins looked at Rudman. He nodded, his lips compressed thinly, his face furious. Jessica returned his jacket. They watched as she and the other two walked away.

'Say their own people will recover the aircraft. Pilot's dead,' Rudman spat. 'All we have to do is protect it until they get here. Blasted army playing at spies. We're left to look after the bits and pieces they don't want.' He called a constable to guard the plane, and they walked back to the car. 'You spoke to the girl. What was wrong with her?'

'As far as I can gather she was in France with one of the Resistance units. Old Churchill's "set Europe ablaze" nonsense. Had a narrow escape from the Germans. Then the Lysander they sent to pick her up crashes here, she gets a bang on the head and thinks she's still in France with the Germans after her.'

Rudman whistled.

'No wonder she took a knife to that man of yours. Lucky he didn't get his throat slit.'

Haskins did not reply. He had left out the bit about her killing Germans. Rudman would probably take that as significant.

'Strange one, that girl,' Rudman continued. 'When I first interviewed her I thought she was a bit simple. Then she has a go at Morely with a knife. Now she turns up here after a trip into occupied France, and probably not for a game of pat-a-cake. What do you think is up with her?'

'I don't know. She was seventeen when the business with Morely started – possibly younger. Girls are impressionable at that age, and I think Morely is a bit of a bastard, to be quite frank.'

Rudman grinned.

'I like frank talk,' he said.

Chapter 15: July 1944

They had stopped in another village, to admire the rusticity, and for him to give a lecture – as she saw it – on how rural England had developed, how the Industrial Revolution had affected populations, and how a new Social Revolution could be expected to bring in greater, unpredictable changes. Now they were on their way again.

'I was rather surprised when you resorted to blackmail,' she laughed.

'Blackmail? Me?' he smiled.

'You. The upright, honest, walking book of morals.'

'Well, it was in a good cause.' She looked at him. Silver threads had begun to appear in his hair. It gave him a distinguished look. She ruffled it slightly. These days he often displayed a boyishness which she had come to like.

'Yes. In the end I rather think it was. That was when I began to wonder if there was anything you wouldn't resort to.' She smiled. 'Poor old Rudman.'

Late July 1944. The Allied armies had landed in Normandy and were still trying to break out of the beachheads, but they were firmly lodged and official statements were positive. The German generals had tried to assassinate Hitler, and failed. The Russians had launched their summer offensive. The Japanese were in retreat. Italy had surrendered the previous September. People were cautiously thinking it might, this time, all be over by Christmas.

Haskins was in two minds. There was little doubt that the Germans would be defeated, and as an historian he knew how quickly armies could collapse. On the other hand the Germans seemed to be fighting viciously and desperately, no doubt spurned on by the fate of the rebellious generals. Not for the first time he wondered about the advisability of the decision at Casablanca to demand an unconditional surrender.

He had not achieved a field or any other posting. Martins was gone some months before, forced out in a reorganisation before the invasion by military and political leaders intent on building the most efficient military machine possible to face the might of the Wermacht and cope with the massive problems and dangers of a sea-borne invasion of a scale never before attempted. Martins had been posted to look after the Home Guard, an obvious sidelining. The day he had left he and Haskins had shared a last whisky together.

'Well, can't complain, I had a long run,' Martins had said jovially. Haskins had wondered what this "long run" referred to; that he had managed to exploit his position without being found out, or that he had been obviously too old and incompetent for the position in the middle of a war, lucky to have got the appointment in the first place? He decided that the question was best left unanswered.

Haskins himself had made what he thought of as a blunder. When the reorganisation had taken place he had hoped he would have an opportunity of landing what he called a "real job". Martins' replacement, a Colonel Miller, a thin man with sharp eyes, had asked Haskins whether he had any preferences in his position in light of the changes.

'I would prefer something which makes a real contribution to the war effort,' he had replied. Miller regarded him with neutral eyes. Neutral eyes which did not trust him.

'You don't think what you're currently doing does that?' he asked.

'No. I haven't for several months. I discussed it with Colonel Martins, but he seemed to disagree.' Miller nodded slowly. He looked at his fingers.

'Did you trust Martins?' he asked. Haskins thought the lack of title was significant.

'In what way?' Miller waved a hand to indicate the inconsequentiality of the question. Haskins doubted it. It had been asked too carefully.

'Generally. Did you have any suspicions that he might be, how should we say, taking advantage of his position?'

'I have no evidence to suggest that,' Haskins replied. It was somewhat of a little white lie. He did have evidence, the whisky appearing from time to time, but there was minor "taking advantage" which could be ignored, and serious "taking advantage". Haskins had no evidence for the latter. Miller appeared satisfied with the answer. He also appeared satisfied with Haskins.

'Well, I don't know if it's what you consider "making a real contribution", Haskins, but I'm afraid it won't be possible to have you transferred. On the other hand we are no longer going to waste time on things like the black market – that's a police business, let them take care of it. Our job, and our only job, is to help enforce security for the big event. You know what I'm referring to, of course.' Haskins nodded.

'The invasion,' he said simply. Everyone knew it was coming. A few knew how dangerous it would be. He was well aware that its like had never been attempted before in history, and failure would be a disaster. Dieppe had shown the dangers.

'Let's just call it the "big event", shall we? Don't like throwing words like "invasion" around, bad for security."

Haskins nodded his understanding, though he thought it a little melodramatic.

'We are going to have to try to keep the whole thing as secret as possible,' Miller continued. 'Oh, I know Hitler knows we're coming, but he doesn't know where or how many. Our job is to make sure that we don't have anyone letting their mouth run loose – careless talk costs lives, as the saying goes, and the – special event – is crucial to the war. We can't risk the Germans finding out what they're up against. Especially in the coastal areas where the buildup is. Your connections with the police will come in very usefully. Civilians tend to report loose talk to the police; if it's army personnel we want to know who and where and what as soon as possible. Understand?'

Haskins nodded. He did not say so, but he was immensely relieved; he would continue to be able to see Rose on a regular basis. Portsmouth would undoubtedly be one of the ports used for troop embarkation, wherever the invasion was – unless they tried something idiotic like invading Norway first. He would not put it past them.

In Portsmouth Rudman had reacted with glee to Martins' reassignment.

'Now we'll see how many leads turn out to be empty,' He had said, literally rubbing his hands in expectation. Haskins had long decided that Rudman had transferred his obsession with Longwood to the black market for the duration, despite his initial contempt. Rudman would always be obsessive about something.

Rose had surprised him.

'Oh, darling, why can't you go on doing what you're doing now? This new thing sounds dangerous. Can't you get re-assigned – for me? I shall worry dreadfully.' He had almost looked at her open-mouthed. He had often wondered how Rose would react should he be injured, or even die. He rather suspected she wouldn't be in mourning for long. She kept him at a permanent emotional distance, despite their physical intimacy.

'It won't be dangerous. It's not as if I'm going into the firing line. Anyway, the old work is out, we're no longer responsible for that.' She pouted like a child.

'You *will* be in the firing line. The invasion troops will be targets, even I know that. At least with the Blitz you knew it wasn't aimed at you. Now they will be aiming at you.'

'I'm not going to be with the troops all the time,' he reassured her. 'Anyway, they have shelters and trenches in the camps, it will be safer than the bombing.' She had seemed unconvinced, but that night she had surprised him with her tenderness. In the darkness she had stroked his chest softly.

'Promise nothing will ever keep us apart?' she pleaded.

'Of course, darling.'

'Nothing. Nothing at all. No matter what happens,' she had insisted.

'No matter what happens,' he replied, surprised. He lay there and wondered what had brought the change on. In the end, as he dozed off, he decided that he must have been mistaken about her all along.

That had been in April. By late July he realised that his job would be coming to an end within a few months; while a certain level of security was required until French ports were available for direct landing from North America, only secrecy about the units being formed in Britain and arriving from America and the Dominions still had to be looked after. He had decided to ask Miller if he could be "demobbed", as the word went, though he wasn't certain how officially he had been "mobbed" in the first place. Still, he thought, one September evening at his house in London, the paperwork was correct, and that's all the army cared about.

Erica had retired to bed early, exhausted after a week travelling the country calling for support for the "final push". She was also beset by worries over Henderby. She hadn't received a letter for two months, which, rationally, she knew was explicable under the circumstances, but she had heard rumours of escaped prisoners being shot, and Henderby was the type to try escaping if he could do it. To him it would be a lark, and he had already tried it once. But the stories of German cruelty and murder which had initially sounded like re-runs of World War I propaganda had begun to receive confirmation. She had thought she had lost him once. She could not bear the thought of losing him again, this time for real.

Haskins sat in his study with the rare treat of a glass of legally-obtained whisky, and looked over the bookcases, pictures and paintings. It was time, he decided, to think about life after the war. About what he was going to do. About getting back to the academic life.

About Rose.

About what they were going to do.

As he sat there the telephone on his desk rang, an unusual event. 'Haskins,' he answered. There was a burst of static over the line. Private calls these days could sometimes be almost impossible. He hoped the military network was better.

'Atkins?' asked someone. Haskins could hardly hear the voice at the other end. The most he could distinguish was that it was a male voice. '... roses ...' the voice said, and then disappeared. The line went dead. He replaced the receiver. Someone, he thought, wanted to speak to an Atkins about some roses. Presumably a garden enthusiast who wished to discuss the dangers of green-fly or whatever it was, though he was a little surprised; everyone was supposed to be "digging for victory", planting vegetables, not roses. Erica had ensured that his own garden had produced a surprisingly large crop of various produce, with both of them taking turns in tending the plants while the other was away. He found himself quite happy pottering around the plants, old bush-hat askew, thinking about how he needed to get back to writing the book on the Spanish-American war he had long planned to do, wondering if he should instead concentrate on a treatise of the role food supplies played in modern and ancient military achievements.

No doubt there was still a requirement for roses on special occasions. Roses could well be a weapon of war. He smiled at the thought. "Raise roses for victory!" he imagined the posters demanding. "Gladioli for Glory! Fuschias for the Future! Hortensias against Hitler!"

He leaned back in his chair and resumed contemplation of the study walls. It would, he thought, be difficult to find a job as an historian after seven year's absence from the university. Without a job it would be difficult to convince Rose that he was a suitable proposition as a husband – if he could, ever.

Would Rose give a fig for whether or not he had a job? If she really did love him?

The walls, he noted, were drab, if not dirty. One day, hopefully not too far in the future, he would engage some decorators. Though, he admitted to himself, he would be lucky to find a single can of paint and do the job himself. Decorators and paint would be in short supply for some years to come.

So long as love isn't in short supply nothing matters, his mind told him.

Once more the telephone dragged him out of his reverie. He expected to find the Atkins-seeking rose-grower again.

'Haskins,' he barked into the mouthpiece.

'Operator? Are we connected?' came a voice he recognised as Rudman.

'Rudman? Is that you?'

'Haskins? Haskins, this is Rudman. Listen, Rose has been ...' The rest disappeared in a storm of static.

'Rudman? What was that? What did you say?'

'Operator?' came Rudman's voice, 'operator, what's happened?'

'Rudman! I can hear you. What's happened? What's happened to Rose?'

'Haskins! These blasted telephones. Haskins, Rose has been – ' He was abruptly cut off. Haskins jiggled the telephone base, knowing that it was futile, but suddenly very scared. A cold fist had taken hold of his heart. Rudman would hardly telephone him at home for some inconsequential reason. He may be obsessive, but that would be beyond him.

Haskins considered his options. He would telephone Rudman immediately.

No, he didn't know where he was telephoning from. He would have to await a return call.

He realised that he was standing, still holding the receiver, and replaced it.

He looked at his watch. A few minutes, and then he would telephone Rudman's Portsmouth police station.

Rudman might well be playing a trick on him. He was still obsessive about Longwood, if he saw a chance to trick people into revealing guilt he might well take the chance.

Rudman was totally unpredictable.

But surely even he couldn't be that malicious.

What could have happened to Rose? A car accident? There hadn't been any reports of bombing recently, but those took days to come through anyway.

A flying bomb? The new German method of bombing England was extremely difficult to predict in its flight-path, especially with the anti-aircraft units on the coast trying to shoot them down.

But unlikely. Most of them were aimed at London.

He was sweating. He realised that he was panicking. He forced himself to sit down and lean back and review the situation rationally.

The muscles between his shoulders were tied into knots.

He checked his watch, it was surely time to telephone.

Only thirty seconds had passed. Why hadn't Rudman called back? Please, please, God, let Rose be alive and well. Anything.

He couldn't think of what "anything" could be, and rechecked his watch. Forty-five seconds. What on earth was Rudman playing at?

The telephone rang again and he snatched at the receiver.

'Rudman, is that you?' he shouted.

'You're through,' the operator announced, and Rudman's voice came over the line.

'Haskins? Can you hear me?'

'Yes. What's happened. What's happened to Rose?'

'She's ... she's been ...' Rudman seemed to struggle to form words.

'What, dammit man, what?'

'She's still alive,' Rudman's voice came through after a few seconds. Haskins realised he had missed part of the sentence.

'What do you mean? What's happened?'

'Haskins, can you hear me?'

'Yes, yes! What the hell has happened?' Suddenly Rudman came through clearly, as if he were in the same room.

'She was making a late delivery. One of those bloody flying-bombs! Jesus, what more can we expect of those bastards? But, listen – Haskins, are you still there? Haskins? Answer me, dammit!'

'I'm here. You said she was still alive. What's her condition?'

Now that he was beginning to know the facts he felt control returning, a cold, comfortless control.

'She's been taken to hospital. Look, Haskins, I know you two ... well, I'm sorry, but things don't look good.' At the back of his mind he realised he was hearing a different side to Rudman, someone who could understand the feelings Haskins had. At the front of his mind he knew that Rose was in mortal danger.

'Rudman? Can you hear me?'

'I'm here.'

'Look after her. Understand? I'll be down as soon as I can. Maybe midnight. Maybe later. But look after her!'

'I'll do that. I'll do my best. I'll be at the station.'

Haskins slammed the telephone down. He needed something to do, and that was to get down to Portsmouth as quickly as possible. Rudman hadn't mentioned which hospital Rose had been taken to, but it wouldn't be difficult to find out once he was there, if he had to ransack every one of them.

A knock came from the door. Erica appeared in her night-gown.

'John? What's wrong? I heard the telephone a couple of times, and then you shouting.'

'Rose has been injured. It sounds bad. A flying bomb. Those evil, evil bastards! Bastards! Bastards!' He slammed his fist down on his desk with each word. 'I'm going down there,' he said with clenched jaws. 'I'll telephone my driver,' he decided, and picked up the telephone.

'John?' asked Erica gently. 'John, I'll drive you down. The car's got enough petrol to make it to Portsmouth. It will take hours to find your driver and get started, even more if he needs petrol.'

'No. I'm going down there right now,' he said, obviously not having heard a word. She came forward and laid a hand on his arm.

'John, I will drive you down,' she repeated. He looked at her.

'You're tired,' he said, in a daze.

'John, you and Rose helped me when I was in need,' she said softly. 'Please let me do something for you, now. Please?' After a few seconds he nodded blindly. 'Go put your uniform on,' she said, 'they still have the odd road-block. And Portsmouth is still a restricted area. It could help us get through faster.'

She watched as he took this in, and then staggered off to put his uniform on.

She thought her heart would break.

She would have to help him through this, without telling him how much she loved him.

Chapter 16: Rose

That was the longest night of my life, he thought to himself as he drove. And the days that followed. He glanced across at her. She had rested her elbow on the windowsill, her cheek cupped in her hands, staring out the window, a woman at peace with herself and the world. He wondered what she was thinking.

'John?'

'Darling?'

'Do watch where you're driving. Do you want me to take over?' He had already switched his gaze back to the road, having narrowly missed driving into a bush.

'Don't be silly. I'm fine. I was just thinking how strange the twists of fate and where they take us. All this talk of Greek muses, I suppose, makes one think of how the Greeks viewed their gods and the fates.'

'Goodness! No wonder you weren't concentrating on the road.'

'What were you thinking?'

She smiled and patted her stomach.

'I was thinking that if you don't watch where you're driving you're going to upset little Johnny here.'

They had thought of naming the expected child Ben, if it had been a boy as she predicted, but she had argued against it. Better that it should be named after its father, just as he had been named after his father, and his father before that.

If it were a girl, they would name it Rosemary.

Neither Erica nor Haskins had said a word during the drive down to Portsmouth. Haskins sat grim-jawed, staring ahead into the feeble light given by the car's dimmed black-out lights. Erica knew he was the sort of man to go silent when hurting. She knew that he would not welcome her chatter. She was glad to be able to concentrate on the road. Driving with such lights made the journey perilous, especially as she was trying to drive as fast as possible. But it would be foolish to add two more to the casualty list through recklessness.

And she did not want to think of Rose. Of Rose. Of John. Of John and herself.

For Haskins the drive seemed to take forever. All he could see in his mind was an image of Rose, laughing. Laughing, singing, happy, but distant. He wanted to be able to say something to her.

But he remained silent.

After three hours they drove up alongside Rudman's police station. He was waiting next to a parked car. He waved them on to follow him, getting into his car. It drove off, leading them to the hospital. Haskins realised that Rudman must have been watching from his office, and raced down as soon as he saw them coming. He was grateful.

Rudman was a strange man.

Haskins would have charged into the hospital demanding to see Rose, but Rudman was obviously familiar with the hospital, and led them through the low-lit high corridors to the doctors' rest room. Two exhausted men in off-white coats and loosened ties lay in armchairs, one with eyes closed and head thrown back, the other staring at the ceiling, a cigarette smoldering in his hand.

'Doctors Goodall and Weybridge,' Rudman introduced them. 'This is Major Haskins, Miss Moreley's fiancé.' The doctors bestirred themselves, stood up and shook his hand. Their eyes were red, their faces drained. It was the early hours of the morning; they must have been working through the night.

'How is she?' Haskins demanded abruptly. The two doctors exchanged a glance.

'We've done all we can,' Weybridge said. 'It's in God's hands now.' He managed a thin smile. 'People often think we're miracle workers, but the real miracle is the human body. We have to thank our Maker for that.' Haskins was surprised to hear Weybridge speak like that. He supposed a hospital was as good a place as any other to give you religion. It was not something he had ever concerned himself with.

'She has multiple injuries,' Goodall explained. 'It would be faster to list the bones not broken. Burns, massive blood loss. No internal bleeding as far as we can see, but the next few days will be critical.'

'So you're saying she hasn't much chance. Only a prayer,' Haskins said shortly.

Both doctors fingered their collars nervously.

'She's young, and fit. It is incredible how some people can recover from the worst injuries,' Goodall said, knowing how feeble it sounded. Haskins nodded grimly.

'Thank you for all you have done. I'm not ungrateful, it's just –'

'We understand,' Weybridge assured him.

'Can I see her?'

'You can look in on her few a few seconds. But she won't be able to see you or hear you. She's completely under with morphia. She will be for a few days. The best thing for you now is to get some rest and be here if – when she comes out of it.'

Goodall led them down silent, low-lit corridors to a single room. The thought struck Haskins that they probably kept the hopeless cases out of sight to avoid disturbing the others. Well, this isn't a hopeless case, he thought defiantly.

Goodall gestured to Erica and Rudman to wait outside while he and Haskins entered. Inside the room a nurse was tending equipment. There was a single high-raised bed in the middle, a bandaged head at the top, the rest of the body hidden by raised white sheets, tubes leading from underneath.

'A minute at most,' Goodall said, more to the nurse than to Haskins, and left him alone.

Haskins approached the bed. The pale face did not look like Rose, ugly bruises showing against a skin the colour of the sheets.

'Rose?' he asked softly. Why he did, since the doctors had already told him she couldn't hear, he didn't know. He just had to say something. He saw her arm lying just outside the sheet, a plaster cast on the forearm. He took her fingers gently. 'Rose,' he whispered, 'it's John. I know you can't hear me, but I want you to know I'll be here for you. No matter how long it takes. You will get better. I know you will. And I'll be there every step of the way.' He paused, and added, 'remember, darling, nothing will ever get between us.'

He felt foolish talking to her, and ran out of words. He stood there miserably, watching her face. It was empty of life. He couldn't even see a sign of breathing. He didn't believe in miracles, and hope as he might, he felt the heavy weight of inevitability crushing him.

Suddenly he felt a slight pressure on his fingers. He looked down at his hand. Rose had pressed his fingers!

'Rose?' he almost shouted. 'Rose you're going to be alright!' The nurse was at his side, gently trying to lead him away.

'Now, Major, time's up. You're upsetting her. Come, she needs rest.' The nurse's gentle touch became much firmer, and with some strength she forced him to the door. He looked back.

'I'll be here, Rose,' he promised.

Outside Erica had jumped up from the bench she had been sitting on. She looked anxiously into his eyes.

'John? What's happened?'

'She squeezed my fingers. She's going to make it.' He realised he was crying, tears streaming down his face. He didn't care.

The doctor looked at the nurse and shook his head sadly.

'Come on,' he said gently to Haskins, 'let's get you a cup of tea.'

If only, the doctor thought, Haskins knew how often desperate relatives and loved ones had thought they had felt movement of the patient, which was clearly impossible. It was some psychological aberration, some mental trick that gave them hope.

A particularly cruel one, he thought. Major Haskins was going to go through hell before he finally had to accept the inevitable.

At least it would not take long. A few days. The woman in the bed wouldn't last much longer than that.

Haskins spent the following days at Rose's bedside for every moment the hospital staff would allow, reading to her, talking to her, describing the gardens outside, anything that came to mind, oblivious to everything else as time slowly ebbed away. Rudman took it on himself to telephone Miller in London and explain the situation.

'Might as well give him indefinite leave,' he had said, 'it will save you the paperwork of declaring him AWOL.' Miller grunted agreement.

'How is the girl? What are her chances?' he asked.

'None,' Rudman replied brusquely. 'I'm afraid Haskins will be useless to anyone until she goes. And then – well, the best thing you can do for him is hand him a rifle and send him to France. Let him take it out on the Germans.'

Miller had stared out of his office window after the telephone call ended. He understood what Rudman meant; when the girl died the only thing Haskins would want is revenge. He couldn't be sent to France as a major, though, not without the training. But he would no doubt be happy to go as a private. Miller ordered a corporal clerk to start getting the paperwork ready.

A pity. Haskins was a good man.

Erica absorbed herself in looking after Haskins. He had no concept of mealtimes or sleep. She made sure he ate regularly, and even, on the first day, had to remind him to shave. Once she had thought she was in love with him. Now she knew she was. She prayed every night that Rose would recover, she deeply wanted Haskins to be happy, but she knew how slim the doctors believed her chances were. If Rose were to die Haskins would need someone to look after him. She could never be unfaithful to Henderby, and loved him as a husband, but there was nothing she could do for him as she could for Haskins now. With the state of rationing, simply ensuring that Haskins ate properly was almost a full time job.

She did not know what the future held, whether Peter would ever return safely. But John was here now, and he needed her.

And she needed him.

Chapter 17: Good for her

'I think we're almost there,' he said. He pointed ahead. 'I'm sure I recognise that curve in the road. Doesn't it lead to a little seaside port?' She peered at where he pointed.

'Village more than port, if I remember correctly,' she said.

'And Longwood is a few miles further on.'

'A few miles,' she said dreamily. They were silent for a while.

'I hope we will find out who did it,' he said. 'Then we can put it all behind us and get on with our lives.'

'Get on with our lives,' she murmured. 'Yes, I like the sound of that.' She stroked his cheek fondly. 'You and me, Professor and Mrs Professor.'

'Took a while. Took ... some pain. But we got there in the end.'

As the days passed what little hope there was disappeared. On the fourth day Doctor Goodall advised Erica to prepare for the worst. He knew such words would be lost on Haskins. He had tried once, but had been effectively shouted down by Haskins. Haskins would need someone to support him when the end came. It was clear that he was already at breaking point. Days spent reading or talking to Rose's inert body, sleepless nights, all had taken their toll. His face was gaunt, his eyes bloodshot. It took all of Erica's willpower to get him to eat even small amounts. They had adjoining rooms at a nearby hotel, and each night she could hear him pacing up and down until the early hours.

'Another one of them getting away,' Rudman had remarked morosely within Erica's hearing on a visit. She had narrowly restrained herself from hitting him. She knew he was referring to Longwood. She realised that it was part of his self-defence mechanism against the things he came across in his job. After all, it was he who had taken the trouble to telephone Haskins, and to wait at the police station to guide them to the hospital.

But it seemed such a callous thing to say.

On the fifth day, a Sunday, Haskins was reading the newspaper to

Rose. He didn't like reading war news, but that was almost all there was, and he couldn't concentrate for long enough to read even the shortest of stories. As it was, with autumnal sunshine creeping in through the windows on the Sunday afternoon, he was almost falling asleep.

'Looks like the break-through has started,' he said, and yawned involuntarily. 'Well, that's good news, isn't it, Rose? The end in sight, that sort of thing.' He thought he heard a noise from the bed and looked up. 'What's that, Rose? You'll have to speak up, you know. You know me, getting old and deaf.' It was a figment of his imagination, he decided, just as that hand squeeze had been. It had never been repeated.

While he would not admit as much to Erica, he could read the writing on the wall. Rose had grown successively thinner even over the five days, and paler, if that was possible. It was just a matter of waiting for the end. He would keep talking and reading to her until it came. Maybe he was only doing it for himself now. But he would keep on.

He looked out of the window. Memories came back. Autumn. Long walks in woodland turning golden brown. The sight of smoke issuing from farmhouse chimneys as the fires were lit against an early chill. Winter. Those wonderful two weeks at Dear Aunt Edith's farm. Rose, laughing like a little girl as they had a snowball fight. He blinked back tears, and took out a handkerchief to wipe his eyes. Silly, he thought. Silly, silly, silly!

We should have got married, he thought. I should have insisted. We could have moved north for the duration. Or west. Cornwall, Devon. A little smallholding in Cornwall would have been ideal. He could have found a way of getting out of uniform. After all, there wasn't much doing now.

After all, there wasn't much to look forward to now.

A noise in the background intruded into his thoughts. He thought of other sounds. Of Rose laughing. Of Rose humming or singing, both the bitter-sweet songs of longing and what she called "the fun ones"

– Beer Barrel Polka, as a comment on when she had been asked to deliver beer in an emergency the one time. Great, heavy barrels. She had been forced to ask the pub landlords to help her move them. It was the only time she had relied on others.

Another noise interrupted his thoughts. This time there was no mistaking it for what it was, a low groan of pain. In the same room. Haskins looked up, terror mixed with joy on his face. He scrambled across to the bed and gently took her hand as a another groan issued forth.

'Rose? Rose! Rose, it's me, John! Rose? Talk to me, Rose!' A nurse had heard the commotion and entered the room. She took Haskins firmly by the arms and tried to pull him away.

'Come, now, Major, it's time for you to ...' She stopped suddenly as she heard Rose moan softly. She looked with open eyes as Rose's arm moved. 'Of all the saints and – Doctor!' She shot out of the room in search of a doctor.

'Rose, I'm here,' gabbled Haskins. 'Speak to me, Rose, speak to me. Darling, say something.' He found himself rudely pushed aside by Goodall.

'Get him out of here, nurse,' he ordered. The nurse gently but firmly ushered him out.

'The doctors need to be with her now,' she said dragging him to the corridor. His eyes shone as if in some fanatic trance. He danced a jig as other nurses and another doctor streamed passed, rushing into the room.

'She's going to be alright,' he said, and then repeated it loudly as he saw Erica come up the corridor. She looked at him anxiously, and then at the nurse, who was smiling broadly.

'Is she ...?' she asked hesitantly.

'She appears to be waking up,' the nurse said. 'It's too early to say anything else, but when they wake up they normally recover.'

'My God,' whispered Erica. She looked at John, and then threw her arms around him. 'Oh, John, I'm so happy for you,' she said, tears streaming down her face. He gave her a bear-hug that made her wince. She didn't mind. She had been plagued by guilty thoughts of what would happen if Rose died and Peter never made it back. Now she felt relieved at discovering that she really was very happy for Haskins.

'Now why don't you two sit down. I'll see if I can arrange a cup of tea,' the nurse said. 'You know we don't normally, but this is a special occasion.' There was a twinkle in her eye. There was a mad grin on Haskins' face. He sat down on the bench with Erica, her hand in his, his feet drumming against the floor.

'John?'

'Yes?'

'I know it's good news, but ...'

'But what? What can be better?' She squeezed his shoulder tightly

'It's going to take a long time for her to recover, you know,' she said softly, 'and she might never recover fully.'

'She will be fine, absolutely fine, she's a fighter,' he answered defiantly. Erica did not reply. She decided that Haskins would adapt as time went by. She really did hope that Rose would make a full recovery, but after such a shock she would probably never be the same. Neither physically nor mentally. It was unlikely that the Rose who survived, if she did survive, would be the same Rose.

It was half an hour before Goodall came out, beaming happily and rubbing his hands. Erica and Haskins stood up immediately.

'Well, she's still in a great deal of pain, obviously, but surprisingly improved,' Goodall said.

'Can I see her?' Haskins pleaded.

'She's very dozy from the stuff we've pumped into her. She might manage a few words, but she'll probably never remember them. Two minutes, maximum.' Haskins nodded an acceptance he didn't mean, and shot into the room. He took Rose's hand. She tried to lift her head, her eyes dull and unseeing.

'Darling? It's me, John. Can you hear me?'

'John,' she said weakly. He could feel definite pressure from her fingers as she tried to squeeze.

144

'Now take it easy. That's an order,' he said, pretending to be gruff. There was a flicker of a smile on her mouth.

'Accident ...' she said.

'Yes, darling, my sweet, you've had an accident. You are very weak and need to conserve your energy. So for a change I will do the talking.' This time the smile flickered in her eyes as well. Tears began to trickle down her cheeks, and he gently wiped them away. He didn't realise that his own cheeks were streaming.

Erica waited outside with Goodall, not wanting to get in the way.

'Well,' said Goodall cheerfully, 'that shows how much we know.'

'I'd given up hope,' Erica remarked.

'Our fault I expect. We did tell you to expect the worst.'

'How – how much of a recovery do you think she will make?'

'Having been wrong once, I hesitate to make another mistake. But,' he added, smiling at her, 'with Major Haskins looking after her I think I can say I'm confident she will make as good a recovery as could be hoped.'

'Is there anything we can do to help?'

'Good food would help. We feel the effect of rationing like everyone else, so any extra would help. Fruit especially. Nothing heavy. And, it's a bit early at this stage, but it's also important to get things back to normal as soon as possible. Little things, such as clothes. In my experience the sooner women have their own clothes the better they feel, even if they're still in hospital.'

'A nightdress?'

'That sort of thing. Favourite photograph, writing paper, whatever. She certainly won't be doing any writing for a few weeks, but sometimes just having their own things near them reassures a patient.'

'Rose was never much one for writing,' Erica commented.

'Good for her,' said Goodall as Haskins came out of the room, wearing an exhausted but happy expression on his face.

'She's sleeping,' he said. 'I waited until she was fast asleep and tiptoed out.'

'Excellent!' approved Goodall. 'I suggest you need to get a rest yourself. I think we're in for the long haul now.'

Chapter 18: The secret

'Here we are, the finest hostelry in the South East,' he said as they parked next to the village pub. The sun was going down. It highlighted some of the drabness of the pub, the unrepaired wear-and-tear of the war years. For all that it was a welcoming sight. Begrimed, yes, but also cheerful and welcoming.

She opened her car door and stepped out slowly and stiffly. Long periods of sitting still left her joints aching. He went to the back of the car to retrieve their suitcases.

'Could do with a lick of paint,' she observed, looking at the little pub.

'Everything could,' he agreed. 'Well, if there's anything you've forgotten to pack, I don't think we'll find anywhere around here selling it.'

'No, I'm pretty sure I remembered everything.'

'Including a nightdress?' he asked suggestively.

'A nightdress!' she laughed. 'Who would have thought that a nightdress could cause so much trouble!'

'Well, you can't really blame the nightdress,' he said, 'now can you? And it did really bring us finally together, didn't it?'

A week after she had woken up Rose was amazing the doctors with her recovery. Although she slept most of the time, aided by painkillers, she was beginning to take solid food, if only small amounts at a time. Haskins joined Erica in non-visiting hours to forage for any small delicacies they might find. With rationing the shops held little, but both of them had contacts who knew of little farms or allotments where judicious bargaining could result in prized apples or pears, or on one rare occasion, grapes.

'We must get Rose some decent clothes,' Erica said on the one morning.

'Clothes?' Haskins was surprised.

'We women are very attached to our clothes, John, you should know that. Besides, Doctor Goodall told me we should see that Rose is surrounded by things she feels at home with. And I can't imagine those hospital sheets are very comfortable. They look as if they've been used and washed for years.'

'Well, I have her keys. Why don't we pop around now?'

'No time like the present,' Erica agreed.

It was strange, Haskins thought as he opened the front door to what Rose had described as her 'little house', which proved to be somewhat larger than normal, part of a semi-detached pair of houses, that in all the time they had spent together he had never been here, only that one visit to next door in his official capacity. He felt somewhat of an intruder.

'You go up to the bedroom,' he said to Erica. She looked at him in surprise.

'Not becoming shy, are we?' she asked.

'I feel a little uncomfortable,' he admitted. 'I've never been here before. It feels like Rose's secret retreat, where she came to be alone and safe.' Erica nodded in understanding.

'While you're down here doing nothing you can dust the furniture,' she suggested, teasing, before trotting up the stairs. Haskins looked around. In two weeks the dust had already become visible.

Two weeks, he thought. Has it really been only two weeks? It felt like a lifetime. More than a lifetime.

He was sunk in contemplation when Erica appeared at the top of the stairs.

'John,' she called softly, 'I think there's something you should see.'

'What is it?'

'Come up and have a look.'

Haskins went up the stairs, feeling somewhat irritated. He really had hoped to avoid spending too much time in Rose's house, or going into her bedroom. It was her inner sanctum, and now was hardly the best time for her to find out that others had been traipsing around without her knowledge, no matter how close they were. She would allow him into her life properly if – when – she was ready, not before. They should have asked her, or at least told her, before coming here.

He followed Erica into a bedroom, and suddenly stopped.

'I bumped against it,' Erica said apologetically, 'I must have knocked the catch loose.' It was a large, wall-mounted mirror, fitted to the shared wall. Except the fittings holding it to the wall were false; it was hinged on the left side, and had swung open. It had concealed a doorway into the attached building. The opposite door was open. 'I just thought I'd better make sure it was locked,' Erica continued, looking a little shame-faced.

Haskins stepped through the doorway, Erica following. The room was bare of all furniture, just the way it had been the night he and Rudman had raided the house.

But it was not totally bare now; cardboard boxes were stacked upon each other. There were no labels to indicate the contents; Haskins opened one to find bottles of whisky. He whistled. He opened another. It contained tins of peach slices in syrup.

'Well I'll be – so that's why we never caught them!'

He laughed out loud. He laughed for so long Erica wondered if he wasn't having some form of attack due to the strain he had been under. He leant against the wall weakly.

'John? Are you alright?' he looked at her, tears in his eyes from the laughter.

'Rudman and I,' he said, trying to get his breath back, 'we kept on going on black-market raids only to find nothing. Rudman thought it was either duff information or a leak. In the end we both suspected Colonel Martins. And all the time it was Rose!'

He broke out laughing again, slipping down the wall until he was sitting on the floor. All the pent up worry, tension and exhaustion of the previous few weeks was coming out.

'You know,' he gasped, 'I was in this very room with Rudman. I remember that mirror.' He nodded towards a mirror which had been hinged exactly as the one in Rose's bedroom, forming the "door" that Erica had opened. 'It never struck me as strange at the time that there wasn't a single stick of furniture in the house, no pictures, nothing, nothing but that mirror.'

He paused, recovering from his laughter. He looked up at Erica.

'And every time we went on a raid I would tell Rose. So it turns out we did have a spy after all. And it was me.'

Erica let him sit in silence. She was appalled at the revelation. All this time Rose had been secretly playing the black market. She wondered how she must have felt.

'John?'

'Yes?'

'What are you going to do about it?'

How would he take the news that his 'fiancé' had been using him?

He looked around.

"Would you arrest him if you had to?" Rudman had asked him of Colonel Martins.

"Of course," he had replied. He could hear his voice echoing in the room. "I think my duty would be quite plain."

That duty was now more clear than ever.

Aye, but duty to whom? asked an old soldier some twenty years or more ago.

Maybe the judge would be lenient with her, considering her condition.

But by the time it came to trial she would have recovered, certainly to the extent where leniency would play no part. Black marketeers received little sympathy these days.

Possibly her work as an ambulance driver during the bombing raids would be taken into account, though those days seemed so far away. That was the strange thing about Rose. At one and the same time she had risked her life to save strangers, yet also deliberately took on the establishment.

Remembering the many tip-offs that Rudman had received, Haskins realised that it wasn't only the establishment that she had taken on.

He could see her now, her jaw pushed forward determinedly, saying "I don't feel patriotic. Why should women? We get fed scraps from the table." He could see her now in court, dressed, as she would be, to the nines, looking defiantly and contemptuously at the judge. She had taken on the world as she saw it, and through a pure accident, had lost.

And now she would be going to jail for quite a long time.

"Promise me that nothing will ever come between us". He had promised at the time. He had made the promise again while she was lying in hospital, unconscious.

He did not lightly give promises. He believed they could not easily be broken, if at all. But where did a promise lie in this situation? It was a promise made against the backdrop of a lie. Not quite a lie, but close. Somehow it all seemed so unfair, he thought. All the worry he had been through, she had survived, she was recovering, and now this.

Unfair. It was not a word he had ever used before. He had never had time for people who bemoaned their lot. "Get out and do something about it" was his motto.

Get out and do something about it.

He came to a decision, and sprang to his feet.

'We are going to have to shift this lot,' he said. 'Somewhere a little safer. Without anyone knowing.' Erica's eyes widened in surprise. He noticed her look. 'Well, after all we've been through you don't think I'm going to hand her over to Rudman, do you? And besides,' he added, 'when Rose comes out she will need loads of good food to help her get better. I'm sure we'll find some amongst this lot.'

She shook her head.

'Professor John Haskins, Mr Prim and Proper, sometimes you really surprise me. You, of all people, handling black-market goods.' He winked at her.

'I call it finders-keepers,' he said. 'Come on, we'll leave it here for now and come up with a plan to get it up to London.'

He was rather surprised at his own behaviour.

They closed the mirror doors carefully, making sure the latches would not accidentally slip again. Erica filled a small suitcase with Rose's night things, and they left, locking the front door behind them. They were intercepted by an old neighbour, obviously suspicious.

'Who are you then?' she demanded. 'Why you have been in Miss Morley's house?' Haskins doffed his cap gallantly, cheerfully. In some strange way the discovery had released much of the pent-up tension from the previous weeks, and the decision to follow an illegal path had made life exciting.

'Major Haskins at your service, madam. I'm afraid Rose – Miss Morley – has had a bad accident. She was caught in the blast from a flying bomb. She's still very ill, but recovering in hospital. Mrs Henderby here, a very dear friend, and I, have come for some of her things to make her feel more comfortable.'

'Oh, my goodness! Poor Miss Morely! I wondered why I hadn't seen here around, driving that lorry of hers. You will give her my regards, won't you? Mrs Jenkins. Number fifteen.'

'Of course, madam.'

'Will she – well, when she's better, that is – well, she can't live on her own. Not after an accident like that. She will need help.'

An idea struck Haskins.

'She won't leave hospital for a good few weeks. When she does she'll be coming to stay at my house in London, with Mrs Henderby. I'm hoping to move most of her things up there in the next few weeks.'

'Oh, good, I'm glad of that. You can't get home-help these days. You know –'

'Very true, Mrs Jenkins, very true,' Haskins said quickly, before she started a long and well-rehearsed complaint. 'We must be off, but I have no doubt we will meet again over the next few weeks.'

'Yes, um, goodbye, nice to have met you.'

Haskins waved as they drove off.

'Move her things up to London,' Erica quoted wryly. 'John, you would make a good criminal.'

'They do say that criminals and police are just different sides of the same coin, and I am sort of being in the way of a policeman,' he replied, grinning happily.

'But John, London – all those flying bombs. The one that ... wouldn't

Rose be safer down here?'

'By the time she's ready to come out the army will have overrun the launching sites,' he predicted confidently.

Erica did not reply. It had sounded like an edict. She had a feeling the army would obey.

They did not tell Rose of their discovery for the first few weeks. She was still far too weak to handle such news. But every other day they went at different times to Rose's house and filled up Erica's car with as much as it could handle from the adjoining house, including some of Rose's things just in case anyone should ask. In any event Haskins had decided, whatever Rose might say, that she would be staying with him during her recuperation. He was not going to take a "no" from her, not now.

Within a few trips they felt they had come to know all her neighbours, who would ask solicitously over Miss Morely. Haskins was able to assure them that she was coming on quite astonishingly, and might soon be able to be handle being wheeled out into the fresh air, should a late summer's day present itself.

Early in October such a day appeared, and Haskins sat out on the hospital verandah with Rose cosily wrapped up, enjoying what was likely to be the last warm sunshine for the year.

'I can't wait to get back to my little house,' Rose said cheerfully.

I'm not surprised, thought Haskins to himself. He decided it was time to broach the subject.

'Rose, Erica and I have set up a room in my house in London for you,' he said. 'You'll need looking after for a good few months after you're discharged.'

'Oh, but John, there are so many things I still have to do.'

'Rose,' he said gently, 'I know about the magic mirrors. And the contents of number 28.'

There was a silence.

'Oh,' she said in a suddenly dead voice, her shoulders sagging.

'Mark of genius, really, mirrors. They reflect things. So no-one wonders if there is anything behind the mirror, because they only see themselves and behind them, without knowing they're looking the wrong way. Quite brilliant, really.'

'I suppose that's it then,' she said listlessly.

'How do you mean?'

Her hands picked at the rug over her knees.

'Us. Everything. I know what I did was unforgiveable – in lying to you, not the – the other stuff. I suppose Rudman will be waiting for me when I get out.' She paused. 'I'm sorry, John. I really am. I know you will have to do your duty. As you see it.'

'Well, I had to think long and hard about this one. One has, as you say, to do one's duty, you know.'

'Duty,' she echoed with a trace of scorn.

'And on this occasion I had to ask myself, "Duty to whom? Duty to what"?'

'I'm sure you made the right decision,' she said, looking down at her hands, her face drained of colour. 'I'm sure you will do your duty as you always have. God, King, and country.'

'Well, in this case I have decided that, under the circumstances, possibly we need to overlook certain things.'

She raised her head, puzzled at the cheerfulness in his voice. Her eyes widened and slowly lit up as she saw the smile on his and realised what he was saying..

'What things?' she asked quickly.

'Everything, really. On two conditions.'

She nodded, a small smile developing.

'I can guess the first. Give up the – unofficial work? Yes, well, I couldn't carry it on anyway. The lorry's gone, and you can't do that sort of thing from a wheelchair. The war will probably be over by the time I'm out of this. There won't be a market left anymore. What's the second thing?'

'That you agree to marry me as soon as you're well enough.'

She gasped.

'Professor John Haskins, that is blackmail!'

'Yes, I know. Terrible, aren't I? Ruthless Haskins, that's what they call me,' he said, smiling. 'Otherwise I will be forced into handing you over to the authorities.'

She smiled back.

'I suppose I have no choice but to accept then. Very well, I do.'

It was an unusual blackmail, where both blackmailer and victim knew he would never have carried out his threat.

He took her hand and squeezed gently. They sat silently in the sun's rays, happy in each other's company. For both of them it was if they were coming home.

'I'm really relieved it's over,' she said, stroking the back of his hand. 'I know you won't believe me, but I really did hate having to lie to you. But how was I to know you were going to pop back into my life when things had just got going rather nicely? I could hardly tell you what I was doing. You would either have to arrest me or share the chance of being caught and sent to prison for not doing so.'

'I do believe you, Rose. I've been thinking it over for the past few weeks. I've realised how difficult it must have been for you. I always sensed a distance between us. Now I know why.'

'No more distance, I promise. I shall become the good little house-wife you want.'

'God forbid. I shall divorce you if you do.' He paused. 'Was it – how shall I put this? Remunerative?' She blushed.

'Yes. Very. Actually, I own both houses, more or less. The trick was only dealing with expensive luxury items, and being careful who the clients were – you'd be surprised at some of the names. Very honourable and upstanding people. But why do you ask?'

'I've been thinking of our future. I'm not going to be able to walk back into my old job at the university after so many years away. Maybe we could try that idea we had at Erica's aunts place – start a vegetable holding. Rationing will be with us for quite some time after the war. Even without knowing a great deal when we start we should be able to make a living.'

'Oh, John! Darling, it sounds nice, but you are such a dreamer sometimes. What do we know about growing vegetables?'

'We can learn, Erica's already taught me a lot,' he insisted petulantly. She smiled as if at a truculent child.

'I think you should have a word with the university first. You never know. Things have changed so much. Please? For me?' Now she was the pleading child. He laughed.

'Alright. How you manage to twist me around your little finger I will never know. Not that I mind, though. Not with you.'

'You charmer.' She sighed sadly.

'What's wrong?'

'Just one more thing to do,' she said. 'One last thing.'

'And what's that?'

'Never mind, darling, it's something I have to handle.'

'Excuse me, Mrs Haskins-to-be, you will have to learn to obey the orders of your husband. And right now I'm ordering you to tell me what's bothering you.'

'John? Please? It's my unfinished business.'

'The – remaining supplies behind the mirror.' She nodded unhappily.

'It would be foolish to risk Rudman finding them now,' she said. He chuckled.

'I wouldn't worry about that,' he said. 'Currently they've taken up residence at the impeccable London residence of a well-known Professor of History. Completely beyond reproach and suspicion.' She gasped again.

'How did you – ?'

'Erica and I told your neighbours we were taking your clothes and such up to London where you would be recuperating. They must think you own an awful lot of clothes by now.'

'Oh, John, thank you. And Erica. I thought I saw a knowing look on her face once or twice, but I was too weak to think about it.'

'I think she sees you as some form of modern Mati Hari. And striking a blow for women's freedom.'

And maybe she's right, thought Haskins.

She had scars the length of her body. She had lost an earlobe. Her face, remarkably, was untouched, or comparatively untouched. There was a nick above an eyebrow which could be concealed by make-up – when the days came again that they had make-up. Haskins guessed that she would probably elect to wear trousers for the rest of her life. There was a weal from ankle to knee on her right leg.

She was well enough to be discharged into his care at the start of December. The lounge of his house had been set up as a bedroom, for her to use until she was fit enough to handle stairs. She insisted on doing her share of household chores as far as she could manage. She sat at the kitchen table helping to prepare the various meals; the distance between the table and stove was within her strength to manage. Erica handled the heavy pots and pans where necessary, the two of them exchanging gossip, Erica from her various committees and Rose from the neighbours when the weather wasn't too cold to venture out into the garden for a few minutes in the morning and afternoon. They discussed and joked about various events, as if they were sisters, or old friends. It was hard work for Rose, and she retired early to bed each night, but the exercise slowly improved her stamina. Haskins returned to this domestic scene in the late afternoon of the day before Christmas Eve. He walked into the kitchen where the two were chatting, the lights already on as winter darkness had come.

'Well, that's it then,' he said, smiling happily. 'I'm discharged. Finished. Ex-major. Just a normal civilian'. Rose stood up in delight.

'Oh, darling, that's wonderful!' She hugged him and he hugged back gently. 'Harder, darling, I'm not a broken little bird anymore,' she insisted. He hugged a little harder, but not too much.

'You're certainly coming on in leaps and bounds – if you know what I mean.'

'I managed to walk down to the shops this morning,' she said proudly. 'Those little ones down the road.'

'Excellent! But don't try to takes things too fast, will you?'

'Of course not, darling. But I have to be ready for a spring wedding and you know what. A legal you know what.' Erica giggled. Haskins blushed and sat down. Rose sat down next to him.

'Yes, well, there is that, yes. Hum. Yes. Um, no news Erica?' She shook her head.

'Not since November.' That was the only letter she had received from Henderby recently, and was already two months out of date.

'Well, to be expected I suppose,' he said. 'Our bombers are pretty much ruining everything they're got. Our troops at the Rhine. The Russians have them in a stranglehold in the East – apparently Stalin's winter offensive has them retreating as fast as they can. I suppose non-military post won't have a very high priority.'

He hadn't told her that he had heard that it was more or less confirmed that fifty escaped prisoners of war had been executed after recapture. They had escaped from Stalag Luft III near a town called Sagan. It was the same camp Peter was in, though fortunately the timing of his letters had confirmed that he was not amongst the escapers.

'I was hoping this war would be over by Christmas,' Erica said sadly. 'I had this dream that Peter would be home, and we would be celebrating our first Christmas together in – what, five years?'

'We'll have our own little celebration,' Rose promised. 'A kind of looking-towards-the-next-one, as it were. After all, it can't go on much longer, can it? Hitler is throwing his last shot as we speak.'

What would become known as the Battle of the Bulge had begun on the 16th. Haskins was confident it would fail, but thought the newspapers and radio were being far too blasé about it.

There was also the matter of the new German V2 rocket; while his prediction that the launching sites for the V1 would be overrun by the time Rose was released was not too far off the mark, the V2 was far more mobile and came without warning. He had heard that figures of deaths reported in the newspapers were grossly under-reported. It was a hard straw to bear for people who had presumed themselves now safe from bombing, and he had not mentioned the stories he had been told to either Rose or Erica, though Erica would have heard much through her own channels. If the V2s could not be stopped, he had decided, it was better not to think about them, and

158

to hope that the end of the war would come soon.

'March, at the latest,' he said.

'Is that an order? To march?' Rose asked coyly. Haskins made a face at her.

'The month of March, silly. You know what I meant.' Erica watched them banter, with a mixture of happiness and sadness in her heart. After the heartache and pain it was if they had resolved to revert to childishness to banish the past. She so dearly wished Peter would come home, and they could do the same.

That Christmas lunch they celebrated with what Haskins enthusiastically referred to as "liberated foodstuff". Rose was permitted half a glass of wine with lunch, despite her petulant demands she be allowed a gin and tonic.

'I suppose you think I'm being childish?' she accused Haskins.

'Rose, my sweetest, you can be as childish as you like with me. I'm afraid that's what love does.' She had stuck her tongue out at him, but meekly accepted the half a glass of wine. Another half-glass was permitted after lunch, as she had seemed to cope so well with the first. It sent her to sleep, and she lay on the couch with her head on a cushion on Haskins' lap. Erica sat in an armchair, and they listened to the radio.

'The pipe?' asked Erica softly. Haskins raised his finger to his lips. Rose has bought him a pipe as a Christmas present.

'The local shops didn't have slippers,' she had said, 'but I managed to convince one to part with this, he seemed reluctant enough.' Haskins could see why; it was a Meerschaum, stamped "Made in Germany" underneath.

'I shall treasure it always,' he had promised.

Erica had given him a pair of socks and a signed copy of her latest book, recently published, inscribed "To John; All my love. You have always been there when I needed you. XX EH, Christmas 1944". She was a little embarrassed.

'What can you give the man who has everything?' she had asked rhetorically. Haskins had assured her that it meant a great deal to him, and he meant it. He had known she should have qualified "All my love" with "Except for that I have for my husband".

For Rose, Erica had found silk stockings, two pairs, which delighted her. She was self-conscious about the scar on her leg.

'I hope these aren't from the black market,' Rose had asked archly. Erica laughed.

'No, unfortunately not. I had to badger some American acquaintances a little.' She would have blushed had the others known how she had described Rose's misfortune, painting her as a "delicate English Rose, struck down cruelly by the German Luftwaffe, confined to her bed". They would have difficulty recognising the Rose that bustled around with a good deal of energy these days, to the child-like Rose depicted as unable to rise from her bed each morning, unable to receive guests, that Erica had suggested. It was just a question of different times, Erica had reasoned to herself.

Haskins himself had struggled over the problem of presents since mid-way through November. He knew it would be a special Christmas, that, however inconsequential and inexpensive the gifts, a great deal of thought was required into what they would mean. Before his discharge he was lucky; visiting an army camp which had long seen the soldiers despatched to the fighting front he overheard two clerk-corporals complaining.

'Fifty-nine!' said the first. 'What idiot ordered so many? Fifty-nine left over. And forty-two signed for.'

'We'll just have to box them up and send them back, I suppose,' replied the second. On a whim Haskins had entered the storeroom he had been passing. Both clerks came immediately to attention, and he gave them a relaxed salute.

'Carry on. Just sniffing around, listening to any problems,' he said. They regarded him warily. Finally the second spoke.

'It's not my place to say anything, sir, but sometimes – well, we know England can't afford to waste anything, and look! They send us a hundred field typewriters! We have fifty-nine left, and forty-two signed out, which means we have one more than we should have.'

160

'Let's have a look at one, then,' he said. The first corporal pulled out one of the offending items. It was slightly heavier than a commercial portable, but well made, and the carry-case was solidly constructed. He knew immediately that Erica would love it. She only had her heavy desk-typewriter, and had often complained of having to work indoors during sunny days during the summer, or lug the heavy machine downstairs.

'The paperwork alone will be a nightmare, sir' said the second corporal, sniffing something in the air, and glancing meaningfully at his companion.

'A true nightmare, sir,' agreed the second, not sure of where things were going.

'Our duty to avoid paperwork, costs too much,' Haskins suggested. The other two agreed volubly. 'I'll take this away as a sample,' he said, putting a pound note on the desk. 'No need for signing or anything.' They agreed that signing for it would indeed be unuseful, if not unpatriotic.

So much for you, Professor Prim and Proper, he thought as he left.

Erica loved the portable.

'I won't ask how much you paid for it,' she had said, kissing him. It was unmistakeably military issue.

'I purchased it for King and Country,' he assured her. Well, something like that, he thought to himself.

For Rose he had bought two things, because one wasn't quite a Christmas present. The first was a pair of specially altered long ear-rings, designed to allow her to wear them hanging below her hair, without the missing earlobe being visible.

'Oh, John, thank you,' she had said tearfully. She knew how much he understood how her altered appearance affected her.

'For special occasions only,' he said. 'I think the clasp will hurt like billy-ho after a while.'

'Here's to lots of special occasions and damn billy-ho,' she replied.

His second, non-Christmas, present to her he offered on bended knee.

'Miss Rosemary Morely, will you marry me?' he repeated his proposition, presenting a diamond engagement ring. It was only a small diamond, all that he and the war could afford.

'Yes, yes, of course I will,' she replied, the tears now streaming down. It was the emotion which had led to the petulance later on. But, thought Haskins, as he and Erica listened to the war news on the radio, Rose asleep with her head on his lap, it was worth it. He raised his glass of 'liberated whisky' to Erica, and she returned the gesture with her liberated gin. The German push in the Ardennes was failing. They were on what they thought was the final run.

Chapter 19: Victory in Europe

The Humber seemed to realise that they had reached their destination, and, after he had parked, fell asleep like an old, tired, grateful and faithful dog. They got out and Haskins went to the boot for their suitcases.

'So I had Terpsichore, you had Clio, Jessica had Urania, Peter had Thalia. Which was Erica's?' Rose asked, stretching. Haskins closed the boot.

'Calliope,' he replied. 'Georgina couldn't make her mind up so Erica chose Calliope because of the epic poetry.'

'And you said it was more appropriate due to the rhetoric. I thought she was going to throw something at you.' He smiled grimly.

'And Georgina was left with Melpomene, tragedy.'

'By that stage I think she had lost interest in the muses. Come on, let's see what they've got for us.'

She led the way. He followed her into the village pub, carrying the suitcases. Whereas, prior to the flying bomb, she had always had a certain way of walking which he might have described as sensuous, now she carried herself as a mature woman, a creature of unimaginable desire and controlled sensuality. I am a woman, her walk said. Of course, he reflected, the baby inside her might have something to do with it.

Inside the pub three men sat drinking, pint glasses half-full in front of them. They looked up suspiciously.

'Pub's closed, one of them said gruffly. Haskins suspected that they weren't too scrupulous about observing opening hours, afternoon closing, a legacy from the Great War.

'Is the landlord around?' asked Rose with an air of command.

'I'm the landlord,' the first speaker said.

'Professor and Mrs Haskins, we booked a room,' Rose announced, as if a sudden fit of grovelling might be in order.

'Ar,' said the man, springing to his feet. 'I'll show you to your room. Please, follow me, let me take those bags, sir.'

Haskins had the urge to tell the man he was quite capable of carrying his own damn bags, thank you very much, but gave up, accepting that the socialist spirit washing through the country had yet to permeate this village. The landlord took them along a ground-floor passage.

'We built these extensions in 38,' he said, 'seemed like a good idea then. What with the Depression almost over, and people spending money on local holidays rather than abroad.'

'And then came the war,' Haskins noted.

'Aye, sir, as you say, then came the war. But it wasn't all bad. We had Yanks staying here after '41, soldiers on leave from the various camps, happy to pay more than the going rate. Wanted a bit of true English life, they said. Well, between you and me, sir, madam, we, myself and the wife, we had to pay the bank, so we was happy to take their money. We had hoped that things would pick up after the war, but it's been a quiet summer, like.' He looked back with an anxious smile. 'Mind you, we do have a full house this weekend. Who knows, maybe it's the start of the rush.'

If you knew the reason for the full house, thought Haskins, you wouldn't be very happy.

The landlord left them with the keys to their room.

'I'll leave you to settle down,' he said. 'Let us know if there's anything wanting.'

'Remember all those hotel rooms?' Haskins asked Rose, looking out the window through threadbare net curtains.

'This is different,' she said, taking off her gloves, and drawing a finger across the top of the desk of drawers. She held up the finger. 'No dust,' she said.

'The last stretch,' he said, continuing his review of the woodlands outside.

'What's that, darling?'

'Something I used to say to my students,' he replied, turning around. 'In an exam the last stretch is the worst, the longest.'

'Erica?'

'Yes, Erica. And the others.'

'But this is the last stretch, John, isn't it? This is where it ends? Or rather, where we can really start our lives?'

'I certainly hope so,' he said, remembering that it had to be one of them.

But which one?

May 8th, 1945, Victory in Europe day. The day before Germany had signed a treaty of unconditional surrender. Spontaneous street parties broke out in cities and towns around Britain; toasts rang out through France. Around the world people of the allied countries celebrated. Haskins returned home late that evening, a broad grin on his face.

'The things they're doing in Trafalgar Square!' he exclaimed. 'Normally you would be arrested for that sort of thing.'

'And what were you doing in Trafalgar Square?' asked Rose suspiciously. He kissed her.

'Certainly not what they were. I don't know whether they were drunk with excitement or relief or just plain drunk. There was a sailor who was definitely three sheets to the wind, but his girlfriend didn't seem to mind – if it was his girlfriend. They probably didn't even know each others' names.'

'And you joined in the festivities?'

'No, I was trying to get back. The traffic was stalled everywhere, streets full of people dancing. The police were doing nothing to stop them – some of them actually joined in.'

'Well, I suppose it's understandable. It's all over now, bar the Japanese. A drink, darling?'

'Yes, I think I will. Whisky, please.'

'I think I shall have a gin,' she said, going to the drinks cabinet. She was now considered to be so well on the road to recovery that the occasional drink was permitted. If "permitted" was the right word; Rose was once again in control of her life. The lounge was once more a lounge, and she had moved to Haskins' bedroom. To their bedroom. The wedding was planned for early June.

'Erica around?' he sat on the couch and stretched his legs, yawning.

'She's upstairs, writing.' She handed him his drink and curled up next to him.

'No news?'

'No news.'

'It will take a while, I suppose. The whole of Europe is one big mess. The Germans were moving all prisoners of war back as the Russians advanced. Impossible to keep proper records, apparently. Not even the Swiss Red Cross could get good information.'

'The old couple at fifty-eight, their son came back over a month ago – he was a prisoner of war,' she pointed out. 'Do you think – well, that he might not come back?'

Haskins thought for a few moments, or rather tried not to think. The possibility was increasing as each day passed.

'All we can do is hope,' he said finally.

She sighed. If Erica could get Peter back it would make facing the future so much easier. Without him there would always be a gap to remind them, a ghost in their midst.

'Did you get your job back?' Haskins' reason for going in to London had been to visit his university to find out what the situation was.

'No, I didn't.'

'Oh, John, I am sorry.'

'However,' he said, grinning, 'I did get another offer. You've never met Harry Phelps, have you?'

'No, I can't say I've heard the name before.'

'He's Chair of Psychology at Walburga College in Portsmouth – it's a rather eccentric institution by all accounts, they think themselves a cut above universities, so I'm told. Anyway, Harry and I used to know each other quite well at one stage. Bumped into him in London purely by chance. Apparently they have several positions vacant, including Chair of History. He said he would put a word in for me. I have a feeling that education will be in the forefront of things in the coming years, what with the changes everyone is talking about. And if I don't get Chair I'm bound to get another post, maybe Research. There will be a lot of documents coming out of Germany soon. The war will provide quite a bit of work in years to come.'

'Portsmouth? Darling, that would be wonderful!' She gave him a shy look. 'I know some people at Walburga. They were one of my best clients. Very demanding in terms of their official dinners.'

He laughed and raised his glass and they toasted each other.

'They might have to re-appraise their ideas of you if I get the job. Still, from the sounds of it they'll take it in their stride.'

She looked at him happily from under her fringe as she sipped.

'But John, that would mean leaving London, wouldn't it? Wouldn't you miss this house. You seem so fixed here.'

'Oh, I think a change would do me good. London is going to be very weary-looking for a while. A good many years, in fact. And we already have a place in Portsmouth, don't we? Might need a little work done in parts though,' he teased. She blushed. 'Would you mind going back to Portsmouth?' he asked gently, stroking her hair. 'After what happened?' She smiled back at him, her jaw firm and unwavering.

'No. I actually want to go back. What happened, happened. I'm not going to let the war haunt me. We were lucky, in a bizarre way. We have something to look forward to. So many others don't.' She nestled into his shoulder and he kissed the top of her head. Yes, he thought, we were lucky, in a bizarre way.

A week later he was sitting in his study going through the documents for his application to Walburga College. They had arrived the previous day – light maroon documents with an impressive crest and ornate letterhead, suggesting an ancient tradition which wasn't going to be changed for anybody's war – and he wanted to get them off as soon as possible. He was interrupted by a knock at the front door downstairs. He uttered an imprecation of irritation. Rose and Erica were out shopping for the wedding, in a desperate attempt to find something that would look, or could be made to look, vaguely like a wedding dress. It would be a small ceremony, conducted by the vicar of the local church, a man prepared, under the circumstances, to overlook the fact that neither bride nor groom had ever set foot in his church before, and probably wouldn't after. Haskins decided to ignore the knock. Whoever it was could come back later.

Another knock came, this time less certain, as if the person wasn't sure whether he had the right address, or whether anyone was in. Haskins flung his pen down and went downstairs to open the door. A thin, grey-faced man in a cheap, ill-fitting suit stood in front of him, nervously twisting a cap in his hands.

'Yes?' asked Haskins, deciding that it was someone down on their luck, looking for any odd job to earn a living.

'John? Don't you recognise me? I haven't changed that much, have I?' A weary grin passed across the man's face and Haskins mouth fell open.

'Peter?' He stared at Henderby for a while, stunned. The only thing recognisable about him was the grin. Suddenly he roused himself. 'Good God, man, come in, what am I thinking about? Come in, come in.' He closed the door behind them and led a frail Henderby through the corridor. 'Come to the kitchen, it's where we all congregate these days. And you look as if you could do with a cup of tea. Or even something stronger.'

'A cup of tea would be welcome. I don't think I could stand anything stronger.'

'Sit down, sit, down,' Haskins urged as he put the kettle on and lit the gas. Henderby sat down slowly and gratefully.

'I wasn't sure whether this was the right address,' he said apologetically. 'I lost the address Erica put on her letters. Lost everything, really. So I went to the Camden Town house, and they told me Erica was here. Everything seems to have changed so much. I wasn't certain – I hope you don't mind?'

He was a shadow of his former self, his old charm only coming through vaguely, uncertainly.

'Of course not,' Haskins replied forcefully. He put some tea leaves in the pot, added the water, and brought it to the table. 'Pretty weak stuff, I'm afraid. We re-use the tea-leaves until there's absolutely nothing left.' After he poured the tea he noticed Henderby's hands shaking as he took his cup. 'You look all done in.'

'Oh, I'm not so bad now. I've been walking all over London. Silly, I shouldn't have done that. They wanted to keep me in hospital, but I've had enough of being locked up. Is Erica –'

'She and Rose have gone shopping.' He looked at Henderby, whose face was recovering a little colour. 'I think I might give her a little brandy before she sees you, she's likely to faint.'

'Do I look that bad?'

'It's not that. Well, not only that. She's been frantic with worry for months. The shock ... well ... I think I might give you one before you meet her too.'

'Why? Has anything happened? What is it?'

'No, no, calm down, everything is fine. I was just thinking that she's likely to throw herself into your arms, and you don't look strong enough for that at the moment.'

'She always was a power-house of energy.' Henderby took another sip of tea, his hands still shaking.

'So, what happened? How did you get into this state?'

'Marching,' Henderby replied. 'Marching ... marching,' he repeated, as if in a dream.

He appeared to be ready to leave it at that, but then continued. 'We were in a camp in the east, and when the Russians began to push the Germans back they moved us west. Once in a train, crammed worse than sardines. But the railway system was falling to pieces, and they needed it for their troops – and other things, or so I'm told – so in the end we had to go on foot.'

He looked at his tea and took a sip carefully, as if he was afraid to finish it too quickly.

'Rations were always minimal, but on the march we just took what we could when we could. And on the march we didn't get Red Cross parcels. We were all pretty weak to start off with. Even the guards – they were mostly old, or not fit for active service. It was the middle of winter and – well, it was a bit hellish, really. Hellish.' The word came out as if he could not quite believe it.

He remained silent for a few seconds.

'A few didn't make it. What with the marching, too little food, dysentery ... Fortunately we were a smaller group, split off from the main lot at some stage. Managed to scrounge bits and pieces here and there. And we didn't attract the attention they did from our own fighters – difficult to distinguish a group of POWs from enemy soldiers, I'm told. The other lot ... too many of them. Too many.'

Another pause.

'Finally come the spring, we made an agreement with the guards; they would march us as far west as possible, and surrender to the English, or Americans, they were dead scared of falling into the hands of the Russians. They didn't fancy the French either.'

He looked at Haskins with a lopsided grin, the one Haskins remembered. He had lost the youthful energy of the pre-war days. But maybe that was temporary. Hopefully.

'You look as if you could do with something to eat,' Haskins suggested.

Henderby held his hand up to indicate "not yet". He wanted to finish his narrative.

'We woke up one morning to find the guards gone. Scarpered. Vanished. Presumably they decided their best hope was to take to the roads and try to get home, wherever that might be. Ditch the uniforms, I suppose. Anyway, there we were in a forest in Germany, the roads with continual traffic, troops in lorries heading for the front, or marching on foot, refugees and other individual troops heading back. The troops heading back, retreating, they were a motley crowd. The clever ones hid in the bushes when they saw a vehicle approaching. The others – well, we saw one lot shot in an open field. Presumed it was for desertion. Not pleasant.'

He took a breath and another small sip of tea.

'We decided the best option was to stay hidden in the forest. The guards had left their rifles, so we had a little protection if needed. Scavenged for food at night. Barns, that sort of thing. And then – after a few days, maybe a week, I suppose – everything went quiet.

No more troops. No more vehicles. No refugees. Nothing. The whole morning. Not a soul. Until a jeep appeared about half a mile away, driving very slowly. Americans. Scouting, they were, trying to find the Germans. One of us, I can't remember his name, volunteered to go down to the road and stand in the middle with a white flag – well, it was some white material, not too clean, but he thought it would do. I would have gone, but I could hardly stand for more than a few moments at a time.'

He paused in recollection.

'Fortunately the Yanks weren't trigger-happy. Soon as they realised we were prisoners of war – ex-prisoners of war – they radioed back for help.'

He laughed suddenly.

'Sent a bloody big Sherman tank first! As if we were likely to attack them or something. Anyway, they were good, the Yanks. Fed us. All the time. Like their food, do the Yanks. And medics. And the rest.' He sighed. 'And that's it, really. They handed us over to our own lot. I spent a couple of months in hospital, somewhere near Paris, desperate to get home, but too weak to try. They wanted to get us home as soon as possible, and the fit ones were sent back as soon as transport was available. I asked one of them to call Erica, I suppose that never happened?'

Haskins shook his head.

'The telephone system is pretty diabolical at the moment. Difficult to make calls in or out of London.'

Henderby nodded.

'The whole of Europe is a mess.'

They were exactly the words Haskins had used to Rose a week ago. Henderby looked at Haskins, embarrassed.

'Look, old chap, I hope you don't mind but ... '

'Well, go on.'

'I have a rather huge favour to ask you. I feel terrible about it, but ... '

'Oh, come on now, Peter, out with it.'

'Well, it's just that I need a place to stay, and I was wondering if, possibly ... '

Haskins realised what Henderby was asking and laughed aloud. After all they'd been through. after all that had happened, Henderby was embarrassed about asking whether he could have a room for the night. Or maybe a few nights.

'Peter,' he said, gripping Henderby's shoulder, feeling the bones underneath, 'don't be an idiot, of course you can stay, and welcome. Not quite a home for a hero, but we make do.'

'I can't say I feel much of a hero. Behind wire for four years.'

'You are, though. A hero. One of the few, as Churchill put it back in '40. ' He stopped suddenly, a smile on his face. 'Anyway, as far as I recall, you're still married to Erica, and she's living here now. I seem to remember her being quite insistent on her conjugal rights.' Henderby blushed, and they both laughed. They stopped as they heard the front door being unlocked. 'Stay there,' he ordered Henderby. He walked through to the front door. Rose and Erica looked exhausted, their empty shopping bags suggesting that their expedition had not been successful.

'I am dying for a cup of tea,' Rose said. 'I don't suppose you've put the kettle on?' she asked Haskins as he came towards them.

'Tea coming right up. In the lounge,' he directed them.

'What's wrong with the kitchen?' asked Erica.

'It's out of bounds for the moment,' he said. 'Now I want you both to sit down. I have something to say to you.'

'John, I'm tired, I don't feel like playing games,' Rose said, 'what is it?'

'Sit down, both of you,' he commanded sternly, and they sat, reluctantly. 'And stay seated.' He smiled, nodded, and went back to the kitchen. Rose sighed.

'Honestly, that man! He can be so childish sometimes.'

'What do you suppose it is?'

'Probably found something for the wedding. Two yards of purple-dyed hessian which he thinks will make a nice dress.'

Erica chuckled.

172

'I've got someone who would like to say hello,' Haskins said, re-entering the lounge. Henderby followed him, a shy, nervous look on his gaunt face. There was silence for a few moments. Rose looked at the stranger in surprise. Suddenly Erica shrieked, jumped up, raced across the room and threw herself on him.

'Peter! Oh, Peter, my darling, darling Peter!' Henderby staggered back under the onslaught, and Haskins pulled Erica back gently.

'Now, Erica, you mustn't maul him, he is one of our heroes back from the war. And I think he needs a little tender care – and a bit of feeding up. Well, a lot of feeding up, really.'

Erica stood back from Henderby, and looked him up and down, gripping his shoulders, tears pouring down her face. She traced a line along his cheek slowly.

'Peter, you're so thin. What have they done to you?'

'Why don't you two sit down? Rose and I will make some tea.' Rose took the hint, and followed him to the kitchen.

'He looks absolutely shattered, poor thing,' she said. 'I didn't even recognise him when he followed you in.'

'Neither did I when he was on the doorstep,' admitted Haskins, filling the kettle from the tap. 'I think he's a lot worse than he realises. The only thing that's been keeping him going is the thought of Erica. Now that he's found her he'll probably just want to fall sleep for days.'

'I remember the feeling,' Rose said, putting her arm around his waist. She kissed him gently. 'I'm glad he's home. It sort of, well makes everything whole again.'

'Yes, it does rather. To a certain extent.'

'I'll make some sandwiches, he must be starving,' she decided. 'We have some bread left, that margarine stuff, and that paste that pretends to be fish-paste.'

'I'll get out four bottles of Guinness. I know we were saving them for the wedding, but this is a special occasion.'

'He'll be fast asleep within ten minutes of that,' Rose pointed out, taking out half a loaf of bread from the bin..

'Yes. Do him good. Erica will tend him like a mother hen. What more could a man want?'

'Not starting a war in the first place. I can't see how anyone could start a war again, ever. Not after seeing what it's done to Europe.'

He sat down at the table, suddenly feeling tired.

'That's what Georgina said back at Longwood, wasn't it?'

'But surely, John,' she said, slicing the loaf carefully, as thin as it would take it, 'not after this?'

'There is a theory that wars happen in generational cycles,' he quoted automatically. 'The generation that wasn't involved in the previous one has only the memories of the survivors, constructed out of propaganda, mostly. So they think it would be rather dashing to go off to the battle front.'

'I wonder how she is these days.'

'Who?'

'Georgy.'

'Georgina?'

'Well ... '

'No doubt Rudman will let us know from time to time.'

'Oh, John, you don't think he will follow us to the grave, do you? I couldn't stand having him turning up every few months, like the avenging ghost at the banquet.'

'He'll give up eventually. He won't be able to prove anything after all this time. Even he will see it's fruitless.'

'Eventually.'

Four weeks later Rose and Haskins were married at the little church. Apart from Erica and Henderby – now looking a little more like his older self, if ever so slightly – there was only a small sprinkling of neighbours, friends and distant relatives. After the short ceremony they returned to Haskins' house for a celebration with some of the dwindling 'liberated foodstuffs'. By the time the June evening came they found themselves alone, back in the kitchen.

'To us,' said Rose, raising a glass. 'Us, the survivors.' They drank to that.

'And to the end of the war,' Henderby said.

Just under two months later the explosion of the second atomic bomb, dropped on Nagasaki, brought to an end a second world war.

Chapter 20: The Second Weekend

Rose and Haskins sat on a couch in the lounge saloon of the pub, enjoying a post-dinner drink. The meal had been surprisingly good; most of the ingredients were local, bypassing rationing, and they either had access to some secret store of rationed items like sugar and flour, or had cunningly camouflaged whatever it was they had used.

'I must see if I can get the recipe for that apple crumble,' Rose said. Haskins laughed.

'If anyone had suggested even a few years ago, that you would say something like that you would have laughed in their faces.'

'Really, John. I have never laughed in anyone's face and I have no intention of ever doing so.' She sighed. 'But I know what you mean. I seem to have become the prim one, and you act like a little boy sometimes.'

'But you love me for it.'

She smiled at him.

'Yes, I suppose I do. You know, I think it's those other academics' wives. You'd swear they were born discussing things like dinner parties and layouts and who sits where. Majorie Phillips – what a name, Marjorie! – and Mary Devondale, they were discussing the correct way to address an archbishop the other day! Who cares?'

'The archbishop, I would imagine. No, I'd keep away from them if I were you. Academic politics is nasty business. Hello, I recognise that young girl who's just come in.' Rose looked at the entrance. A young woman had walked in, looking around as she walked to the bar. She saw Haskins and Rose, and Haskins waved. The woman nodded back.

'Not so much of a young girl, more like a young woman. Pretty thing, though,' Rose sniffed. Haskins chuckled.

'Do I detect the presence of that green-eyed monster called jealousy?' he asked.

'Of course not. Not at all.'

'Good, because I can assure you I have nothing but academic interest in that young lady, she's far too dangerous for anything else. That, my dear, is Jessica.'

'Jessica? Jessica Goodchild? The muse? Surely not.'

'Jessica the muse, and Jessica the woman who came back from occupied France and almost killed one of my men.'

'She's certainly grown up – and out.' Jessica was approaching them. She wore a plain blouse and skirt with slightly high-heeled shoes, all of which accentuated the figure that had developed out of the anaemic young girl they had previously known.

'Mind if I sit down?' she asked shyly, gesturing with her drink at an armchair.

'Go ahead,' said Haskins. 'We were just discussing how much you've changed. You look blossoming.' He gasped as Rose put an elbow in his side. 'I suppose we must have changed as well. It has been a long time,' he added quickly.

'It's alright, Jessica, I'm still trying to teach him some manners. It's just taking a while,' Rose said.

Jessica smiled, wanly, for the first time since she had entered the lounge. It was, Haskins realised, probably the first time he had ever seen her really smile.

'I don't mind. I was thinking the same thing, really, how both of you have changed.' She looked at Haskins. 'You look much younger than when I last saw you.'

'Ah, when you were trying to kill one of my soldiers. I probably looked older because of the fear,' he joked.

'Good for you, girl,' said Rose, 'I hope you gave him a good lesson.'

'Help, help, I'm surrounded by murderous women,' Haskins mimicked a cry.

'John, really, stop it!'

'You look – well, I don't want to sound rude, and this might sound stupid, but you look what I'd call pregnant,' Jessica said to Rose.

'I am,' said Rose.

'Two months,' confirmed Haskins proudly. 'Hard work, but I finally managed it.'

'A little bit of advice, Jessica,' Rose said, 'never get married. There is some trick of nature whereby, when the rings are slipped on the fingers, the man's sensibility genes somehow travel through the air and the woman ends up being the sensible one.'

'You're married?' Jessica gasped. 'To him?'

'What do you mean "to him"?' asked Haskins in a wounded, little-boy voice.

'Of course I'm married, I would hardly be in my condition otherwise, now would I? And, yes, to him, as you so eloquently put it.' She gave Haskins a glare.

'Oh, I am sorry, I seem to have put my foot in it. Only –' Jessica took a deep sip of her drink and leaned forward. 'Only, the last time I saw you,' she said to Rose, 'I thought you were the hell-raising type who could never be tied down in marriage. And the last time I saw you,' she turned to Haskins, 'you were a major in uniform, the rank made you look somehow older. I'm sorry, I'm being a bit rude, aren't I?'

'Not at all, Jessica,' Rose said. 'What with everything we've been through I think we're entitled to be a little honest with each other. I presume you're down here for this Longwood business?'

Jessica nodded and took a sip of her drink.

'Yes. I wasn't going to come at first. After all, it didn't hold any good memories for me – the opposite really. Then I heard from a friend that Robért was going to be here.' She looked at Rose in embarrassment. 'Look, I know he's your brother, but – well, he treated me very badly. I heard that he was a bloated drunk these days, and wanted to see him and rub his nose in it. Hoping that it would close the issue, in a way. I'm sorry.' She finished her drink quickly.

'Nothing to be sorry about, Jessica,' Rose assured her as the young woman stood up, 'I heard what he did and I have no intention of defending him, even if he is my brother.'

'Sit down,', said Haskins, 'I'll get another round in. What are you having?'

Jessica sat down again quickly, automatically, as if obeying an order.

'Thank you, it's very kind of you. A small cider, please. Apparently they don't have any gin.'

'Yes,' said Rose as Haskins walked over to the bar, 'if we'd known that we would have brought some ourselves. This cider is passable, I suppose, but hardly in the same class as a good stiff gin.' Jessica smiled.

'That sounds like the old Rose,' she said. 'Sorry, that sounds a bit rude.' She looked at her. 'Someone told me that you were rather badly injured during the war.'

'We English use quite quaint phrases, don't we? "Rather badly injured". I think, "at death's door" would be closer, quite literally in my case. I was in a coma for five or six days. The doctors and nurses had given me up as lost. If it hadn't been for –' there was a catch in her throat. She nodded towards Haskins at the bar, paying for the drinks. 'They told me afterwards how he had sat every day at my bedside, reading and talking to me. If it hadn't been for him I believe I would have slipped away. So, you see, I owe him my life. In the full meaning of the word.'

'Is that why you ... married him?'

'Oh, no. You see, I do love him. And I believe he loves me.'

'Who's that?' asked Haskins cheerfully, coming back with a drinks tray. 'Do I have a rival? Give me his name and I will challenge him to a duel!'

'Silly,' Rose said, ruffling his hair as he sat down, 'you know I was talking about you.'

'Cheers,' said Haskins, raising his pint glass. 'Here's to the end of rationing and the return of good whisky.'

'Gin,' Rose corrected him.

'Whatever.' He looked at Jessica. 'I suppose she's been telling you the story about how I saved her life?' Jessica nodded. 'Yes, she tells everyone that story sooner or later.'

'I do not!' insisted Rose, punching him in the shoulder. He cried out and held his arm in mock pain.

'You see the real reason I was there every day was simple,' he said to Jessica. 'We had had an argument before the accident, and I was determined we should finish it – I knew I was right and I was

180

damned if I was going to let her get out of it that easy.'

Jessica laughed.

'You both seem very happy,' she said.

'We are. Very. We've been very fortunate, all things considered.' Haskins leaned back and put his arm around Rose's shoulders.

'I don't think I will ever be lucky in love,' Jessica said sadly, looking into her glass for an answer to a question she wasn't sure of. 'Not after Robért.'

'Of course you will,' Rose assured her. 'Just because you fell into Robert's clutches doesn't mean all men are like that. In fact you are lucky; you got out of them. Next time – and there will be a next time – you'll know what to look for.'

Jessica seemed unconvinced.

'Why do you call him Robért?' asked Haskins. She shrugged.

'My mother is French. My father is called Robert. Mum always calls him Robért. It just seemed natural. He seemed to like it.'

'Ah, so that's why you were chosen for France. I wondered about that.'

'That, and the fact that I looked very young for my age. They thought the Germans wouldn't suspect a moody young girl.'

'Did you go back? Afterwards? After that time?'

'No, not after – that time when the aeroplane crashed. It was my second time. They said that the Germans would recognise me if I tried a third. I knew they really thought I had cracked up, but they didn't want to say so.'

'I think you were extremely brave,' Haskins said.

'It wasn't bravery – more like madness. I was so angry with – Robert – I was ready to do anything.' She finished her cider. 'Well, I'd better be off to get my room. An early night, I think. Thanks for the drink.' They watched her leave.

'So,' asked Rose, 'are you still going to tell me that she could have done it?'

'It depends whether you view it in terms of possibility or probability.' She sighed.

'Sometimes I really wish you weren't a professor.'

'Well, it's simple. Possibility: could she have done it? Yes, she had the potential opportunity, and she has shown the capability to kill under certain conditions. Probability: how likely is it that she did it, based on our understanding of her character? Pretty unlikely, I would say.'

'And motive?' He shrugged his shoulders.

'Who knows? She found Robert with the maid, kills the maid, Georgina walks in, so she kills, or thinks she has killed, Georgina.'

'And Robert? What is he doing during all this?'

'I don't know. Maybe he had already had his way with Emily, and had left the room. Maybe it was a figment of Jessica's imagination in the first place. Look, I agree it's tenuous, but I'm working from first principles – eliminate, if that's the word to use, those who could not possibly have done it, and Jessica does not fall into that group.'

'Come on, Sherlock Holmes, I'm tired. Time for bed.'

'Good idea.' He finished his drink. 'I tell you something, though. We don't have a clue who it was, and I'll wager neither does Rudman. Hopefully after this weekend he'll give it up as a bad job.'

Chapter 21: Saturday, 1946

Jessica was on her way out for a walk the following morning, small bag over shoulder, when she met them going in for breakfast.

'Oh, you remember I mentioned that someone had told you of your accident?' she asked Rose. Rose nodded. 'I remembered who it was last night. A friend of Nigel Johnson – the one who made out that he was a socialist before the war. He was a commando in one of the training camps I was at. I bumped into his friend in Oxford Street a few months ago.'

'I wonder how he knew,' Rose said.

'Maybe he heard from your brother. I hear the three were drinking partners when Johnson was in London.'

'Any idea of what happened to Johnson?' asked Haskins. Jessica made a face.

'Someone said that he'd been on the Dieppe operation. Hopefully a German sniper shot him.'

'Not your favourite person?' She shook her head emphatically.

'I couldn't stand him. He liked to dominate people by making them scared of him, talking about how many Germans he'd killed with a bayonet, that sort of thing.'

'He did that with us,' Rose said. 'Not a very nice person.'

'Well, let's hope he doesn't turn up here. I'll see you later.' They waved goodbye as she left, and headed into the saloon lounge.

'That's something I will never forget,' Rose said with determination.

'What? Meeting Johnson?'

'No. Robert. Not once in all the time I was in hospital did he visit. One measly little card, one measly line saying how he would like to be there and the rest explaining how he was too busy to make the journey.'

'Would you have like him to be there?'

'No. But I would have expected it. Hello, there are Erica and Peter.' The other couple were sitting at a table in the corner. They waved and Haskins and Rose joined them, the women embracing, the men shaking hands before sitting down, Rose next to Erica, Haskins next to Henderby.

'You're looking absolutely blooming, Rose,' Erica said. 'Anything we should know?'

'Yes. Two months.' Erica clapped her hands.

'Oh, congratulations!' Henderby looked puzzled. He raised an eyebrow at Haskins. Haskins used his hand to indicate an enlarged stomach.

'Congratulations, Rose,' Henderby said. 'What are you hoping for, a boy or girl?'

'I don't mind, really.'

'We've agreed that, whichever it is, we'll practise having the other for the next one,' said Haskins. 'With the emphasis on the practise.' Rose blushed and Henderby laughed.

'John!' said Erica, trying not to laugh. 'Really, Rose, you are going to have to train some manners into him. He seems to have lost them.'

'I'm trying. Hopefully the experience of fatherhood will do something for him.' The landlord's wife bustled in to take their breakfast order – porridge, toast and/or eggs, no bacon today. They settled on eggs and toast.

'Porridge reminds me of school days,' Henderby grimaced. 'Boarding school. Stuff tasted foul.' They laughed. Haskins noticed that it was to pre-war days that Henderby had referred – was he trying to link those and the present to blot out the war?

'I was saying to Peter,' Erica said, 'how surprising it is that we haven't seen each other since January.' Haskins and Rose had left London for Portsmouth to allow him extra time to acclimatise himself and prepare for a new term. It was just as well; colleges and universities were finding themselves overwhelmed with applications from newly demobbed soldiers who had skipped further study until the war was over.

'Yes,' said Rose, 'you must come down to Portsmouth sometime. We have plenty of room.'

'I was going to say the same about your coming up to London,' Erica replied, 'but I suppose it's easier for us to get away. Ooh, look, those look scrumptious. I don't think I've seen so many eggs together since before rationing.' Two plates had arrived, ladies served first.

'What time did you get in last night? We must have just missed you,' Haskins asked.

'Just after ten,' replied Henderby. 'We noticed Robert leaving.'

'Robert? Leaving where?'

'Here. The men's bar. We presumed you knew he was here.'

'He didn't mention anything, but then we haven't spoken since – well, the last time we were here,' Rose commented, layering her toast thickly with butter from the unusually large amount on offer. She noticed Haskins watching, smiling. 'I'm eating for two,' she told him, 'and baby needs his butter, not that awful margarine substitute.' She turned back to Henderby. 'How was he looking?'

'Fairly plastered, actually, staggering a bit. God knows how. Maybe the cider around here has more of a kick in it than the weak stuff they call beer in London.'

'Mmmm. Yes, but, how did he look overall? Same as always? Last time I heard he was laying it on quite heavily on a regular basis.'

'Difficult to say in the lighting. He's definitely put on a lot of weight. We wondered where he was staying.'

'Probably cadged a free stay at Longwood. I doubt he's got any money to spare,' Rose said off-handedly, starting a second slice of toast. The next plates came and the men tucked in with relish.

'Mustard!' exclaimed Henderby. 'When did I last see mustard?'

'I wonder where they get it. Such an out-of-the way place,' mused Erica.

'Precisely,' said Haskins, trying to gesture south while buttering toast. 'The sea close by, little unknown port, plenty of sailing craft lying around after the war.'

'Smugglers?' asked Rose, alarmed. 'Do you think it's safe for Jessica to have gone for a walk on her own like that?'

'I think Jessica could give them a surprise or two if they try anything. Anyway, smugglers rarely work during daylight. And if they did, they'd pretend to be normal fishermen. They'd hardly take any notice of a holiday-maker wandering around.'

'I hope you're right,' she said.

After breakfast Rose and Haskins decided to follow in Jessica's footsteps along the coastal path, while Erica and Henderby opted for a less rigorous stroll along the beach.

'One thing I don't understand,' Haskins said as he pounded along the path, taking in the sea breeze, 'is why Robert is down here at all. If he has become alcoholic as seems to be the case, why not stay in London? Why make the long and difficult journey, presumably by train – and they're still pretty unreliable – to somewhere completely off the beaten track, with only the likelihood of a single local pub, and that half an hour's walk away?'

'John, could you try to walk a little slower? It's not a race, you know,' Rose complained. He slowed his pace. 'Maybe he realised he was drinking too much and wanted to get away for a while?'

'Sorry. Didn't realise I was walking so fast. I suppose it's a possibility, but it seems unlikely to me.'

'Maybe he remembered that last weekend. Plenty of free booze.'

'Now that's more likely. Finds the free booze isn't available anymore and resorts to cheap cider in the local pub.'

'Do you think we should be able to see Jessica from here?' Rose asked. They had reached a little summit, and the path, coast and sea stretched out below them, a higher summit behind.

'Not unless she was really dawdling. She had an hour's start. No, what interests me is why people have come here. The four of us are hoping to resolve a mystery so that we can put it behind us. Jessica wants – or claims she wants – to humiliate Robert. So, back to the question; why is Robert here? For a free drink, or because he's worried someone might find something out? If it's a free drink, and there isn't any available, will he return to London today? Before our four o'clock rendezvous?'

'Well, I'm glad you've taken us off your list of suspects at least.'

'I very much doubt whether Rudman has, though.'

They returned to the pub in time for lunch. Erica and Henderby had already started on large sections of meat pie and gravy, with potatoes and vegetables.

'I'm famished,' declared Rose, flopping into a seat next to them. 'The slave-driver here has had me charging up hill and down dale.'

'Good exercise,' Haskins said, 'in a few months you'll be glad of it. That meat pie looks rather tasty.'

'It is,' Erica said through a mouthful. She swallowed. 'Mmmm, delicious. The landlord told us that he'd stocked up for a summer of holiday-makers, but hardly any had turned up, so we're reaping the benefit.'

'Ah,' said Rose, 'so that's the explanation. No smugglers, then. Sherlock Holmes was wrong again.'

'Sherlock Holmes?'

'John. He's been going through every possible theory of who killed Emily and tried to kill Georgina.' The landlord's wife came through to take their orders. They asked for the same as the others.

'So have we,' said Henderby, 'but I must say we've come up a total blank. Plenty of theories, no evidence.'

'John was saying last night that he doesn't think it will ever be solved, weren't you John?' Haskins nodded.

'And hopefully Rudman will give up and leave us in peace,' he agreed.

'I suppose that's all we can hope for,' Erica said. 'What with the war and everything ... I mean it would be good to have justice for Emily and Georgina, but after all the atrocities of the war, and without any evidence ...'

'I agree,' said Rose. 'Where's Jessica? Has she already eaten?'

'I thought she was with you two,' Erica said. 'Weren't you following the same path? Wouldn't she have to turn around to come back?'

'That's what we thought, but we presumed we'd missed her somehow. John, do you think we should do something? She didn't have breakfast, so she isn't likely to want to skip lunch. Maybe she's hurt herself.'

Haskins thought for a few moments, his fingers drumming the table.

There were all sorts of reasons Jessica had not come back, and he didn't regard skipping lunch as impossible for Jessica.

'That looks marvellous,' a voice behind them said. Haskins almost jumped.

'Jessica!' Rose cried. 'We were getting worried about you. Where have you been?' Jessica dropped into one of the seats, and ordered lunch as two steaming plates arrived.

'I cut off the path and went up the tall hill,' she said. 'I wanted to have a look at Longwood before going there this afternoon. Guess who I saw in sitting in the garden.'

'Who?' asked Erica and Rose simultaneously.

'Robert, and Nigel Johnson.'

Henderby whistled.

'Not the most savoury characters to be seen in company,' he said. He looked at Rose, embarrassed. 'Sorry.'

'Don't be. I am not my brother's keeper. Jessica, are you sure it was those two? It's quite a distance to recognise two people.' Jessica patted the bag she had carried.

'I took binoculars. A throwback from training.'

'Now that's something we hadn't considered,' Henderby said, 'suppose the two of them were in cahoots? One of them held Georgina down while the other –'

'Peter!' interrupted Erica. 'Not while people are eating. Really!'

'Sorry,' Henderby apologised. He looked around the table sheepishly.

'Oooh, yummy!' Jessica said, looking at the arrival of her lunch. 'I have to starve myself to keep my figure. I think I shall take a break today. You know,' she continued, cutting off a piece of meat pie and drowning it in gravy, 'I can never decide which is better, French or English food.'

'So any plans for the future?' Rose asked, hoping to move the conversation away from further discussion of Georgina and Longwood.

'I'm studying psychology. I'd like to qualify as a child psychologist – somehow, working with children seems worthwhile.'

'Dodgy field, psychology,' Haskins commented. 'Some brilliant minds, but quite a few charlatans floating around. Where are you studying?'

'A place called Walburga College. I don't know if you've heard of it? Their psychology department has a very good reputation – very forward thinking.'

There was an intake of breath from Rose, and Haskins chuckled.

'You could say that I know of it. I'm Chair of Research, History. Have been for six months or so, now. I'm surprised we haven't bumped into each other.'

'Me too, very surprised,' said Rose in a voice that carried more meaning than the words suggested.

'I suppose it isn't unusual,' Jessica commented, appearing to miss Rose's implied suspicion. 'After all, the psychology faculty is right at the end of campus – I don't know where History is.'

'More or less dead centre,' Haskins replied. 'You're right, though, I can't recall ever having visited the psychology faculty – or many others, though. Far too much work to do in my own area as it is. The amount of documentation coming out from Germany is incredible. It will take years to collate it and to try to assimilate all of it in some intelligible way.'

'What is this – Walburga? – College like?' asked Erica.

'Eccentric. Very eccentric. Named after Saint Walburga, also known as Gaudurge, Vaubourg, or Walpurgis – and "Bugga", something many students seem to find rather amusing. You might have heard of Walpurgisnacht in Germany – though Walburga is said to have been born in Dorset, and the College insists on that – it's a celebration of the arrival of summer, supposedly based on a pagan tradition. Part of the College's traditions side more with the pagan side. I think the general feeling is that authority is to be academically tested at every opportunity. Not of course by the students – or at least, only within accepted boundaries.'

'Sounds fascinating,' Erica said, a faraway look in her eyes.

'Oh, oh,' Henderby laughed, 'she's off now. I can see her next book

coming; The Ladies of Walburga: Students On The Rampage.'
Erica smiled.

'Well, maybe. At least it's something to look forward to.'

'Amen to that,' said Rose. 'Here's to looking forward.'

After lunch Haskins and Henderby went for a walk along the beach. Rose retired for a lie-down, claiming exhaustion after the morning and the lunch. Erica wanted to note down some ideas she had had during the morning for her latest novel, which would now contain pirates. Jessica decided to spend a couple of hours in the pub garden, reading a book.

'So, what do you think?' Henderby asked excitedly.

'About what?'

'About my idea. That Johnson and Morely are in this together. It makes sense. Both were on their downers. Neither is what you would call morally upright. Since then both have proved capable of violent acts.'

'Not really evidence, though, is it?'

'What more evidence could you want?'

'I'm a historian, Peter, remember. I would need rafts more evidence. Not even a signed confession would be sufficient.'

'But we will never get a signed confession. You can bet on it. Instead we have to accept what we have. They might not end up hanging, or going to jail, but they would be excluded from society for the rest of their lives.'

'I rather doubt that that would bother them. For some people it might even make them attractive.'

'Damn world's gone to pieces,' Henderby said moodily. 'You know, at the time, I wondered how anyone could do such a thing.'

'And now?'

There was silence before a reply came.

'Back in '40, I'm in my Spitfire, revelling in the machine, lovely aircraft, like a prize race-horse. So they tell us to go out and shoot the Germans down. No problem, it doesn't feel like killing, it's two competitors in their fighters, better one wins. You don't see the blood or anything, just a smoke trail, and hopefully the other man gets out in his parachute. But it doesn't feel like war, not like you're actually killing someone, another human being, you see what I'm saying?'

Haskins nodded.

'But something changed?' he suggested. Henderby nodded gloomily again.

'Forget the fighters, they told us, go for the bombers. Well, tactically we understood it, but it went against all we believed in – their bombers didn't stand much of a chance against a Spitfire.' He laughed. 'Silly, to think of it now, now that we know what they ended up doing. Back then it was almost chivalry. A gentleman's combat, high in the sky, clean, no-one else involved.' He kicked angrily at a bit of beach sand. 'First bomber I took on, I can remember it as if it were this morning. It was a morning, in fact. Took out the rear gunner as we were told to – a Heinkel, I think it was. God!' He shivered. 'Blood all over the place. Splattered around inside the windows he was firing from. He didn't fire after that.'

'Put you off the whole business, did it?'

It took a while for the answer to come.

'That's the funny thing. I loved it. I looked forward to the next one. I enjoyed shooting out their gunner and then their engines. That's why I bought it so far out, close to the French coast, chasing after one I thought I could just get. The sight of blood ... ' They continued walking in silence. Haskins suspected that this was the first time Henderby had told this to anyone.

Again and again! he thought angrily. Every time in this whole mixed-up affair it came down to images of blood. The question was who had tasted blood first by murdering Emily and trying to murder Georgina, and who had stumbled into it because of the war. Henderby, he remembered, had been up suspiciously early for a man suffering a tremendous hangover, and the attentions of Erica.

And Erica had been up even earlier. Would she not have stayed in bed with her lover?

Good God, he thought, I know these people so well, we have been through so much together, why am I thinking these thoughts?

Henderby looked at him.

'I know what you're thinking,' he said lightly.

'Oh? What's that?'

'You think it could have been me, don't you?' Suddenly he laughed loudly, almost hysterically. 'The funny thing is, I think so as well! I can't remember that night! Did I break into the bedroom and steal the tiara, killing Emily and almost killing Georgina at the same time? I don't know, I can't remember!'

Haskins stopped abruptly, and faced Henderby.

'You haven't told Erica about – having to kill the German machine-gunners, have you? Since you got back?'

'Of course not, I'm not that stupid,' Henderby sulked. 'I'd only just got back with her, I didn't want to lose her again. She would think I was mad. Maybe I am.'

'Peter,' Haskins said gently, 'I want you to do me and yourself a favour. When you get back to London, sit down with Erica and explain how you felt.'

'And risk losing her?'

'Not much of a risk. You weren't with her when she thought you had been killed by the Germans, and we were facing invasion. She wanted them to come, she wanted to kill at least a couple of them in exchange for you.'

'She did?'

Haskins squeezed his arm.

'Ask Rose, she'll tell you.' The wind was picking up, and he realised it was time to head back. 'Peter,' he said gently, 'I only caught a few months of the last war, but I saw then, and I've also seen recently in the one we've just finished, what it does to people. Outside you look fine, but inside it will take a lot longer to recover. You have to talk to people you trust. Cry the tears you need to. Wash it out of your system.'

'Cry?'

'Peter, when Rose was in a coma in hospital I could have watered Kew Gardens on a daily basis. We live in a new world. It's time to accept that we are only human.'

Henderby turned and looked out to the sea.

'You know how often I've wanted to cry? But kept myself in because men don't cry?' He turned slowly back to Haskins, smiling weakly. 'I'll give it a go, John. I'll speak to Erica. Thank you. Thank you for listening. I'll never forget.'

'Time we headed back,' suggested Haskins.

'Just a second.' Henderby took out a handkerchief and blew his nose, then wiped his eyes with the backs of his hands. 'Sea spray,' he explained. Haskins nodded, and they began walking back.

But who was he walking back with? he wondered.

Chapter 22: Afternoon

'Walk or drive?' asked Rose. It was three in the afternoon and they were getting ready for their four o'clock appointment at Longwood. She was checking her appearance in a mirror, carefully applying scarce lipstick. Haskins looked at her. She was wearing a body-hugging black dress that she had made herself, emphasising her curves, "before they become bumps", the Christmas silk stockings covering the scars on her leg. The expertness she had shown in sewing had surprised them both.

'Walk, I think. It's not that far, and we don't want to waste petrol. Will you be alright in those shoes?'

'If we walk I'll put them in a bag and wear flat soles. You can carry the bag.'

'Your wish is my command, oh great and mighty one. Shall we go down?' She looked at him disapprovingly.

'You could have brought your good suit. And that revolver in your pocket, really John. I'm surprised you didn't bring that silly old hat along.'

'I'm a history professor. I'm expected to wear sports jackets and odd trousers.' He had almost brought "that silly old hat along". He liked that "silly old hat". The comment about the revolver he ignored.

'Hmmph. Just an excuse. We women spend ages making ourselves look good for you men, and you just slob around in any old thing.' He felt like pointing out that not so long before she would have taken five minutes to "get ready". He decided it would not be a good idea.

'Come on, let's go downstairs and see if the others are ready.' She picked up a black wrap, put it around her shoulders, and they went down. Henderby, Erica and Jessica were waiting in the saloon lounge, idly passing time in occasional nervous conversation. There was a gasp when Rose and Haskins walked in.

'Looks like a funeral gathering,' muttered Henderby. All three women were dressed in black. They looked almost like three sisters.

'Of course!' exclaimed Haskins, 'Blackout material.' Rose frowned at him.

'Well? Some of the early stuff is quite comfortable. And it's the only material left to make a decent evening dress. Just as well I didn't throw ours out.'

'Where did you have yours done?' asked Erica of Rose. 'It looks smashing.'

'I made it myself. Rather proud of that,' Rose admitted, enjoying the praise. Haskins looked at Henderby, and they rolled their eyes. 'That's enough of that, you two. Here, you can carry this.' She pushed the small bag containing her evening shoes into Haskins' arms. Henderby lifted his hand to show that he too was doing porter work.

'Shall I carry yours, since I'm already sherpa?' Haskins asked Jessica. She shook her head.

'I'm only wearing flat-heels. Could never get the hang of real high-heels.' Rose took her arm.

'Come, my dear, Erica and I will teach you sometime. You have lovely legs, men will fall head over heels with you – pardon the pun – when you learn to show them off.' The three women led the way out into the sunshine, the men following, each with one hand in pocket, the other with a bag slung over the shoulder. The women looked set for an evening ball, the men for a stroll on a rather neglected beach.

'Have to admit to being a little nervous,' Henderby said to Haskins as they dawdled behind. 'What do you say to a woman who was almost murdered? Makes me feel almost as if I were the guilty one.'

'I know how you feel,' Haskins said, though his face showed no such emotion. 'Funny how you can face some awful task without flinching, yet this ... ' He didn't finish the sentence.

'Nice day, though.'

The strong autumn sunshine lit upon the dappled leaves of trees, golden brown leaves just beginning to show amidst the green as they turned towards winter, the fields recently harvested. It was an incongruous sight when matched with their current task.

'Wonder how Constable would have painted this scene,' Haskins said. Henderby laughed.

'Picasso might make a better choice. Erica wanted me to wear a suit. Fortunately I forgot it back in London. Glad to see we share the same approach.'

'I think our wardrobes might be the first thing on the list when rationing ends.'

Henderby sighed.

'Our brave new world, socialism and austerity. You know, I bumped into one of the chaps I was in camp with, the other day in London. He said they were going to start an association of ex-prisoners of war. I was thinking of joining.'

'What about your old unit? Surely they'll have an old-boys club of some sort?'

'That too. It's just strange. I hated the war, hated being behind wire, but now ... the future doesn't seem to hold much, apart from Erica. And you and Rose, of course.'

'It's understandable. The same thing happened after the last one. It was such a powerful, shared experience it dominated everyone's lives even afterwards. Look at the annual services on the 11th of November.'

'The eleventh day of the eleventh month,' quoted Henderby bitterly. 'They'll have to add names to those memorials.'

'Maybe that's why we're on our way to Longwood now. A shared experience.'

'Frightened me witless at the time,' Henderby admitted. 'Most gruesome thing I'd encountered until then. And I didn't even see the bodies.'

'Just as well, it was a horrifying sight. You also had a hangover at the time.'

Henderby grinned.

'Now that's a memory I enjoy. Not the hangover of course. The way Erica ... well, how can I put it?'

'Made her attraction to you forcibly obvious?'

'Yes, that's rather diplomatic. I'm rather glad she did too. She's an amazing woman.'

'Makes you wonder who the hunters really are. Well, there we are, the driveway to Longwood house.' The others had stopped and waited for them to catch up. Rose took Haskins' arm, as did Erica Henderby's, as if for protection.

'Into the valley of ... ' Henderby began. 'Well, maybe not the best quotation.'

'Let's get it over with,' said Rose. They began walking up the long, curved drive, Jessica on the left of Haskins and Rose, Henderby and Erica on the right. The walk, each thought, seemed to take forever, the top of the house slowly coming into view, then the upper bedrooms, and finally the whole house, the patio, the garden where they had sat seven years before. There was no-one sitting outside now.

At the front door they paused while Rose and Erica changed shoes. Haskins knocked on the door, and it was opened after an interval by Mrs Murgle, a much older Mrs Murgle, her face lined as if with years of worry.

'Mrs Murgle?' I don't know if you remember us?' Haskins asked.

'I remember your, sir,' she said peering up at him. 'Miss Georgina is expecting you. Please come in.' They followed her into the lounge. 'I'll let Miss Georgina know you're here.' She left them standing. None of them seemed inclined to sit.

'Nothing's changed,' remarked Erica. The lounge looked exactly as it had seven years before, two worn couches facing each other, armchairs around in profusion, the French windows open, sun streaming in, yet appearing to stop suddenly, as if the room did not want it.

'Needs a lick of paint,' Haskins noted, feeling it a trite remark to say. Almost everyone used it these days, often at least once a day. The walls were almost grubby, the curtains faded and in need of a wash. 'I wonder when the army moved out.'

'Maybe they didn't use this part of the building,' suggested Rose.

'Bound to have done,' Henderby replied. 'Ideal for a map room.'

'Which means that everything was put back exactly as it was after they left. Down to where the furniture was. I remember thinking that that little table really didn't fit there.'

'Intentional, I rather think,' said Haskins.

'But why?' asked Erica.

'Inspector Rudman requested it,' a voice said behind them, making them jump. They turned to find Georgina standing in the doorway.

Had she intended to surprise them it had worked. There were gasps from Rose and Erica. Georgina was dressed completely in white, white dress, shoes and scarf thrown around her neck. Her blonde hair seemed almost white. The only incongruity were the glasses she wore, tinted deep blue, as if to hide her eyes from the world.

'Georgina,' Haskins finally said, breaking the mood. He walked over and kissed her on the cheek. 'How are you?' he asked softly. Her face, he noticed, had hardened over the years. There was no trace of the woman who at thirty had acted like an eighteen-year-old. When he had kissed her she had drawn back and her body had stiffened, as if physically repulsed, and had permitted him the briefest of kisses. He stepped aside to let the others follow in the formality of greetings. It was not a welcome.

'Please, sit down. Mrs Murgle will bring some tea in shortly.'

Laced with cyanide? Haskins thought. Georgina's bearing showed nothing but deep-seated hatred.

They each sat down uncomfortably, the women on the left couch, the men on the armrests, away from the worn chair that seemed to announce that it was the chair of the mistress of the house. It duly proved to be as Georgina sat down, her back straight, her bearing stating that this was a necessary, but regrettable, interview.

They sat in silence for over a minute, the tension growing, becoming almost palpable. Behind the blue-tinted glasses it was impossible to tell who or what Georgina was looking at, indeed even whether her eyes were open. Rose clasped Haskins' hand for comfort. In his mind he decided that if nothing happened in the next minute they would leave.

If Georgina wanted melodramatics, she could have them on her own.

The tension was broken by the entry of Morely and Johnson. Morely merely nodded at them and dropped himself into the nearest chair, issuing a belch and muttering "stupid business"', before lapsing into silence, looking unseeingly at the carpet in front of him. He was bloated, fat and red-eyed, the picture of a dissolute drinker, almost oozing alcoholic fumes.

'Well, so here we are all again,' said Johnson, looking at them from the couch opposite. His eyes lit on Jessica, and travelled up and down her body, leering. 'Nice,' he decided finally. She merely looked back, dismissively, as if to say she recognised his type and was not afraid of him. He turned his attention to Henderby. 'So, Henderby, I here you were in the bag as well,' he said.

'As well? They got you?' Johnson nodded arrogantly.

'Dieppe. Bloody mortar knocked me out. Not before I'd taken a dozen of them, mind you.'

'Not quite the same story your comrades tell, is it?' asked a voice from the doorway. They turned to find Inspector Rudman looking at Johnson speculatively. Johnson glared back.

'They're lying!' he spat.

'All of them?' Rudman asked from the doorway. 'The two who were picked up by the Germans in '40 at Dunkirk and claim your reports were falsified? The ones who say that you lay hiding in Dieppe until it was safe to surrender? The ones from your prison camp who claim that you were a stool pigeon for the guards?'

'They're lying,' Johnson repeated, but with less vigour, staring at the carpet, the look on his face that of a man caught out.

'Well, I'm sure the commission of enquiry will decide who has being telling which stories,' Rudman replied, coming into the room. 'And I hope to hear certain stories today, stories about a weekend in 1939. One of which will be a lie. And I will know which one.'

'Inspector, you have our statements from back then,' Haskins said. 'I doubt if any of us can remember precisely where we were or what we did seven years later.'

Rudman looked at him for a few seconds.

'Preciseness is not what I'm looking for, Major,' he said finally.

Johnson flinched at the title, Haskins noted. He wondered why Rudman used it even though he knew Haskins was long demobbed. To create tension, he decided. That was Rudman's plan, to wind up the tension until someone broke.

'Indeed,' continued Rudman, 'the question will be who remembers too much? Who remembers too little? Who has a story they made up seven years ago, and can they remember it?' He paused, a grim smile on his face. 'But we have another little activity happening. You see, back in '39 we forgot to check one obvious hidey-hole for that tiara, which, no doubt you will remember is at the heart of this case. Find the tiara and you find the murderer.' He paused to let this sink in. 'Or murderess,' he added slowly.

'And where would that be?' asked Rose, making plain that she thought Rudman was overdoing his performance. Rudman merely smiled his wolf-grin.

'You see, we presumed that the murderer would hide it somewhere it could be retrieved. We did not take into account the possibility that it might have been put somewhere almost impossible to retrieve without being obvious. In the boiler, for example.'

'The boiler?' asked Erica in amazement. 'Why would anyone put it into the boiler?' Rudman concentrated his unblinking eyes on her.

'Not "put", Miss Ringold – or should I say, Mrs Henderby. "Throw". Into the flames, probably as far back as possible. Along with any blood-stained clothes which might need destroying. Nice large boiler, has to be for a place this size, almost tall enough to walk into, you could throw something far into it quite easily. Of course, we would have got around to checking the boiler in normal circumstances, but the little matter of the war intervened, did it not?'

'You think it's still there? After seven years?' Henderby asked incredulously. Rudman's gaze shifted to him.

One by one, thought Haskins, he's putting the pressure on one by one.

'Now that would be a little ridiculous, would it not, Mr Henderby?,

No, you see a man used to clean the boiler every other day, chap called Roy Larkin. Couldn't do it while we were here, but he's a very conscientious man, our Roy, carried out his duties at the first possible moment. Very good memory, as well. He remembered shovelling out what he thought were a set of melted wires. Wondered what they were, and who threw them in. But not curious beyond that, just tipped the whole lot onto the ash-heap at the back. Now in the normal course of things the ashes would have been dug into the garden during winter, but we weren't in normal times, were we? Come the war, come the army; the ash-heap was added to, but nothing was taken away.'

'And you think you'll be able to find it?' asked Rose.

'Oh, yes, Mrs Haskins, we'll find it alright. I have a constable sifting through it as we speak.' He laughed without humour, a quiet, almost manic laugh. 'They think I'm fanatical about an unsolveable case, my superiors. Would only give me one constable. Said any more would be wasting resources. So it will take time. But we'll find it.'

'But even if you do,' Rose persisted, 'what can it tell you? After seven years in an ash-heap.'

'Wars are strange things, Mrs Haskins, very strange. So much death and destruction. Yet so many inventions. Jet aircraft, rockets, even medicine. There's talk about landing on the moon. Computers, as well, I hear them called, quite amazing machines. And also forensic science. Oh, yes, it's amazing what we can recover these days, such as fingerprints. And the murderer actually did us a favour. You see, fingerprints are caused by the oil your hands produce. And oil in fire burns a very neat and long-lasting impression. I think we will find something very interesting.'

'But surely the silver would have melted.'

'Yes, but not diamonds, Mrs Haskins, not diamonds.'

'Most of us handled the tiara,' Erica pointed out. 'I'm sure I recall holding it at one stage.'

'Yes, but do you remember what Miss Riley ordered her maid to do before putting the tiara away?'

'Of course!' said Haskins. He didn't believe a word of Rudman's scientific explanation, but he now saw which way the man was going. 'What were here words? "Polish it until it shines. I want all those nasty fingerprints cleaned off." Something to that effect.'

Rudman nodded, smiling. It was a smile without a hint of humour.

'Precisely. So when we recover the fingerprints we will have the murderer – or murderers. Somehow I doubt that they were sensible enough to wear gloves.'

There was silence as they took it in. Rudman looked at each of them in turn, looking, Haskins presumed, for a sign that one of them was worried. He didn't seem to find one. Most of them looked surprised. Morely looked lost. Johnson seemed indifferent. What Georgina thought behind the glasses was impenetrable. Delight at the thought of impending revenge, no doubt, Haskins thought. The silence was interrupted by a cough. A constable stood at the French windows, carrying a small box. His uniform was coated with ash and dirt.

'Excuse me, sir, I've found it.' Rudman clapped his hands. 'And there's something else, sir.'

'Excellent!' exclaimed Rudman, ignoring the constable's addition. Well, bring it here, man, hurry up!'

'Er, the carpet, sir.' The constable indicated his filthy boots.

'Dammit, man!' Rudman exclaimed, and muttered something about the bloody carpet. He strode over to the constable, ripped the box from his arm, and returned to the coffee table. All eyes were on the box as he knelt down and slowly lifted the lid, placing it carefully alongside. He took a white handkerchief from his jacket pocket and used it to lift a melted mass of dirt-covered silver and diamonds from the box, lifting it high to catch the light. There were two or three sparkles from the mess, little suggestions of what it had once been. There were one or two gasps. 'Perfect,' Rudman breathed. He looked into the box and cocked his head. 'Hello, hello,' he said thoughtfully.

'I tried to tell you, sir,' said the constable at the French windows, aggrievedly. Rudman gently put the remains of the tiara on the box lid, and used his handkerchief to pick another item from the box.

The magician's trick, thought Haskins. See this handkerchief? Watch the handkerchief. Do not watch my hands.

Rudman slowly withdrew a more solid object form the box. Despite being engrained with dirt its form was clearly visible. A knife. This time the audience were riveted. There were no gasps.

'So, that's where it went,' Rudman said, his voice so low as to be a whisper. 'So much for our Mr Larkin. Not so observant after all.' He held the object in his hands for some seconds.

Haskins noted that the handkerchief hid most of the knife. All the observers could tell was that it was definitely a knife. He wondered whether it had come from Rudman's kitchen the day before, being suitably dirtied to make the illusion real.

'Now there's a piece of luck,' Rudman said. He appeared to hold it up to the light, turning it around a few times. 'Thrown too far in, landed at the back, I would say, hardly singed. This will definitely give us something. Our murderer made a bad mistake with this.'

He knelt there for some seconds, like a supplicant before a holy relic, before finally returning it slowly to the box, adding the mess of tiara, and replacing the lid. He stayed kneeling, looking at the box as if in a trance.

'And now?' asked Haskins, fascinated at what he saw as a complete charade. There was no doubt Rudman's audience were transfixed.

'And now,' echoed Rudman, as if he were trying to think. He stood up slowly, and carried the box to a chest of drawers against the wall behind Johnson. He placed it on top reverently, and turned around slowly. 'And now we face the final act. I'm afraid I am going to have to ask you all to stay here overnight. I'm sure Mrs Murgle could arrange your accommodation.'

'I have no intention of staying here, ever again,' Jessica said vehemently. 'And there is no way you can make any of us stay, unless you arrest us now.'

Rudman gave her a long, slow stare.

'Quite right, Miss Goodchild, quite right. I can't force you to stay. I understand why you would not want to. But I think you especially know you can't fight your fears by running away. Or is there something else you're afraid of? Perhaps someone else is afraid?' he asked, looking at them in turn.

Haskins debated the options. He had no urge to stay at Longwood. He could now see what Rudman's plan was. Presumably having them stay overnight helped raise the tension, and added more ears and eyes to hear and see. He was quite willing to stay, but disliked the idea of Rose staying. But if he stayed and Rose went back to the village pub she would be on her own there.

'No?' asked Rudman finally. 'Good. Now the last time I called the experts in they never arrived. So this time I'm going up to London to make sure they come down. Let's see.' He consulted his watch. 'I will leave at six o'clock. Constable?'

'Sir?' The constable looked even less enamoured at the prospect of what was likely to come.

'Get yourself cleaned up, I'll be needing you for guard duty tonight.'

'Very well, sir,' said the constable dejectedly, and left to carry out his task of hygiene.

'Now. I should be back in the early hours. Until then I will leave the evidence in this room with the windows and doors locked. The door into the passage will be manned by the constable. I advise you all to make sure your own doors are locked. Any questions?'

Very neat, thought Haskins, the bait dangling before the fish – or shark – and the little suggestion about people locking themselves in. Rudman obviously expected at least one person to make a night-time expedition.

'Good. Right, now I think I have time for some interviews, one at a time. You first, Professor Haskins. The rest of you may wait in the dining room – or wherever you wish. Just make sure that you're available.'

I've been demoted, thought Haskins. Or promoted. No longer "Major". I wonder why that is.

'I think I could do with some fresh air', Rose said, squeezing Haskins' hand before leaving. They filed out silently, Georgina to her room,

Johnson and Morely to the dining-room, the others into the garden, as if needing to get away into the sun. Rudman closed and locked the French windows, and then crossed to close the main door. He came back and sat next to Haskins, taking out a pen and notebook.

'Bit of camouflage. Try to look as if you're answering my questions.' He paused. 'I took it from your look you didn't quite believe me.'

'It was an excellent performance, I have to say. You deserve an award.'

'But you didn't believe it.'

'No. I don't believe you can recover fingerprints from that mess. I doubt if that knife is the real knife. Come to that, I don't believe the tiara was miraculously recovered only this afternoon.'

Rudman grinned broadly and quickly brought his hand up to his mouth to cover it.

'No, we found that in the first few days. It was difficult to pretend that I would be so incompetent not to have the boiler searched, but it's amazing what people will believe. And the knife isn't, as you suspected, the original. Couldn't get anything off it or what's left of the tiara. Not a shred of evidence. That's why I had to set up this little cameo.' He looked at Haskins. 'Last shot, this one. If this doesn't work I'll have to give it up. Unless whoever it was has a mental breakdown and confesses, and that seems pretty unlikely.'

Haskins was surprised. Rudman had given such a good performance of a man obsessed with the chase that Haskins presumed he would never give up. Rudman laughed as he saw the surprise on Haskins' face. 'Oh, don't worry, I am quite realistic about this. If nothing turns up, that's it. Do you think they bought it? The performance.'

'I think so. You will not be going up to London, I take it?'

'No. It will appear as if I have left, but I shall, of course, be waiting in this room for any possible late-night visitor. However, there is one thing about which I was completely honest, and there is a favour I need from you.'

'I wondered why you were telling me this. I thought I was still on your list of suspects.'

'Oh, you are, you are. But so far down, and – well, I knew you wouldn't take the bait anyway, so even if it is you it makes no difference.'

'What's the favour?'

'Well, when I said that I was only allowed a constable I was telling the truth – my superiors also think I'm a little mental about this case. I haven't told them precisely what I'm doing here. In fact the only other person who knows about this little cabaret is the constable – gave quite a good performance himself, as it happens. Digging out that ash heap, knowing there was nothing to find.'

'He certainly had me fooled – dull, apathetic, bored, not a very bright spark.'

'Yes, it's entirely possible, after such a long day, that he will fall asleep on a chair in the passage. In fact I think I can guarantee it.'

'Allowing a person or persons unknown to unlock the door in the dead of night and steal the tiara?'

'Precisely. Unless, of course they come through the French windows, which would be my bet. There were always a few sets of keys lying around for that, if I remember correctly.'

Haskins had no doubt about Rudman's memory. He had probably refreshed it from his notes several times recently.

'Yes, in case someone was going down to the pub and expected to be back late,' he replied.

'Exactly. Now my problem is quite simple; I only have one set of eyes, and I've never been good at staying awake after midnight – unfortunate for a policeman, but there you are. What I'd like you to do is to stand guard with me for the night. I would look like the most supreme of idiots if I get this right, and fall asleep to wake up and find the evidence gone. And I like to think that I am aware of my own weaknesses. We can stay awake till midnight and then take shifts until dawn, if necessary. Be a bit like old times, I suppose. You have your revolver, I notice.'

'Yes. Makes a bit of a bulge, doesn't it. I hope I won't have to use it.'

'You'll do it then?'

After a pause for thought Haskins nodded.

'This whole thing has cast a shadow over our lives for the past seven years. If there's anything I can do to resolve it – and bring a murderer to justice, then, yes, I'll do it. I shall have to explain it to Rose, though. I don't think she'll like it very much.'

'Don't tell her anything other than you're off to do a job for me,' Rudman said. Haskins looked at him in surprise.

'You don't suspect her, do you?'

'I suspect everyone, Professor. Put it this way; if you tell her and nothing does happen, won't you spend the rest of your life wondering?'

'I can live with that,' Haskins said firmly. 'She is my wife and I love her. I will tell her exactly what I am doing. I am not going to risk my marriage by not telling her.'

And besides, he thought, I've already broken the law for her once. Twice would not be a problem.

Rudman shrugged, knowing he would not change Haskins' mind.

'Well, if you insist. But please make sure that it's somewhere out in the open where no-one can hear you. This is a smoke and mirrors trick, everything depends on people believing the illusion.'

'Don't worry, I'll be extra-careful. Walls do have ears, I know.'

'Good man. Right, let's continue with the theatre of the macabre. I'd like you to ask your wife to come in – by herself, of course.'

'Why Rose next?'

'Standard police tactic. Interview the other partner straight away. Prevents them from discussing their stories in the interval.' Rudman smiled. 'Don't want to throw the whole game at this stage by doing anything out of character, do we?'

'Very well.' Haskins stood up.

'Any time after eight,' Rudman said. 'Make sure that no-one except the constable sees you. He'll be waiting. He'll let you in as soon as he sees you.'

'I'll see you later then. Good luck.'

'You too.'

Outside the others were sitting on the lawn, each lost in their thoughts. Erica lay with her head in Henderby's lap, eyes closed. Rose and Jessica were each absent-mindedly tugging at the grass.

'Your turn,' he said to Rose. She stood up slowly, unwillingly.

'What does he want to know?' she asked.

'Oh, just going over the statements we originally made,' Haskins replied, wondering how he could lie so fluently. 'Is there anything you've remembered since, that sort of thing. Don't let him intimidate you. That's exactly what he's trying to do.'

'I won't,' she said determinedly, and set off for the house. Haskins flopped down next to the others.

'Looks like it's going to be a long night,' Henderby commented.

'You can say that again,' Haskins replied, lying on his back and closing his eyes. 'A very long night.'

Chapter 23: Night guard

Dinner, had there been what could be termed dinner, would have been a desultory affair, with appetite for neither food nor small talk. Georgina had a plate sent to her bedroom, where she locked herself in. Rose, Erica and Jessica declared that they had already eaten too much that weekend, and decided on an early night, Haskins and Henderby agreeing. Erica suggested that Jessica join herself and Henderby for the night, but she declined, not wishing to get in the way, and stating her confidence both in her ability to handle anything that came along and the protection of a solidly locked door. When Haskins locked their door he could hear the sound of other locks turning. It was, he decided, a very strange night.

Only Morely and Johnson sat in the dining room, and that was more to share a bottle of whisky than for any food. Both sat silently, Morely's interest in talking long gone; Johnson appeared to have lost interest in his war stories. Haskins lay in bed, their room dark but for the low moonlight, waiting for them to finish, Rose trying to sleep alongside. As their nightwear was at the pub they had taken off only their shoes before climbing into bed.

Shortly after nine o'clock he heard Morely and Johnson walking unsteadily up the stairs, into their separate rooms, and then two more locks turning. He waited for ten minutes in the semi-darkness, until all was silent, before gently shaking Rose's shoulder. She was still awake.

'What is it?' she asked.

'Ssh,' he whispered in her ear. He had failed to find an opportunity earlier to get her to one side to explain the situation. Now he realised he was in the "walls have ears" situation. 'Don't say anything, just listen,' he whispered as softly as he could. 'Rudman has asked me to do a little task for him.' Earlier, while waiting for the others to go to bed he had agonised over what he should say to Rose, realising that explaining that he would be downstairs with Rudman, both armed and waiting for a murderer to appear, would hardly be likely to inspire a relaxed night's sleep. On the contrary, at best she would spend the night worrying, at the worst she would insist on accompanying him. Indeed, had she not been pregnant he might have welcomed her presence.

'What do you mean, a little job?' she asked, concern in her voice.

'Ssh, keep your voice down. It's alright, it's nothing dangerous, but I have to pop out for a while. I want you to lock the door after me, and keep it locked. Don't open it for anyone but me, understand?'

'No, I do not understand,' she whispered back angrily, 'what is it you have to do?'

'Dammit, Rose, keep your voice down,' he hissed. 'Look, I shall only be gone for a few hours – maybe longer. Please, just trust me. Will you do that?'

He could see her eyes worryingly trying to search his face. Finally she gave a small nod, and touched his cheek gently.

'Very well, John,' she whispered, 'I do trust you, you know I do. Darling, please don't do anything silly, though, promise me. Please.'

'I promise.' He kissed her. 'Remember, lock the door after I leave.' They slipped out of bed and she waited while he put his shoes on. She hugged him and kissed him.

'Be careful, my sweet,' she said. 'I love you.'

'I love you too, Rose. Don't worry, I shall return safe and sound. You just keep the door locked. Promise me.'

'I promise.'

He unlocked the door as quietly as he could, and then walked out as if he were on his way to the bathroom, but making sure his shoes made little noise. The passage lights had all been left on. He cast a casual glance around, noted that the passageway was empty, and headed quickly downstairs. Behind him he heard a faint sound of a lock turning.

In the bedroom Rose checked that the door was firmly locked, and then leaned with her back against it, eyes closed. What, she wondered was John doing? The tiara and that knife? Could he be going to – no, that was impossible. He had nothing to do with the business, she knew that. It was utterly and completely impossible.

Please, please, John, she prayed, be careful and come back to me safely.

Haskins made it down to the door to the lounge without anyone appearing. The constable, sitting on a chair, looked up, nodded, and quietly unlocked the door. It was quickly and softly relocked once he was inside. He looked around to acclimatise his vision. Light shone through the windows, curtains drawn back, equally creating light and casting dark shadows.

'Forward a bit, and to your right,' a voice whispered. He moved slowly and carefully forward, feeling for any items of furniture which might lie in his way. A hand grasped his shoulder. 'Well done,' Rudman whispered. 'No one saw you?'

'No. I'm pretty sure about that,' he whispered back. Rudman had placed himself in the darkest patch of shadow, against the wall behind a couch pushed out from the wall. 'What now?'

'Do your knees creak when you stand up?'

'Not that I'm aware of.'

'Mine do, something chronic,' Rudman whispered. 'We'll take it in turns, you stand for half an hour, me sitting on the floor. Can't stand the whole night, we'll be good for nothing if anything happens.'

'Right.'

'I'll give your leg a tug when it's time to change. Two sharp tugs means I've heard something. Two kicks from the person standing up means the same. Apart from that, do nothing. Don't worry about the lights, I have a torch here in case anything happens. Got it?'

'Got it.'

'Good luck.' Rudman slid down to the floor quietly, though Haskins suspected he heard a faint sigh of relief. He wondered how long Rudman had been there. Presuming that, after his widely announced "departure" at six, it had taken him an hour to slip unnoticed back into the lounge, that meant at least two hours.

How, Haskins wondered, do you keep alert and ready for an intruder while standing in the same spot? He tried to remember any tricks he had learnt as a young soldier, but failed. As a subaltern-to-be he had stood little guard duty, and even that had been patrolling from one spot to another. Standing still for any length of time, straining to remain unnoticed, was a different matter altogether.

He checked his watch to see the time, but found it impossible to tell in the dark. Holding it in the light was clearly out of the question, the movement could be spotted by someone else watching from outside. He decided he would have to guess when half an hour was up, or just change over when he felt he needed a rest.

He tried to remember how they had reached this situation, but found that his mind wished no such thing. It was as if his mind wished to blank it all out until the murderer was caught. Or not. Did he hope that someone would enter the room? Who would it be? Morely? Johnson? Erato or Polymnia? Or someone else?

Once again he found he did not want to think about them.

There were nine muses, he thought, but no muse for murderers.

The new house. Rose and he had bought a new house, with a sea-view, before the war ended, while house prices were still low. They had held on to the semi-detached until prices rose, which they were now doing. Erica and Peter were renting his London house, and Rose had mooted the idea of buying properties to let, something for her to do as her own business. Erica checked other rents monthly to make sure they were paying the going price. She could afford it, she pointed out, they could not afford to lose dear friends over something as trivial as money.

Something as trivial as money! Good old Erica. Only she could say something like that.

Yet wasn't that more or less what Georgina had suggested when showing off that tiara?

One of his tasks in the next few months was to decorate a nursery for their child. With what he didn't know. A tin of paint cost a fortune, if you could find one. Fortunately it would be a while before the child understood what a coat of paint meant.

Rose preferred wallpaper. Haskins had never given such domestic issues much thought before, merely getting a painter in every few years to paint his house exactly the same colours as before. After all, they were covered by maps and pictures anyway, weren't they?

He stiffened suddenly. Almost simultaneously he gave Rudman two gentle nudges with his foot, and Rudman pulled his trouser hem twice. There had been a noise from the patio outside the French windows. Rudman stood up, very slowly and gently. His knees did indeed emit slight creaking sounds.

'Hear it?' asked Rudman in a low voice.

'Yes,' Haskins replied in a whisper. They stood silently. They could see the French windows, and a small area of patio immediately in front. There was no sign of movement, nor any further noise..

'Fox,' suggested Rudman. They watched and listened for another minute. 'I'll take over. Knees were becoming dead stiff down there.' Haskins sat down, careful not to make any noise. He doubted that half an hour had passed, but it seemed a good time for a change.

On the floor he could see almost nothing. The couch in front of him blocked his sight, and also meant that he couldn't stretch out his legs. He realised that sitting down would mean a different type of stiffness if it carried on for any length of time.

What he actually needed was a stool of some form, but it was a little late for that, even for thinking about.

Thinking. He would, he decided, recite mentally all the kings and queens of England, and then, those of France, Germany and any other country or empire he could think of. For some reason King James the first came immediately to mind, who was also King James the sixth due to the union with Scotland.

He wondered why he had thought of that.

Possibly because someone there was more than they appeared to be. Two different things.

He was on his feet before Rudman kicked him. There was no doubt this time, there had been a distinct sound coming from outside the French windows. Shadows flickered and played across the patio, but he could not see whether they came from the trees or some more sinister source.

'This is our man,' whispered Rudman. 'Get ready. Dead silence.' Haskins wondered what police nose led him to this conclusion. Beside him he could sense Rudman take out his revolver and hold it ready, arm pointing upwards. He followed suit. He hoped this wasn't the time he discovered whether those five bullets would work.

But it was an undeniable fact that he and Rudman were awaiting someone who had murdered another person, someone who would undoubtedly be prepared, armed, and ready to kill again. This time he wasn't facing unarmed black marketeers from a distance. This time he would have to make a split-second decision.

He could feel his heart racing. He realised he was holding his breath in, and forced himself to breathe normally. It felt as if the sound was echoing around the room.

There was silence for a few seconds, possibly minutes. There was definitely something moving on the patio. And then, suddenly there was a face at the French windows.

'Do we shoot it or send the dogs after it?' asked Haskins in a low voice, trying not to giggle. He felt like laughing, hysterically. The face at the window was that of a fox, it's eyes, muzzle and whiskers quite clear in the moonlight.

Rudman breathed out slowly, and slowly lowered his revolver.

'Hope it stays there,' he whispered. 'If it moves suddenly we'll know there's something else out there, almost definitely human. Foxes don't like humans.' Haskins did not reply. After Rudman's previous confident prediction he was beginning to doubt the police officer's hunches.

They put their revolvers away, and stood waiting. Haskins found himself stifling a yawn. The fox padded away silently into the night.

'Any idea of the time?' asked Haskins.

'About eleven. I think,' came the whispered answer.

Great, thought Haskins, Rudman has no idea of the time either. We'll be here until daylight.

If it was eleven o'clock, he realised, the next hour was the most crucial. Rudman had predicted that he would be back by the "early

216

hours", which could mean anything from one o'clock onwards. To ensure a safety margin for getting and disposing of the remains of the tiara the murderer, if they were to come, would have to do it in the next hour.

He sensed Rudman standing on tip-toe, and then slowly letting himself down. He did the same, wondering what Rudman was looking for. Then he understood; it was a policeman's trick for moving body-weight and relaxing muscles while not moving too much. He had seen police constables do it before, without realising why.

They stood silently, every so often one would rise on tiptoe, then slowly down again. Haskins felt another giggling fit threaten. They must look, if anyone could see them, like a version of two nodding-donkeys. Rose would have found it hilarious. He began to wonder how ridiculous the situation actually was. If no-one came they would both look like idiots. No wonder Rudman hadn't mentioned his scheme to his superiors.

Time was passing. He desperately wished he knew how fast.

Psychology was key to timing, he thought. If it was Johnson, he would come at eight minutes to, eleven minutes past, or some arbitrary time, but not on the hour, or half or quarter hours. Normal people gravitated to such times; a trained ex-commando like Johnson, whatever he had done or not done, would avoid such times. Morely; he would be there closer to the hour or half-hour, he decided – if Morely was sober enough to note the time. Jessica would be like Johnson. Peter – Peter, he always felt, made up in charm what he lacked in subtlety; Peter had been awarded Thalia, the muse of comedy. Peter would probably come crashing through a window after falling out of a tree.

It could not possibly be Peter.

But once again he could not think of any of the others in a distanced manner. Even the thought of Jessica was purely based on the notion of training, not really on Jessica. There was Jessica the trained killer, a concept, and Jessica, the attractive young woman he knew as a person. Jessica was no doubt capable of killing should the situation force it upon her, but murder?

It was impossible.

Five minutes? Fifteen minutes? Fifty? At least twenty, he decided. That made it, at most, another forty minutes to midnight, not more, probably less.

He wondered what Rudman was thinking.

He wondered if Rudman was thinking. Was he of that strange type who could make their minds go blank when required, only re-engaging when action was demanded? Maybe he was wondering what he would be having for breakfast.

Breakfast. More lashings of eggs on toast with real butter. Maybe even a rasher of bacon, the landlord's wife had said that they were hopeful for a full Sunday English breakfast, eggs, bacon, toast, fried tomatoes and mushrooms, but probably not the sausages, unfortunately.

What on earth was he doing here in the darkness with a loaded revolver in his jacket pocket thinking of eggs, bacon and the rest?

Sausages would be nice. It was ages since he had a really good sausage.

Suddenly Rudman stiffened. Haskins concentrated. Had there been a very slight sound outside? Outside the French window or in the passage? The French windows! There was definitely a human figure at the windows this time, clad in black, doing something to the lock! In a trice both men had their revolvers out.

There was no doubt that this was it.

Unless, thought Haskins wryly, they were about to catch a blissfully unaware common or garden burglar.

They pressed their backs tight against the wall.

The windows opened, a slight breeze flowing into the room. Haskins could smell the sea air, redolent of seaside holidays, walks on the cliffs, everything but the black-robed figure entering the lounge. It closed the door soundlessly and then glided silently along, straight to the desk of drawers on which the cardboard box lay. There was definitely now no doubt. Only one of their group could know that the box contained anything of value. The figure stopped before the desk of drawers, its back towards them, hesitant as if listening, before picking up the box in both hands.

There was a click as Rudman switched on his flashlight. The figure was bathed in electric light.

Haskins gasped.

He could not see who it was.

But it was clearly a woman.

Dressed in black, head shrouded in a black scarf.

Oh, my God, No, he thought, feeling sick.

Black. Black dresses and scarves.

It had to be one of the three – Jessica, Erica or Rose.

His heart thumped madly. It couldn't be Rose, surely? The couch opposite hid the woman's legs. The figure that could be seen could have been any of the three.

Terpsichore, Urania or Calliope. Which one? Which one?

Was it wearing silk stockings?

'Turn around very slowly and carefully, please. You know who I am, and I'm armed. I also have Major Haskins next to me, and he is armed too.' The figure stood still for some seconds, and then slowly, very slowly, turned around, the box in her hands. Only the eyes showed, and these were slits, closed against the torch beam.

'Switch the lights on, Major, if you please. Let's see who our mystery visitor is.'

Haskins did as he was bidden, careful edging his way to the left and then to the light switch at the door, his revolver pointing downwards at an angle.

He didn't know who the figure was, but he did know he did not want to shoot them.

He switched the lights on.

Now the figure was half side-on to him, staring at Rudman, an armchair hiding her legs. The side-view gave him even less to determine her identity. Initially he could swear it was Jessica. Then it could have been Erica.

It could not possibly be Rose.

The sinking feeling came again.

It could not possibly be Rose.

He was all too aware that it could be Rose. His heart was still beating madly. He could not trust himself to speak.

'Take the scarf off, please,' Rudman requested. The figure stayed standing, box in hands, not moving. 'Very well, if that's the way you want it. Just remember this revolver is loaded. Any funny business and I will shoot.' He emphasised the word "will".

He edged his way around the couch and approached the figure warily, holding his revolver pointing directly at the woman, careful not to make himself a target should Haskins have to fire. He reached out a hand for the trailing end of the scarf.

Suddenly a knife shot out, in the woman's hand, the box falling to the floor. Haskins noted in a split second that she must have been hiding it behind the box. But Rudman was ready for it. He brought down his revolver butt onto the woman's wrist before the knife reached him. There was a yelp of pain and the sound of the knife imbedding itself into the floor. The woman stood holding her wrist in pain, her only hope gone, Rudman blocking the one exit, Haskins the other. Her shoulders slumped. She seemed to have surrendered.

'Now, let's see who we have here,' Rudman said grimly. He took hold of the scarf and whipped it off the woman's head.

Haskins gasped.

His hands clenched involuntarily.

His trigger finger pulled too far and his revolver went off.

The lounge echoed to the thunder of the shot.

'Do try to keep control of your firearm, Professor,' Rudman said mildly. 'I'm sure the carpet has never done anyone any harm.' Haskins stood with open mouth, unable to think sufficiently to be grateful the bullet had gone into the floor. 'And,' continued Rudman, 'you could have injured Miss Riley here.'

Melpomene!

Georgina glared at Rudman, her long, faded golden tresses hanging across her shoulders, made more white by the black dress she was wearing. 'Take a seat, Miss Riley, right there. Slowly, now, that's the way. Now I think it might be an idea if I put these handcuffs on, just in case you get any more silly ideas.'

Georgina made no resistance as Rudman forced her firmly into the chair, and snapped handcuffs on to her wrists. She sat nursing her injured wrist and glaring at the space in front of her.

'You can tell the constable to come in, Professor, he seems to be quite distraught out there. Maybe he has forgotten that he actually has the key.' Haskins suddenly realised that the constable was banging on the door, there were loud cries asking what was going on from upstairs, and someone was running downstairs. He turned to the door and called for the constable to come in. The lock turned rapidly. The constable entered, clearly nervous. He had not been issued with a firearm, and obviously did not relish entering the room unarmed.

'It's alright, constable,' Haskins reassured him, 'my revolver went off accidentally. Oh, hello, darling, I didn't wake you up, did I?' he asked nonchalantly. Rose was in the doorway, wide-eyed, bare-footed, alarmed, out of breath from running downstairs.

Haskins felt like singing out of sheer relief.

'John, are you hurt? John?'

'Now, now, no one is hurt my dear. Well, not really. Though I thought I gave you strict orders to stay in your room until I returned.' She threw him a look which told him all he needed to know what she thought about his strict orders. She looked behind him.

'And what is she doing in handcuffs?' she asked, seeing Georgina.

'I think I'd like to know that too,' he replied. 'Come and sit down, Rose, you're blocking everyone else.' The doorway was filled with the others, Henderby, Erica, and Jessica. Haskins noticed the absence of Morely and Johnson. Fast asleep in a drunken stupor, he presumed.

'Yes, come in and sit down,' called Rudman. 'We are about to start the final act of our little drama.'

They filed in and sat down, all facing Georgina, fascinated by the sight, keeping back in case she was dangerous. Henderby and Haskins sat on the armrests of their wives' chairs, an arm on their shoulders for protection, much as they had done earlier. Georgina stared ahead of her, her face a picture of hatred, her stance suggesting a wild animal not quite cowed.

'Now, Miss Riley,' Rudman continued, 'would you like to tell us exactly what happened that night seven years ago?'

She said nothing, staring ahead as if she had not heard.

'Very well, let me kick it off for you. You killed your maid, Emily Watkins, by stabbing her in the chest. Care to tell us why?'

Georgina remained silent.

Haskins knew that if she kept silent, or denied the murder, a competent lawyer could break any case Rudman might bring. Rudman desperately needed a confession.

Then, in a quiet, bitter voice she spoke.

'You would not understand,' she said.

'Oh, I don't think you give us enough credit, Miss Riley. Emily Watkins was not only your maid but also your lover, not so?'

Georgina seemed to ponder this.

'Yes,' she said finally, almost as if hypnotised.

'You had an argument,' prompted Rudman.

'She was my lover ever since she was sixteen years old,' Georgina continued, ignoring him. 'I showed her a life where women did not need men, where we could be happy with what we were. For five years we were happy together.'

'I doubt whether she had much say in the matter,' Rudman commented dryly. 'What happened? Did she tell you she had found a man and preferred him?'

Georgina appeared to have missed Rudman's insinuation.

'No,' she said slowly. 'She said she was in love with another woman. That she did not love me anymore.'

The others looked at her in shock, wide-eyed and silent.

'So you had a fight, ripped her clothes, and stabbed her.'

'It was not like that,' she replied after another pause. 'I said that you would not understand.'

Rudman waited for an explanation. Finally it came.

'She liked to be forced into submission. She enjoyed it. I took the knife and forced her to undress, thinking that she would change her mind, that giving her what she liked would ... But she kept begging me to stop. I realised that she was serious. She was standing on the bed.' Her eyes seemed far away, as if recalling that night. 'She always did that. Stood on the bed while ...' She sighed, and gathered herself. 'I stepped back and she fell.' She looked at Rudman for the first time. 'It was an accident,' she said, 'an accident. You cannot hang me for an accident.'

Rudman did not reply. His face showed clearly that he intended to try.

'What happened then?' he asked. Georgina resumed staring into space.

'I knew no-one would believe me. They don't understand us. I had to make it look like a robbery. My nightdress was covered in her blood. I had to get rid of it.'

'So you took the nightdress off, cleaned the blood off yourself, put on a clean nightdress, and took the other and the tiara and threw them in the boiler,' Rudman said. She nodded.

'But your throat', gasped Rose. 'Surely you didn't ...' Georgina ignored her.

'No, she didn't cut her own throat, did you, Miss Riley? Someone else did that to you.'

Georgina nodded slowly.

'Who was it?'

She said nothing for a while.

'Frieda,' she answered finally. There were gasps around the room. 'Frieda was the woman Emily had fallen in love with. Frieda was one of us. Frieda was also my lover. She came in after I had got rid of the tiara and the nightdress. I told her what had happened, I thought she loved me enough to help me. I was wrong.'

'Why did she not just report you to the police?'

Georgina shrugged.

'She was in love with Emily. I had not realised that. She told me she was going to make me pay for her death. I pleaded with her, I told her it was an accident, how we couldn't ruin our lives over the girl, how we would be happy together in America.'

'She didn't believe you?'

Georgina shook her head.

'She held me by my hair. She forced my head back, used the knife to cut my throat, and then threw me down.'

'Forwards, fortunately for you, if that's the right word. Your head fell forward, blocking the flow of blood. Even so, you were lucky she didn't cut deeper.'

She made no response to her luck.

'So she wasn't really Jewish after all,' Rudman continued.

Georgina let out what could have been a bitter laugh.

'Oh, yes, she was Jewish.' For the second time she looked directly at Rudman, her mouth twisted in a sneer. 'We met in Berlin in 1933. Berlin then was the best place in the world. Hitler was not yet in power. Or, at least, the bad times had not started. There were nightclubs for everyone. That is where I discovered who I was. I was twenty-four, she was seventeen. She showed me what love really is. Because she was Jewish she could not let her parents know her true feelings as a woman. After I left Berlin and returned to America in 1934 we wrote to each other.'

'That was when you took Emily on as a maid,' Rudman suggested. She nodded.

'Frieda knew she could not live under the Nazis, both as a Jew, and as one of us. Things became worse every day. She smuggled a letter out, explaining how she planned to slip across the border. I was waiting there. I brought her to England, knowing that people would believe what I said. But England was too small a place for us. In America we could find somewhere remote and live the lives we were intended to live.'

'Thus the story of the marriage.'

'It would have been a marriage. Just not the sort you think of.'

'Doesn't seem to make any difference now, though, does it.'

She looked down at the handcuffs on her wrists, eyes unseeing.

'No. It doesn't.'

Chapter 24: Daylight

The sky was beginning to lighten as they walked down the road back to the village, the married couples holding hands, Jessica with her arms wrapped around her as if to ward off the early morning chill. The police van had left with Georgina in it. Their statements had been taken. Rudman was finally happy.

'How did he work out that Emily was Georgina's lover?' asked Henderby.

'I told him about something I had seen that night,' Rose replied. 'I should have told him before, but I wasn't sure of what it was. Initially I thought it was Georgina and Frieda in a passionate embrace, but then decided that I must have mistaken that for one of them whispering into the other's ear.'

'And Rudman decided to rely on your initial feeling?' asked Henderby.

'Yes. Took a hell of a leap in logic to connect Emily and Georgina, though,' said Erica.

'Not really,' Haskins said. 'Rudman played his cards close to his chest right until the last.' There was a sound of derision from Rose. They had already had a full and frank discussion about his failure to tell her what he was going to do, and he had thought he had, on balance, reassured her sufficiently. Only just. 'That knife they found the day after, the pruning knife in the bushes. That worried him, he couldn't help but feel that it had played a part. When they found the other in the boiler he was convinced it was a double murder – or an attempted double murder – but he had no proof. He always had his doubts about Georgina. Claimed to be a "copper's intuition". Personally I think it was two things; firstly, he told me once that, in his words, "there is someone missing from this whole business". I couldn't work out what he was talking about – at the time I thought he was making absolutely no sense. In fact he was referring to Georgina's supposed husband-to-be. If she was about to marry her childhood sweetheart, why no word from him when she didn't turn up? She was in a coma at the time, she could hardly claim that she had let him know she wasn't coming.'

'But the war broke out a few days later,' Erica pointed out.

'Hardly enough to stop a telegram getting through. Yet no telegram came, no urgent request for information. No contact made with the police to find out where their bride was, just Georgina's later assertion that the wedding had been called off after she failed to return on time. Yes, not exactly the most solid of evidence, or even non-evidence as it were, but Rudman found it significant.'

'And secondly?' asked Rose, used to his ways.

'Secondly, he always thought Georgina's choice of guests revealing. You could either think of her as benevolent, or feeding on other peoples' insecurities.'

'I did warn you about that, darling,' Rose murmured.

'Yes. You did.' He smiled. 'I'm rather glad I married you, you know.'

'Me too. Rather.'

'Well,' Haskins continued, 'when she stole in for the remains of the tiara, I think Rudman put two and two together – or maybe even two and three – and came up with the magical four. Obviously she knew – or thought she knew – that hers must be the only fingerprints on it – and on the knife. Which means that she was the one to throw it into the boiler. Which means either she murdered Emily, or knew who had murdered her, and was setting up robbery as the reason for the killing. The alternative to robbery was a crime of passion.'

'I think Rudman said it to get her talking,' Rose said. 'He wasn't sure if he was right, but took a chance. He would have badgered her into telling the truth sooner or later.'

'Why was she so bitter towards us?' asked Jessica. 'She knew none of us had done anything to her.'

'I think she hated the entire world for what had happened,' Haskins said. 'She felt that everything was a result of what she would call the rest of the world not understanding. If they could have been open about everything that night would never have happened. And when it did, it tipped her over the brink.'

'You could almost feel sorry for her,' Henderby said.

'I can't,' Rose replied briefly. 'She let us be walking suspects for all that time. She could have owned up after recovering, explained that it was an accident – if it was, which I doubt.'

'But then Frieda would have been arrested,' Erica said. 'I think Georgina still loved her in a way.'

'Pretty strange sort of love,' Henderby commented. 'If a woman tried to kill me I would take the hint.'

'Even me?' teased Erica.

'Especially you, my darling one,' he replied fervently. The others laughed.

Haskins breathed in deeply. He had always enjoyed the tang of sea air, and now, in the first flush of dawn, he felt more at peace than he had in years.

'I think we're finally coming home,' he said.

Home, to peace, he hoped. Despite everything the future looked rather good. While worldly treasures might be in short supply, it mattered little compared to the love of a good woman.

Or a not so good woman.

He squeezed Rose's hand. She squeezed back, smiling at him.

'Time to settle down,' she said. 'You'll have to start acting like a responsible father soon.'

'I suppose so. I can't see it being easy bringing up a family with the Socialists in power.' He sighed. 'I would have preferred to see Churchill's lot getting back in, but I can't see that happening again.'

Other novels by Bill Dughaille:

The FFSG series (aka the Wellbury Chronics)

Summers

The first in the FFSG series.

Detective Sergeant Frank Summers is a man on a mission: to keep his head down, stay out of trouble and enjoy the relaxed atmosphere of the easy-going, genteel town of Wellbury, his new posting. It's a town just made for him, where, he believes, even the criminals take bank holidays off. But, while perceptive in his professional life, he tends to miss the subtleties in his private life. In this case he fails to realise that his own tranquillity is being threatened by three women and a philanderer. The fact that the women in question are his boss, his constable and the local pathologist adds just the touch of danger to his life that he had hoped to avoid. The philanderer has been dead several decades. The women are very much alive. And ticking.

The Eighty-five-percenters

The second in the FFSG series.

Detective Sergeant Frank Summers is faced with an unexpected crisis as the staid citizens of the genteel town of Wellbury rapidly descend into disorganised anarchy after a sociology professor announces on radio that eighty-five percent of the population will die in a coming cull. The prediction appears to be coming true as apparently total strangers are felled one by one according to a list of the ten-most-disliked Wellburians, from nagging neighbours to estate agents ... and the police, at a poorly performing number ten. But Frank fails to realise that there is a graver danger closer to home. Three women have decided that he is their responsibility: his boss, his constable and the local pathologist have agreed to become best of enemies. Now they intend to re-arrange his fate the way it should be. And they aren't asking anyone's permission.

Fakes, Fraud and Deception

The third in the FFSG series.

Detective Sergeant Frank Summers is in the doghouse, despite having recently arrested an internationally sought con-artist. And since he is in the doghouse he has no intention of pointing out that there is something very strange about the attractive French police woman who has come to interview the arrested man, not to mention the two detectives claiming to be from Scotland Yard. Oh, no, he is going to stay well out of the way this time. Definitely.

Jokers

The fourth in the FFSG series.

The doctors have pronounced Detective Sergeant Frank Summers physically fit following recovery after his shooting, but his colleagues fear that his sense of humour was extracted along with the bullet. They are, as always, more than willing to interfere in his life in the pursuit of a good cause. If that wasn't enough, a bunch of criminals calling themselves the Joker Gang are laughing at him, the university students are creating mayhem during their rag week, and someone called The Shocker is trying to kill him. The only advantage is that it take his mind off of the ultimatum the three women in his life have given him, one that he has only until the Sunday to resolve. Or leave town.

Prophecies

The fifth in the FFSG series.

Detective Sergeant Summers is under a hex, otherwise known as his colleagues. First they don't want him to get married, then it is imperative it must happen. Then they decide that a prophecy has been made which threatens the wedding. They don't believe in prophecies, but aren't sure that prophecies understand that. So they'll have to Do Something About It. And if their bumbling efforts aren't enough to ensure he never makes it to the altar, he has to cope with visiting aliens and resident ghosts. He does have tiny Squishy to protect him, but what match can even this plucky little kitten be against a prospective mother-in-law?

Loonymoon

The sixth in the FFSG series.

The Inspectors Summers have tied the knot and embarked on their honeymoon in a small family-run hotel in Normandy. She has very definite ideas of what she wants out of a honeymoon: to set a seal on their love, and to form a foundation for life-long devotion. He just wants to nick a French police officer's kepi. He had a Bobby's helmet nicked from him once by a French girl while he was on crowd duty one New Year's Eve in London, and now he intends to return the favour. Neither is about to achieve their aim unless they can solve the mystery of the woman in the bath and the missing heroin. Which means pitting their minds against the French Inspectors Simenon. That's Mr and Mrs Simenon, whose marriage has gone beyond the rocks and is now beating itself to death against humdrum reality. One or either or both or neither could be the guilty crumpet. More importantly, is their marriage a portent of what could become of the Loonymooners? Ultimately the decisive question could well be: which side do the peas go?

Others:

The Window

Jim Allbright, ex-bobby and now easy-going window washer, innocently responds to an advert for window washing placed in the newspaper by the local council. The response is a torrent of paperwork, political correctness and a computer system doing exactly what it was told to do, but not quite what was intended. But if the system cannot be beaten, the interchange of letters can be used to have a little fun and get to know some of the people struggling behind it. There's Sandi, who signs herself as "(pp the Administrator)"; her four-year old little angel Helen; Graham, a shadowy computer programmer who definitely has too much time on his hands, and a slew of Project Managers and Senior Administrators eager to ensure standards are upheld no matter how many problems they create. Against a run of bad luck and circumstances Jim and Sandi aim to meet up one day, eventually. Hopefully. The window might even get washed. Maybe.

Diary of a Sane Man

In a cross between 'Last Of The Summer Wine' and 'One Flew Over The Cuckoo's Nest', set against a backdrop of the brave new world of New Labour's end of honeymoon, Fred is the Last Cynical Optimistic Realist.

Believing that he's found the perfect niche – three square meals a day plus all the newspapers he can read just for occasionally pretending to be mad – he's not going to be the one to rock the apple cart. Oh, no.

Safe from the wiles of women and the woes of the world, he's not going to rock the boat. Oh, no.

No, he's just going to sit and observe, and comment quietly on the insanity of life outside.

Well, maybe just little one tug of the loose strand of wool on life's jersey ...

Did you know they elected a monkey as mayor in Hartlepool?

Firelight

A modern-day tale of an ordinary family gathering at Christmas; the good, the bad, the dysfunctional and the forgotten.

George Browne and his wife Winifred have retired to a large, run-down pile in the country. Rumour has it that it was once the abode of a mad aristocratic family with a penchant for Satanism, and that both they and their victims still haunt the corridors. Other rumours are that it was a lunatic asylum for much of the nineteenth and twentieth century, and bodies of the inhabitants are buried around the large gardens in unmarked graves.

The Brownes are an unremarkable retired couple who, depending on who you might ask, have bought it as an investment, or alternatively as somewhere with enough bedrooms to accommodate their children, grand-children, and the little baby great-grandchildren. Too often in the past excuses have been made at special times, the most common of which has been of the "I don't want to put you to any trouble" variety. That excuse can no longer hold water.

Now it is approaching Christmas. Winter has set in, but the house is snug with oil heaters and real fires. As the various relations arrive, or don't arrive, it becomes clearer why invitations might have been refused in the past. The men of the family believe in having their way. The women of the family are strong-willed in their own different ways, and have various means of getting what they want.

The guests of the family - friends, boyfriends, girlfriends, wives and husbands - discover that their partners have a totally different side to them as the explosive hatreds of long-nurtured fights and feuds simmer to the surface before quickly boiling over.

One evening Winifred Browne encourages them to each tell a story as they sit in the lounge with the large fire warming them, the television off, no access to broadband, computers or mobile connections. Reluctantly at first they begin. As each evening passes:

with different members taking turns, they announce in stories the feelings and hopes they cannot voice in public.

Finally it's the turn of Winifred Browne. Her story will be the one that tells them who they are, where they come from, and maybe why they have turned out the way they have.

For further details on these visit:

www.dughaille.info